ROSEMARY
for Remembrance

For my husband

May

Thursday 2/10/2011

Rosemary
for Remembrance

{a novel by}
Mary Netreba

TATE PUBLISHING & *Enterprises*

Rosemary for Remembrance
Copyright © 2011 by Mary Netreba. All rights reserved.

No part of this publication may be reproduced, stored in a retrieval system or transmitted in any way by any means, electronic, mechanical, photocopy, recording or otherwise without the prior permission of the author except as provided by USA copyright law.

Scripture taken from the *Holy Bible, New International Version*®. NIV®. Copyright© 1973, 1978, 1984 by International Bible Society. Used by permission of Zondervan. All rights reserved.

This novel is a work of fiction. Names, descriptions, entities, and incidents included in the story are products of the author's imagination. Any resemblance to actual persons, events, and entities is entirely coincidental.

The opinions expressed by the author are not necessarily those of Tate Publishing, LLC.

Published by Tate Publishing & Enterprises, LLC
127 E. Trade Center Terrace | Mustang, Oklahoma 73064 USA
1.888.361.9473 | www.tatepublishing.com

Tate Publishing is committed to excellence in the publishing industry. The company reflects the philosophy established by the founders, based on Psalm 68:11,
"The Lord gave the word and great was the company of those who published it."

Book design copyright © 2011 by Tate Publishing, LLC. All rights reserved.
Cover design by Kristen Verser
Interior design by Chelsea Womble

Published in the United States of America

ISBN: 978-1-61739-684-7
1. Fiction, Historical
2. Fiction, Romance, Historical
11.01.17

Dedication

To our precious heavenly Father, whom, I have no doubt, made it possible for this book to be published.

Acknowledgments

I would like first to thank God for answered prayers. Lord, when you do a work, it is complete. My life will never be the same. Thank you for carrying me through some of the most challenging trials I have ever had to face while writing this book; none of which would compare to what you have done for me when you gladly suffered for my sake and for all.

I would like to thank the wonderful people at Tate Publishing for all their help in the publication of the book.

Chapter One

MARCH 11, 1908

"For I know the plans I have for you," declares the Lord, "plans to prosper you and not harm you, plans to give you hope and a future."

Jeremiah 29:11 (NIV)

The early March day started out unseasonably mild, with the temperature hovering in the lower fifties, unusual for this area of Pennsylvania. For eight-year-old Rachel, it looked as if spring had finally begun to make its long, much-anticipated arrival on the mountains of Blue Knob.

As Rachel stepped down from the front porch, she carefully avoided the broken wooden step Jack said he'd fix but never did. Her stepfather never had any intention even once of keeping his word. The broken porch step was just one of many on the list of broken promises.

Rachel stood at the bottom of the steps, pausing for a moment to enjoy the pleasant feeling of warmth on her face. It wouldn't be long. Spring was almost here. Her heart filled with hope as she closed her eyes for a moment to breathe in the smell of the slowly warming earth. It was that wonderful first smell of the earth coming back to life again after months of being frozen over with the snow and ice of the winter season that Rachel so looked forward to. The first scent of this promise of spring would last only for a few days. Then the earth would bring forth new life from underneath the ground as it pushed its way to the top, reaching for the warmth of the sun above to make it grow.

Spring meant this and so much more to Rachel. Spring meant the relief of the unbelievably frigid blasts of wind that blew across the mountains every winter, quickly freezing over everything in its path. The majestic evergreen trees, their pine-needled branches softly covered with sparkling white snow, and the frozen, bare limbs on ice-coated trees would shimmer on moonlit nights, giving the appearance of an impenetrable winter fortress able to withstand any onslaught the harsh winters might bring their way.

But for the people of Blue Knob, the winters on the mountaintop could be almost unbearable, particularly for those households who already lived in deep poverty. For Rachel and her family of two younger sisters, Maggie and Jennie, and their mother, Julianna, and Jack, her stepfather and father of Maggie and Jennie, there was never enough warmth, clothing, or food to get her family through, especially with Jack's drinking. Most of any money that he did earn doing odd jobs for others when he was sober went to the bottle. Rachel shook loose the depressing thoughts. Being sad would mean she couldn't enjoy her day.

Rachel opened her eyes, determined not to let that happen. All around her, everywhere she looked, the promise of spring helped make her heart a little lighter. The most recent snow had melted, leaving the ground saturated, but it would dry up soon enough. Rachel looked up through the still-bare limbs of the trees. The sky was a beautiful, soft blue. Fluffy white clouds hung gently suspended as they lazily moved in the slight breeze.

Rachel sighed. She couldn't wait to put her hands in the soil and start planting the seeds of vegetables, flowers, and herbs she had saved from last autumn. With delight, Rachel noticed the leaves of daffodils barely peeking up from the ground, seeking the warmth in the air above them. It wouldn't be long until the spring flowers were in full bloom. Rachel looked farther on as she heard the noisy commotion of two feisty robins battling for their breakfast, providing humorous entertainment as she watched for the final outcome. Rachel smiled to herself. It looked like the worm was winning. *Good,* she thought. *That's who I was rooting for anyway.*

With her spirits completely lifted, she started out on her almost-daily journey to work as a domestic for the Nettles. Actually just Mrs. Nettle, since Mr. Nettle had died several years earlier, much to the regret of all who still had to work at the Nettle home. Mr. Nettle had been the only one to keep the harsh Mrs. Nettle at bay when one of her moods came over her. The day Mr. Nettle died was a true loss in more ways than one. With Mrs. Nettle's moods unchecked, it meant more misery for everyone around her. Her nasty temperament was known far and wide across the mountains of Blue Knob and most of Blair and Bedford County.

Even though Rachel was only eight years old, she was expected to pull her weight and contribute to her own household. The very meager income she received from Mrs. Nettle was barely enough for food. And Mrs. Nettle made darn good and sure Rachel knew it too, as every payday she'd look down her nose at Rachel, careful to drop the coins one by one in Rachel's little hand, as if contact with it would contaminate her somehow. It must have grieved Mrs. Nettle terribly to part with her money. Rachel couldn't understand why Mrs. Nettle didn't seem to like her very much.

Rachel's frame was small and delicate. Although her heart-shaped face was like her mother Julianna's, her blue eyes and light brown hair were not. That, of course, could only mean one thing. Rachel looked like her real father. This fact alone made it easy for her stepfather, Jack, to hate her. Every time he looked at her, his hatred and resentment grew. Rachel's small frame took many beatings when Jack was drunk or angry about something, or nothing at all. Usually, this went hand in hand. He blamed Rachel for his having to be married to her mother. In Jack's mind, it was Rachel's fault he was trapped, Rachel's fault there was no more money, and Rachel's fault that his life wasn't better. He claimed she was the one who drove him to drink. The fact that Jack had always been a drunk was not an admission he would ever acknowledge.

And it was during these times of Jack's drunkenness that Rachel paid the price for it. There were times when it didn't stop there either, especially when Rachel wasn't around for the first lashing from the "special" belt that Jack kept for beatings only. He'd keep the leather belt with the large silver buckle hanging from a transom between the kitchen and dining room, its threatening presence a constant reminder for Rachel and her sisters, Maggie and Jennie, to stay in line or else. Unfortunately, "or else" could be anything, or nothing at all. One didn't have to do anything to deserve a beating from Jack Walters. She just had to be there. And when Rachel wasn't there, Maggie and Jennie would pay the terrible price.

Rachel shook her head as the memory of their last beating came to her mind. The lighthearted feeling she had only moments earlier was replaced with her almost-constant worrying about her younger sisters.

These were such terrible thoughts on such a beautiful morning! Rachel looked up at the sky again. After a prayer of protection for her little sisters, Rachel straightened her shoulders, stubbornly stuck her chin out, and, with determination, started walking as she reminded herself this was still going to be a good day.

Chapter Two

The sky was turning an odd shade of bluish gray as Rachel made her way across the Baileys' field to the Nettles' property. Clouds began to roll in continuously, one on top of another. As she passed through the Baileys' pasture, Rachel noticed that their usually docile milking cows seemed especially agitated. Their soft, gentle moos sounded woefully longer and more insistent as they became increasingly louder. Several of the black and white cows were looking directly at Rachel as they mooed. Even their shoulders appeared to be shaking in dread. They seemed afraid, their eyes large and round with apprehension. Rachel looked around nervously. *Maybe there's a vicious wild animal lurking nearby,* she thought. *A coyote, or maybe even a wolf.* As this thought occurred to her, she felt something butting up against her leg. "Ah!" Jumping back and nearly out of her skin, Rachel looked down at her attacker in shocked surprise. Her relieved laughter filled the air. One of the Baileys' old roosters had wandered off from their farm and stood looking at Rachel arrogantly as if she had disturbed him. His black and white feathers gave him a proud appearance as he puffed up his chest. Lifting his head up slightly he gave one "Er er errr!" His crowing voice was raspy with age. But the rooster seemed satisfied as he turned away from Rachel to strut his way back to the Baileys' farm.

Rachel smiled at her strange encounter. Looking toward the mooing cows, she couldn't help but chuckle at them. "Cowards!" she shouted at them as she turned away and resumed her walk through the pasture to the Nettles.'

Wrapping her shabby black cloak around her a little closer, she picked up her pace, attempting to miss the soggier areas of water that began to seep into her worn boots. Rachel could see the Nettle home in the distance. She was almost there. Rain was beginning to fall, softly at first. Rachel turned her face toward the sky. She loved the feeling of the spring rain on her face.

But the rain and wind were picking up with more intensity as Rachel found herself kicking up her heels much quicker. By the time she reached her destination, she was soaked through to her clothing underneath, and her only thought was to be inside to get warm and dry again. Rachel pushed open the heavy oak door to the servant's entrance in the back of the Nettles' massive home. Standing for a moment in the mudroom, the water dripped freely from her cloak and onto the floor. She took off her dark, worn cloak and shivered. Hoping it would be dry before it was time to go home, she hung the cloak up on two hooks, spreading the tattered fabric to dry. She didn't know how long it would take for the clothes she was wearing to dry, but it couldn't be soon enough. Rachel turned and stepped into the enormous kitchen of the Nettle home. The warmth felt welcoming and Rachel stood for a moment, enjoying the feeling. Cook was in the kitchen, having already been up and about for several hours. She was pulling out loaves of freshly baked bread from the cast-iron stove.

Cook was a sweet, chubby woman in her fifties. Her cheeks always seemed to be pink, and she had a permanent smile on her face. Her twinkling, blue eyes saw more than anyone realized. Cook had a heart of gold and a strong sense of humor that got her through each day working for the miserable Mrs. Nettle.

The aroma of the freshly baked bread was heavenly as it reached Rachel's nostrils. Her mouth started to water. She hadn't had any breakfast at home. The only food in the house was the small amount of bread she had left next to the still-sleeping Maggie for her and Jennie to share. Rachel knew Maggie would share with their sister. Maggie loved Jennie the way Rachel loved both of her little sisters.

Rachel hoped Cook would find a way to sneak one of the newly baked loaves to her. It didn't happen too often, but it wasn't because Cook didn't try.

Mrs. Nettle was a mean, bitter, unhappy, selfish woman who ran her household with an iron fist. She was very proud of the control she felt she had over others. She kept an eye on most everything, including how much flour was to be used for the bread and how many loaves she thought could be baked with it. She would even count the number of dry beans Cook bought at the general store to determine how much soup it would make. Mrs. Nettle went on a rampage just one week earlier, determined that Cook could make the same amount of bread with less flour.

"Na, Mrs. Nettle. It can't work that way. All the ingredients hafta work together, and too little flour won't work," Cook told her.

But Mrs. Nettle insisted she was right and hinted that if Cook didn't listen to her, she might not have a job the next day. So Cook did as she was ordered. Feeling very triumphant, Mrs. Nettle was actually smiling the next day as she personally oversaw her instructions being carried out precisely by Cook. She watched with pleasure as the flour was measured out one cup less per loaf. She wasn't smiling, however, when the loaves came out of the oven, sunken in the middle and very dry. Cook dropped the pans heavily onto the table as if to exaggerate how wrong Mrs. Nettle's opinion of bread-making was. Cook had to bite her tongue to keep from saying, "I told ya so." Because the loaves didn't turn out as she thought they should, Mrs. Nettle grabbed the towels Cook used to keep from burning herself as she pulled the loaf pans from the oven.

Not knowing how to use the towels properly, she burned herself on the pans as she threw all the loaves of bread out the back door and screamed at Cook, "Look what you made me do!"

Cook knew not to say anything but stood silently with her hands clasped behind her back. Her tongue still ached to say, "I told ya so," but instead, she said, "I have some salve for them burns on yer skin, Mrs. Nettle, if ya want it."

Mrs. Nettle ordered Cook to get the salve for her and grumbled that she would do it herself, then turned on her heels and stormed out of the kitchen and up the stairs to her bedroom. The next morning, in an unusually good mood, Mrs. Nettle came down the stairs, through the kitchen, and out the back door to look for the loaves she'd thrown out. Her hands were feeling much better from the salve Cook had given her, but she was upset that the loaves from the day before were gone. They could've been used for something. She was sure. As Mrs. Nettle came back into the kitchen, Cook simply said, "Them birds musta been hungry." Mrs. Nettle said not a word but walked out of the kitchen and back up the stairs and stayed in bed the rest of the day. She didn't know that Rachel had taken the loaves. And this morning, Rachel had left the last of it with her little sisters, for when they woke up.

Mrs. Nettle hadn't checked on Cook's baking since then. Cook placed the loaves of freshly baked bread on the wooden table. Reaching for the crock of butter to spread on top of the loaves, she smiled as she looked over at Rachel reassuringly. Nodding her head to the loaves of bread on the table, Cook said, "Them's not the first batch this mornin.' The first batch didn't turn out so well, and ya know Mrs. Nettle don't want nothin' to do with those." She tilted her head sideways and gave a conspirator's grin. Cook's heart ached for the girl.

Rachel looked in the direction of the corner cupboard. *Aha.* Their secret hiding place for freshly baked bread and anything else that Cook felt Mrs. Nettle wouldn't be happy with. But even if the bread passed Mrs. Nettle's inspection, Cook still would have tried to help Rachel.

Rachel breathed a sigh of relief and gave a grateful smile to Cook. She knew that tonight, she, Maggie, and Jennie wouldn't go to bed hungry.

"Rachel! Rachel!" Mrs. Nettle's shrill voice sounded angrier than usual this morning. Rachel shuddered, wondering what imaginary wrong she did this time. Rachel knew that harsh tone of voice. So did the entire Nettle household. When Mrs. Nettle was in one of her moods, she made a point of making everyone around her work harder, fussing with every detail, criticizing, belittling, and demanding the chores be done all over again. Rachel remembered the last time Mrs. Nettle sounded this angry. She made Rachel scrub the kitchen floor on a day it wasn't usually done. Rachel had worked extra hard that day to scrape into the corners to remove the imaginary dirt from the linoleum floor. But Mrs. Nettle wasn't pleased. After inspecting Rachel's work, Mrs. Nettle insisted she saw a spot of dirt still on the floor—though no one else could see it—no one meaning Cook, two parlor maids, the horse groom, and the butler, whom Mrs. Nettle selected to witness her degrading inspection. All of them steeled themselves for what they knew was coming. Why, they asked themselves, did Mrs. Nettle always have to find something to pick at Rachel about? She was, after all, still a little girl. Mrs. Nettle had screamed at Rachel and then, taking a bucket of coal that was next to the stove, flung it across the kitchen floor, demanding that Rachel do it right this time or else. She stormed out, little knowing that each eyewitness to her nasty temper did their part to make sure the mess was entirely cleaned up.

Finney, the horse groom, an older Irish gentleman with wiry, gray hair and handlebar moustache who'd been with Mrs. Nettle since when her husband was still alive, patted Rachel on the shoulder and told her, "Ah, lassie. She's not always been this bad. Just since the mister passed on. He knew how to handle her."

"Rachel!" Rachel was abruptly brought back to reality at the sound of Mrs. Nettle's harsh voice. Cook and Rachel could hear Mrs. Nettle's heavy footsteps coming toward the kitchen. Rachel drew in her breath as she and Cook quickly exited the kitchen to meet their employer in the hall. Neither of them wanted Mrs. Nettle snooping about the kitchen today of all days.

Rachel held back a shudder when she saw Mrs. Nettle. She and Cook saw the real source of her anger. They both stopped suddenly, standing side by side. Rachel's heart skipped a beat.

Cook held her breath at the look of hatred pouring out of Mrs. Nettle's eyes. *This one's goin' ta be a bad one, this is,* thought Cook with dread as she stood close enough to Rachel to offer some form of protection from their employer.

Mrs. Nettle was dressed to go riding. While her new, gray velvet riding habit looked elegantly made, it did nothing to flatter her figure. It couldn't hide the wide hips or the thin, rounded, slouching shoulders. It certainly couldn't hide a face of bitterness and self-inflicted disappointment. Mrs. Nettle was ugly. Her hair was still dark, but there were more wiry gray hairs showing through every day. She had it pulled backed severely in a tight bun, done so with many decorative hairpins to hold it in place. It only emphasized her unattractiveness. There wasn't even one wisp of hair out of place. It wouldn't have dared. Her dark, piercing eyes with deep lines around them and her long, pointed chin made her look even more frightening to Rachel today. Mrs. Nettle's unhappiness at being unable to ride since it had started to rain meant someone was going to pay. And it wouldn't be the horse that she would take her anger out on. Mrs. Nettle looked down her long, slightly crooked nose at Rachel.

"Why are you so late?" she demanded. Rachel was actually ten minutes early, but she didn't dare say anything. Rachel knew she was doomed no matter what she did. She simply looked down at the floor, arms hanging loosely at her sides, and waited for whatever punishment Mrs. Nettle decided to use.

"Well, girl? Answer me! Why are you so late?" Rachel continued to look at the floor, steeling herself for what she knew would be next. Mrs. Nettle grabbed Rachel's upper arm roughly. She didn't seem to be aware that Rachel's arm was too skinny from lack of nourishment. It hurt as she dug her fingers into the soft flesh. Cook took a step closer to Rachel, knowing what was to come next.

Mrs. Nettle screamed, "Look at me, stupid girl! Fine. Maybe when you're through today you'll have had enough to think about it so it won't happen again. After you're done with the wash, you can clean the kitchen with Cook. And make sure you do it correctly this time." Mrs. Nettle's voice rose to an even shriller shriek that sent chills down their spines.

Cook's cheeks were turning deep red with anger over the mistreatment of Rachel. If she'd stepped in to help, the results would've been the same or even worse. Mrs. Nettle turned sharply on her heel, the rustling sound of her gray velvet riding skirt swishing as she stormed up the staircase.

Cook looked at Rachel, who stood quietly with her head down. Guilt washed over her that she didn't step in and do something. Rachel didn't cry, though her lower lip was quivering. *There is something so different about Rachel,* Cook thought. Sometimes Cook could almost swear she saw a grown woman hiding in Rachel, and at other times, still the precious little eight-year-old girl that she was.

Although badly shaken inside, Rachel knew somehow that this day would still turn out all right, no matter how bad things might have seemed at the moment. *The worst thing that could've happened today already did,* she thought to herself. Usually after these fits of rage, Mrs. Nettle would spend the rest of the day in bed. So at least for the rest of this day, all should be quiet in the household.

There were times in Rachel's young life when she would sense a gentle presence surrounding her, a presence that she not only felt and could hear in her heart but a presence that made her believe there was a glorious future ahead of her if only she would hold on a little longer, which she always did. Each time it happened, Rachel felt a renewed hope, knowing she wasn't alone. It also gave her a sense of optimism absent only moments earlier. It was almost as if she was somehow being rescued from something without her actually being aware of what it was.

Rachel drew in a deep breath and straightened her shoulders with determination. She turned to re-enter the kitchen through the swinging door. Cook followed. The pity she felt for Rachel was mixed with anger at Mrs. Nettle's unkindness. Cook knew it would be impossible for Rachel to do what Mrs. Nettle expected along with her regular chores. Instead, Cook went to work helping Rachel with the laundry and the kitchen. They would leave the stove until the baking was done.

Cook began to worry as the day progressed from warm to windy and rainy. Every time she glanced out of one of the kitchen windows, the weather seemed to take a turn for the worse. The temperature was steadily dropping outside, and the rain was turning to snow. *This doesn't look like the early spring onion snow*, she thought. The onion snow usually arrived about the same time as wild onions would start to peek up from the ground. This early spring snow was different. Cook turned away from the window once again and walked back over to the cast-iron stove. She brought out the last several loaves of freshly baked bread from the oven and placed them on a towel on the large, wooden table. Pausing from her work for a moment, she turned to glance out the window again. The snow was thick and heavy and blowing wildly. It seemed to almost pummel its way to the ground. Cook was very puzzled. It was also too early to be a twig-bender, as the mountain people called it. Twig-benders usually happened about mid-April. Neither the onion snow nor the twig-bender lasted very long and melted very quickly. This snow was actually slamming itself against the windows and stuck in place, making it more difficult to see outside. From where Cook stood, it looked as if the whole world was turning white. Rachel was busy washing the empty bread pans that were stacked up by the sink. Cook had a bad feeling in her bones that something about this weather was amiss. But inside the Nettle home, all were snug and warm.

The Nettle home was a Queen Anne Victorian that the generous Mr. Nettle had built for his wife as a wedding gift twenty years earlier. Mrs. Nettle, of course, wanted to make sure her home was better than any other home in the mountaintop community. She was on site constantly, from the groundbreaking all the way to the finishing touches. Her constant nagging about every detail drove the designer and builders almost out of their minds. Several men walked off the job as a result of her demands. To Mrs. Nettle, she was supervising. To the men who stayed on the job, she was a nag. Many changes and alterations to the original house plans were somehow manipulated into exactly what she wanted. It had cost more and took longer to build the home, but Mrs. Nettle didn't care. No one was going to have a finer home than she and Mr. Nettle—no one. It still bothered her that a less costly, more simply designed Victorian on the mountain was favored as the better of the two. Little did Mrs. Nettle know that the same builders who had walked off the job on her home were the same men who helped build the other Victorian.

"It doesn't even have the same quality as ours," she would repeatedly say in frustration to her husband, who would pat her shoulder reassuringly and simply reply, "There, there now, dear."

The Nettle home was still very well made, however. Very few drafts made their way into the home. Outside, the snow continued, becoming thicker and heavier as the day progressed. One could hear the high-pitched winds whooshing and whistling all around them. It was becoming even worse. Cook could barely see out of the windows when she looked yet again but noticed the sky was becoming darker. Night would be upon them soon. Cook had a room in the servants' quarters in the attic, but Rachel would have to make her way across the Baileys' field to get home. Cook knew by the sound of the wind that there would be large drifts of snow outside. Before long they wouldn't be able to see out the windows at all because of the deepening snow.

Cook made the decision to let Rachel go before Mrs. Nettle came downstairs to inspect their work. *Mrs. Nettle is taking her sweet time too,* thought Cook sarcastically. Although she and Rachel were both exhausted with all the extra work, Cook decided she would clean the stove herself, never mind Mrs. Nettle being angry about Rachel leaving early. Surely Mrs. Nettle knew that Rachel had to walk home in this weather but seemed not to care what happened to her. Never had Cook in her entire fifty-odd years of life known anyone as selfish as Mrs. Nettle. She didn't care about anyone but herself and, of course, her stomach. Cook knew that Mrs. Nettle wasn't about to fire her over letting Rachel go home early. She enjoyed her food far too much. *And no other cook would put up with her either,* she thought.

"Rachel, come quickly. I'll take care of that," Cook said. Rachel turned away from her chore of washing the last of the pans, bowls, and utensils from the day's baking with relief. Her chapped hands felt as if they were on fire. Rachel took a towel and gingerly dried her hands, placing the towel near the sink. She walked across the kitchen toward the mudroom where Cook stood, waiting. Cook took Rachel's flimsy cloak down from the hooks it had been hanging on. Thankfully, it was dry. She wrapped it around Rachel and brought the hood up over her head.

This will never do, Cook thought. She could feel how threadbare the cloak was. Holes that had been sewn together were coming apart. Rachel would freeze in no time if this cloak was all she had to keep her warm.

"Take this," Cook said as she handed Rachel two loaves of freshly baked bread she had taken from the table earlier and wrapped in cloth. Rachel could feel that they were still very warm. Cook decided she would instead give Mrs. Nettle the bread that had been hidden in the corner cupboard earlier in the day.

"Keep 'em hidden under your cloak. And take this as well." Rachel was holding on tightly to the loaves of bread she was given as Cook wrapped her own cloak around Rachel, drawing the hood up over Rachel's other hood. The cloak was heavy and too big for Rachel, the length of it almost past Rachel's feet, but it was warm.

"Keep your hands under the cloak with the bread ta keep them warm, and hurry. That old bat might be down here any minute."

Rosemary for Remembrance

Rachel stifled a chuckle. She'd never heard Cook talk about Mrs. Nettle like this. Feeling grateful, Rachel pressed against Cook's chubby frame. They walked the few steps to the back door of the mudroom together. Cook opened the door. The first blast of cold air took Rachel's breath away as she stepped outside. She turned around to face Cook to say goodbye. Cook looked so worried. Perhaps she should sneak Rachel upstairs and allow her to sleep in the servants' quarters. But Mrs. Nettle made the rounds every night to check up on her help and would discover Rachel there. Knowing Mrs. Nettle, she would make Rachel leave immediately. Judging on how the snow and wind were blowing, the storm would only get worse. It would be best to let Rachel go now and hopefully get home as soon as possible.

"Goodbye, Cook. And thank you so much for the bread," Rachel called out. Cook nodded, her heart filled with regret and worry as she closed the door. Rachel turned away from the Nettle home to start her journey back. Another blast of cold wind hit her and almost knocked her off her feet. Rachel huddled deeper into the cloak, doing her best to keep the hood from slipping off her head. Her eyes watered as the snow, mixed with sleet, stung the exposed areas of her face. Never could Rachel remember feeling this cold. Never had she seen a winter snowstorm like this. It was unimaginable. Rachel's watery eyes could barely make out the Baileys' field that she had crossed earlier in the day. Rachel knew she must keep moving, and as quickly as possible. Rachel took a step, her worn boots filling with snow. The snow packed itself around her ankles and calves. The sting of the cold hurt. The wind was tearing at her outer cloak, making it very difficult to move. This combined with the snow packed around her ankles made her feel chilled all over. Her hands under the cloak were still warm, and Rachel was grateful for this.

I must keep going, she told herself with every difficult step. It was one slow step at a time, which seemed to take forever; but Rachel kept the thought in her mind of bringing home the bread for Maggie and Jennie. They'd be so happy to see it.

The wind miraculously stopped briefly. Rachel could see that she was about halfway through the Baileys' field. Her delicate, slender build could barely move from one step to the next, but still, she made it this far.

I must get home to Maggie and Jennie, she told herself. The relief of not having the wind blow at the moment was a blessing that Rachel felt very thankful for. The sudden gust of wind that followed seemed to come out of nowhere and caught Rachel completely by surprise. The wind hit her with such force that it slammed her light frame down into the deepening snow and ice, knocking the air out of her lungs. Rachel, stunned by the helpless feeling of being on her back, looked up at the sky. Her heart pounded in fear. Struggling, she managed to get up on her feet and realized two things. First, the precious loaves of bread she held so protectively under her cloak were gone. Second, the visibility was down to almost zero and Rachel had no idea where she was or which direction to go. Fear turned to full panic as Rachel dropped to her knees and started to dig desperately in the snow with fumbling hands that were turning numb from the bitter cold. She had to find the loaves of bread. She had to. Rachel was unaware that she was crying. She wanted to surprise her little sisters with her gift. She wanted Maggie and Jennie not to go to bed hungry. Her hands and feet were completely numb. The tears on her cheeks began to freeze. Time passed and stood still at the same time. Exhausted, Rachel fell onto her back, unaware she'd done so. Her shivering became violent. Her thoughts were confused and her movements more sluggish as the deep cold and numbness overtook her.

I'm so tired. Is it time to go to sleep? Tired... Her shivering stopped as new warmth enveloped her. Rachel felt so warm, so tired. When she woke up, she would be home with Maggie and Jennie. *Tired,* she thought. *Warm and tired.* Rachel drifted off into a deep, dark, dreamless sleep.

Chapter Three

Jonathan Bailey pulled on the leather reins of his chestnut-colored Appaloosa. The horse stopped and Jonathan sat for a moment, thinking about what to do next. Drawing his coat collar up around his neck a little higher, he removed his hat for a moment and shook loose the snow that had collected around the rim. He pulled his hat down tightly on his head again. As he sat, he squinted his eyes against the biting cold winds, struggling to see through the blinding snow.

This is no ordinary snowstorm, he thought. His Appaloosa gelding had great endurance, but the animal was becoming exhausted, his legs tired from the effort of making his way through the many drifts of thick, heavy snow. Fortunately, Jonathan and his father, Elias Bailey, had the foresight to gather their livestock into the barn before the worst of the storm hit. Their earliest warning had been the cattle's constant mooing.

"Something doesn't sound right," Elias told his wife, Ellen. "Animals can be a lot smarter than humans." Taking their behavior as a warning that something was amiss, he and Jonathan had worked together and brought all the livestock in. The storm that hit came upon their region with increasing intensity. It was getting dark by the time they returned to the homestead. Both riders and their horses were near exhaustion. But Jonathan had gone out once more on his own, telling his father he wanted to make sure all the livestock were accounted for.

I can't help it, he thought. Jonathan had a nagging feeling about something unusual he had spotted earlier. It was something dark against the white of the snow. Maybe it was really nothing, but the sense of urgency Jonathan felt prompted him to continue on in the hope of finding the same spot. As he and his horse, Victory, moved forward, the gusts of wind thankfully died down momentarily, clearing his vision long enough for Jonathan to recognize that he was in the same area where he had first spotted the mysterious black item. Yes. There it was, barely peeking out of the snow. Although Victory was a horse of great endurance, he became reluctant and stubborn, neighing in protest as Jonathan urged him closer. Jonathan, however, had only to nudge his heels slightly into Victory's sides to urge him forward. He got down from his horse and walked toward what looked like a dark piece of cloth. Jonathan almost turned away, feeling somewhat foolish. But the nagging feeling that something was wrong made him crouch down on his knees anyway. More dark cloth appeared as he dug at the snow with his hands. The cold quickly grabbed at his fingers, making them stiff. But Jonathan was able to hold onto the cloth. As he gave a sharp tug, the cloth and what came out of the snow drift left him stunned. He sucked in his breath.

"What?" Jonathan found himself looking down at the face of a child, a little girl. With a start, he realized the little girl was Rachel Walters. She crossed their field every day. She was unconscious, half-frozen, and barely alive. *Or not at all*, he thought. It was difficult to tell for sure. Jonathan wasted no time and quickly picked her up. She was as light as a feather as he placed her over the saddle. When he was in the saddle again, he pulled Rachel up into a sitting position, side saddle. Opening his coat, Jonathan pulled her small frame against him for warmth. She moaned softly. Relief ran through him. *She's still alive*, he thought. His horse, though exhausted, didn't seem to mind the extra weight, almost as if Victory sensed how important his task was. Together, horse, rider, and tiny passenger slowly made their way back to his parents' farm. Rachel let out a soft moan again. Jonathan thanked God. *At least she's still alive*, he thought. The harsh, cold winds once again picked up as they approached the Baileys' farm. As they neared the house, Jonathan yelled out several times at the top of his lungs. "We need help! I found someone! Help!"

    Ellen Bailey was busy adding wood to the iron stove in the kitchen, stoking the fire until the new wood caught. Closing the heavy iron door, she stood up. The sound of something outside caught her attention.

    Probably the wind, she thought.

    "Help!"

    This time, Ellen clearly recognized her son's voice. Elias Bailey had been piling more wood into the fireplace when he also heard his son's call for help. He quickly made his way back to the kitchen as Ellen was yanking the back door open. A blast of icy wind hit her full force, almost causing her to stumble as the wind took her breath. Elias was right behind her and steadied her for a moment before brushing past to help his son. What they both saw took them by surprise. Jonathan had someone with him! "It's Rachel," Jonathan said. Elias reached up and scooped Rachel into his arms to take her into the house. Jonathan rode Victory back to the stable for shelter and to give him extra hay and water. Ellen Bailey followed her husband up the stairs to the bedroom next to Jonathan's. Because of the frigid cold, Mr. Bailey had a fire going in every fireplace in the farmhouse. Ellen quickly crossed the room ahead of her husband and pulled back the covers. He gently placed Rachel down on the large feather bed. Both husband and wife held their breath as they looked at her. For a moment, they thought she was dead. She was so still. But a moan escaped her lips. Her face and hands were bluish from the attack of the blizzard. Elias and Ellen looked at each other. *How long had she been out in the cold?* they wondered.

Jonathan had quietly stepped into the room. He saw the worried look on his parents' faces and felt awash with guilt. *Why didn't I check the first time I went out? I could've saved her. It looks like it might just be too late.*

A small murmur escaped Rachel's lips. Jonathan went weak with relief again. His eyes watered over. *Thank you, God,* he said silently. He glanced at his parents again. They looked very worried. Jonathan's heart started to pound in his chest. "Is she…is she gonna be all right?" Jonathan asked. Ellen shooed her son and husband out of the bedroom. When the door was closed, she walked over to the bed and started to peel away the wet cloak and clothing from Rachel. She was so small and thin that her ribs stuck out from lack of proper nourishment. Ellen let out a sad sigh and slowly shook her head in pity for the child. She didn't know if it was too late or not.

Chapter Four

The miserable blizzard of 1908 didn't give up for the next two days and nights. With unrelenting fury, it attacked the mountain region of Blue Knob and its people. Many farmers who didn't take heed of the early warning of the storm failed to bring their animals back into their barns early enough. They lost much of their livestock in the blizzard. Unfortunately, a few farmers were found frozen to death as well.

Rachel was still in her own unconscious world, unaware of all that was happening around her as a high fever took over. She shook uncontrollably under the bedcovers. The battle of bringing her temperature down seemed almost hopeless. Ellen Bailey stayed by her side almost constantly, wiping her fevered brow with a cloth dipped in cold water. She worried that Rachel might not make it. But Ellen also believed that the most powerful weapon in any battle was spiritual, praise-filled prayer, which she wielded mightily. She sang hymns. She held Rachel's little hands. She talked to Rachel of the future God had for her. She had no idea if Rachel could hear her or not, but she had to try.

Rachel would cry out in her sleep for her mother and sisters. The blizzard had kept Jonathan from traveling across their fields to Rachel's home to let Rachel's parents know she was with his family. *They must be in a panic,* he thought worriedly. This also made him feel guilty. *What if Rachel died?* he asked himself. *What would I say to her family, knowing I should've paid heed to my first instinct when I saw the dark cloth in the snow?*

Jonathan stayed by Rachel's bedside as much as he could, helping his mother take care of her. Ellen's back ached from bending forward to wipe Rachel's brow. Her head was throbbing from lack of sleep. She was beyond the point of fatigue, but still, Rachel's needs were so great that these aches and pains of her own were a shadow.

Jonathan prayed along with his mother as they kept their vigil through the night. Rachel was so delicate and weak that each time he looked at her small, malnourished frame, he didn't think she would make it. So he prayed harder. And his mother kept praying and talking to Rachel. On the third day of their vigil, Rachel opened her eyes for the first time to find herself looking up at the ceiling, confused and disoriented. Jonathan was sitting on the rocking chair beside the bed, watching Rachel carefully. His mother had gone downstairs to fetch more water and drink a cup of coffee. Jonathan stopped rocking and stood up. She was awake. He closed his eyes for a moment. *Thank you, Lord. Thank you for bringing her back.*

Rachel heard his movement and turned her head slightly at the sound. The first person Rachel saw was Jonathan. Her vision was a little blurred at first, but as it cleared, she found herself looking into the softest, kindest eyes she'd ever seen. Jonathan's eyes were a warm brown with flecks of gold. She smiled softly at him. Jonathan smiled back. The relief that went through Jonathan almost made his knees buckle. Jonathan felt so thankful he wanted to cry.

She's going to be all right. Jonathan lifted his head up in silent praise. *Thank you, Lord,* Jonathan spoke in his heart. Overcome with gratitude that she would be all right, Jonathan looked down again at Rachel.

Something he'd never felt before stirred deep in his heart. Jonathan couldn't understand what this feeling was. *Thankfulness certainly,* he thought. But there was something else. It felt like a promise, a hope for the future. Of what, Jonathan didn't know. One thing was for certain. Rachel needed someone to look out for her. Jonathan looked down at Rachel again. She had closed her eyes and would sleep for another day.

The second time Rachel awoke, Jonathan's mother was watching over her. Ellen was rocking slowly in her rocking chair, humming a tune from a hymn book. Rachel couldn't remember which song it was, only that she'd heard it before when she and her family went to church, which wasn't too often.

Ellen Bailey had the same kind eyes as Jonathan. Rachel remembered who they were. This family was in church on Sundays. Rachel would see them whenever her stepfather was sober and wanted to put on a good appearance for his family. Rachel's brows knit together as she tried to remember their names. It took a few moments, but the name came to her.

The Bailey family, she thought. *But what am I doing here?* The Baileys always seemed so happy when Rachel saw them in church on Sundays; not like her family, where Jack put on an act, expecting his family to do the same. Jack wanted everyone in church to believe that he and his family were good, faithful people of the Word. It was the only time he was ever sober. It was also the only time that he seemed to treat Julianna with respect. At first, even Julianna was fooled. He would gently place his hand on her back as he escorted her down the aisle to their pew. Jack acted the perfect gentleman, allowing his wife and children to enter the pew ahead of him. He would sing the loudest from his hymn book. His "amens" were clear and loud enough for all in attendance to hear. Jack Walters wanted to make darn good and sure everyone knew he was a good man with a good family. The Walters' good name still meant something in this community too, and it had to stay that way. Mostly, however, Jack just couldn't wait for church to be done with so he could start hitting the bottle again.

Mrs. Nettle always made sure to sit in the pew directly behind his family. She'd sneak looks at Jack over the top of her hymn book. Her dark eyes would shoot daggers at Julianna and her girls. *Such a waste,* she thought. *Whatever made Jack think to marry this woman? No wonder he took to drinking.*

Mrs. Nettle would give them a once-over, taking inventory of Julianna and all the reasons she was so wrong for Jack. First, Julianna was just too thin, her skin too pale. And those hands; rough and red, they were completely awful. No real lady would ever allow her hands to look like that.

After her assessment of Julianna, Mrs. Nettle would continue on with Rachel. She hated Rachel. *This one,* she thought as her brows knitted together angrily, *will turn out just like her mother. This one…* Her thoughts were interrupted by the off-key sound of the church organ, which irritated Mrs. Nettle further. *Why could they not have found someone who knew how to actually play that stupid organ?* she asked herself. Her thoughts returned to what should be done with Rachel.

Rachel would feel Mrs. Nettle's eyes on her. She could feel the hatred pouring out of this woman and wondered why Mrs. Nettle always had to sit behind them.

One Sunday when Rachel's family was in church, Rachel turned in her pew to watch the Bailey family walking down the aisle. She caught Jonathan's eyes for just a moment. He smiled at her. Mrs. Bailey smiled too. Rachel looked down at her hands. She was so embarrassed to be caught watching the Baileys. But he did smile at her. He didn't hate her like Mrs. Nettle hated her.

The Baileys were genuinely nice, kind, good people. Rachel would continue to sneak looks at them every time she was in church. The Baileys would sit in their pew across the aisle from Rachel's family. As she watched them—mother, father, and son—Rachel would feel such an ache in her heart, a loss for something she never had; but she didn't know what it was. The feelings couldn't be put into words.

Mrs. Bailey always looked so nice. She wore pretty dresses that were modest but flattering and feminine, using her own skills as a seamstress to create the style right for her. Her soft, brown hair was always swept up off her neck in a flattering twist, with little wisps of hair framing her face. On her head she wore stylish, wide-brimmed hats that seemed to match beautifully each outfit she wore.

Rachel would then cast a sidelong glance at her own mother. She wondered why her mother no longer looked pretty like Mrs. Bailey. Rachel had seen photographs of her mother as a very young woman. Julianna had been more than pretty; she had been beautiful, with a full head of auburn hair and merry green eyes that smiled at the camera. The smattering of freckles across her nose made her look positively charming. Although the photographs were in black and white, it did nothing to deter her beauty or the genuine happiness that came through. The woman sitting next to Rachel in church looked nothing like the woman in those photographs. It wasn't Julianna's beauty alone either. It was the joy that seemed to bubble out of her eyes as she looked into the lens of the camera. Rachel never saw that person in the mother she and her sisters knew. Rachel saw a sad woman who seemed to be lost from them.

These thoughts all played in her mind as Rachel took a closer look around the room she was in. She lifted herself up on her elbows. Her neck felt very stiff as she moved her head side to side. The room was plain and simple, with scrubbed, wide-plank floors. There was a colorful, woven rug of green, blue, brown, and yellow near the bed. The bed itself was a large four-poster with a feather mattress. The patchwork quilt covering the bed was well made by the hands that put it together. It felt warm and soft and smelled delightful. Rachel tried to place the delightful smell and realized the quilt must've been rinsed in lavender water. There was a feather pillow behind her head. Rachel had never slept on a pillow before. It felt wonderful. She wanted to sink down into it and not come up.

Rachel never had a bed to herself either. She, Maggie, and Jennie had to sleep in the same bed. Jennie was always placed in the middle for protection from the cold of the harsh winters. The body heat of her two older sisters would help keep her warm. For Rachel, it felt very strange to be alone in a bed, in a room she didn't recognize, in the home of people she barely knew.

And why am I here? What happened to me? Rachel looked down at herself and saw that her clothes had been replaced.

She was wearing one of Mrs. Bailey's nightgowns, too large for Rachel, but comfortable and clean with the same scent of lavender. Rachel's cheeks blushed pink with embarrassment, knowing that Mrs. Bailey had to remove her clothes first.

Mrs. Bailey stood. Turning, she reached for the water pitcher on the stand beside the bed and poured water from the pitcher into the cup. She bent forward and held the cup to Rachel's lips. Rachel felt very thirsty. Instinct made her grab for the cup. With shaky hands and the help of Mrs. Bailey, she gulped most of the water down. Mrs. Bailey poured another cup and gave it to Rachel.

"Slowly this time, Rachel," she said.

Rachel did as she was told and then dropped her head back onto the pillow. She felt exhausted and worried about her sisters. "My sisters, Maggie and Jennie. Where are they?"

"Jonathan will be going over to your home later to let your family know you're all right. We thought we lost you for awhile there. What were you doing out in that snowstorm, child?" Mrs. Bailey asked gently.

Rachel looked away from her kind, questioning eyes. She didn't know how to answer. She felt so weak and tired. *It won't do any good to tell Mrs. Bailey what happened,* Rachel thought.

She'd never understand why Rachel had to leave the Nettle home in the middle of a snowstorm. And Rachel's mother told her once to never speak ill of anyone, especially Mrs. Nettle. She spoke to Rachel with such conviction that Rachel knew to take heed and listen to her. Her mother rarely spoke as it was, so Rachel knew that what was said to her was very important. Mrs. Nettle could and had made life more than miserable for many people in their mountain community. She seemed to take special delight in looking down on those less fortunate than herself, flaunting her wealth, fine clothing, and beautiful home. Many people on the mountain held hopes that one day Mrs. Nettle would get her just desserts for all the harm she'd done. They hoped they would get to see it. But they also saw that even though Mrs. Nettle had all that money, it didn't buy her peace of mind or happiness. She was truly the most miserable person imaginable.

Rachel's thoughts were thankfully interrupted by the knock on the bedroom door, saving her from having to answer Mrs. Bailey's question.

"I'll be right back, Rachel," Mrs. Bailey promised as she patted Rachel's shoulder lightly before turning to walk across the room, the heels of her shoes tapping lightly on the wide-plank floor. She opened the bedroom door to find Jonathan holding a tray of steaming chicken soup, buttered bread, and hot tea with plenty of sugar.

Jonathan smiled at her. "Just a feeling I had. That's all." Jonathan looked past his mother's shoulder at Rachel and smiled. "So you're awake. You know, Rachel, you gave us quite a scare."

Jonathan talked lightly, but inside, he'd been worried sick. He couldn't get the image of pulling Rachel's little form out of the snowdrift from his mind. The guilt he carried that he might not have reached her in time that night haunted him still, even though he could see she was going to be all right. Jonathan crossed the room to Rachel's bedside. Rachel sat up to get out of bed, but Mrs. Bailey walked back across the room and gently placed her hand on Rachel's shoulder.

"Stay put, Rachel," she told the girl as she fluffed the pillows and then placed them behind Rachel's back again.

Rachel felt acutely embarrassed that Mrs. Bailey and her son, Jonathan, were treating her so well. She still didn't know how she got there. She had never had a meal in bed either, even when she was sick. At home, it was expected that Rachel would still do the chores and take care of her sisters whether she was sick or not. Rachel never knew that people could eat in bed. It felt very strange indeed.

"Jonathan, will you stay with Rachel for awhile? There are things I must attend to downstairs," Mrs. Bailey asked her son.

Jonathan nodded. He didn't know how his mother did it. She never seemed to slow down. She once told him that every day was a gift from God. It shouldn't be squandered but cherished, since each day could be the last one. At the time, Jonathan smiled at her way of thinking, not taking what she said too seriously. *After all, I'm a young man. I have plenty of time,* he thought. But looking at Rachel, being in this room with her, and knowing the close call she'd had, Jonathan understood what his mother was trying to teach him. What would have happened to Rachel if he'd squandered his time, if he'd decided to forget about what he saw and instead stayed home for a hot meal and the warmth of the fireplace as the storm raged on? How would he have felt then? He looked at Rachel and felt the same overwhelming guilt wash over him again.

Jonathan leaned forward and gently placed the tray of hot food on Rachel's lap. The aroma of chicken soup was heavenly as it reached her nostrils, and she suddenly felt very hungry. As he was leaning forward, Rachel studied him. Jonathan had soft, brown hair that curled slightly around his ears. He was tall and lanky for his age. When he placed the tray on her lap, he moved in such a gentle, caring manner. Rachel had the faint memory of someone warm and strong holding her closely to him. She couldn't ever remember being held with such care. Rachel realized without being told that Jonathan was the one who rescued her and brought her here. After making sure the tray was balanced on her lap, Rachel looked up at him again. He looked down at her. Rachel had the same feeling she had the night she was rescued. She tried to put a word to her feeling.

I feel…safe. That's what it is, she thought. *Jonathan makes me feel safe.*

Jonathan turned and pulled the rocking chair closer to the bed so he would be facing her and sat down.

The aroma of hot chicken noodle soup suddenly made Rachel's mouth water. Picking up the spoon on the tray, she dipped it into the bowl. She tried not to eat too fast, but she was so hungry. Jonathan slowly rocked in the rocking chair and watched her. Rachel looked lost in one of his mother's nightgowns. The sleeves rolled up several times over, showing little hands rough and worn and arms that were too thin from lack of food. Her hands were trembling from fatigue and hunger, making some of the soup drip from the spoon. Jonathan's heart lurched in empathy toward this little girl who had to grow up too soon.

Jonathan leaned forward to help her. "Here. Let me, Rachel." He spoke softly as he gently took the spoon from her hand, dipped it in the soup, and started to feed her. To Rachel, this was most embarrassing too. But from the sound of his voice, she knew he cared. And she was very hungry. Jonathan tried to hold back a smile. Rachel had the soup off the spoon when it was barely to her mouth. She ate every bite and then sat back on her pillows. The trembling had stopped, and she suddenly felt very sleepy again. She nodded off without realizing it.

Jonathan carefully and quietly removed the tray from Rachel's lap so he wouldn't wake her. She was so delicate he was amazed she'd survived. Yet, he knew in his heart why she did. God had answered their prayers.

He saw Rachel and her family at church sometimes on Sundays, although not every Sunday. Jonathan didn't know why. Her family never talked with anyone, including his family, either before the service or afterward. The one thing Jonathan remembered clearly was that Jack Walters certainly was loud enough while he was there. Jack sang off-key, causing church members around him to shudder as they steeled themselves against his scratching voice, which would become even worse when he sang the higher notes of the hymns. And during the sermons, Jack would thump his Bible as he loudly called out, "Amen." Jonathan didn't know what the circumstances in Rachel's young life were, but he had the feeling that Rachel needed a friend. They were both still children, although he was twelve and Rachel was eight years old.

But there is something very special about Rachel, Jonathan thought. Jonathan decided from that moment on that he would be Rachel's friend. Jonathan would make sure Rachel had someone to depend on. Judging by how thin she was, he would make darn good and sure she never went hungry again.

Chapter Five

Rachel was no longer alone. She had an ally in her new friend, Jonathan Bailey, and his parents. While her life at home was no better, and certainly working for Mrs. Nettle was just as difficult, it was more tolerable just knowing she had a friend in Jonathan.

When word got back to Mrs. Nettle about what happened to Rachel in the blizzard, she showed no concern or sympathy whatsoever. Her only concern was for herself and how it would make her look. She wasn't about to have anyone thinking she had almost caused Rachel's demise. Mrs. Nettle gave much thought to how she could turn this problem around to her benefit while making herself look good at the same time. The third Sunday following the blizzard, when all the snow had finally melted and spring began its official entrance, the town folk could once again move freely about. The church was full that Sunday, all except for the Walters family.

Rachel had planned to take her sisters to church by herself, but their mother was sick in bed again. Jack had decided to start his drinking a little early and wandered off to who only knew where. Rachel was disappointed. She wanted so much to go to church. And she would've made sure to steer clear of Mrs. Nettle. Maybe the Baileys would've allowed her and her sisters to sit with them. But it was not to be.

But Mrs. Nettle made sure she was in church that Sunday. Mrs. Nettle informed everyone after the church services that she had insisted Rachel go home early. Her voice sounded full of concern and regret. "I told her, 'Rachel, the weather is becoming much worse. I insist you leave early today'." Mrs. Nettle was emphatic as she continued. "Do you think she would listen?" she asked as her voice started to rise. "I told her that a spotless house was not as important as her safety. I told her to go home." This last part of Mrs. Nettle's sentence was said tearfully, although no one could see any actual tears in her eyes. She dabbed at them with an elegant, expensive-looking handkerchief with a large, monogrammed golden *N* in the corner. Only the Baileys saw the look of sheer hatred pouring from Mrs. Nettle's eyes. The look she gave the Baileys dared them to refute her words.

No one would've argued with Mrs. Nettle, however. It wouldn't have done any good anyway. Some of the church members shook their heads in disbelief and walked away disgustedly. Many of the ladies, none of whom liked Mrs. Nettle, rolled their eyes. As they followed their husbands out of the church, they whispered to one another so Mrs. Nettle wouldn't hear.

"Do you think maybe there's some truth in what Mrs. Nettle said?" one of the younger women asked.

Another woman, much older, thought about it before answering. *I might have lost my looks,* she thought, *but praise God I didn't lose my sense of humor.* She answered back loudly as they exited the church, "If there is, it would be the first time ever on this mountain."

The burst of laughter from all who heard her answer reached Mrs. Nettle's ears. Her hollow, sinking cheeks were mottled red in rage at being made fun of. *How dare they?* she thought to herself. *This is all Rachel's fault.* Mrs. Nettle thought for a moment before a malicious smile crossed her thin tight lips. *Yes,* she thought. *I'll make Rachel pay for this.* Her thoughts brought a strange sense of satisfaction. Mrs. Nettle felt oddly comfortable in her hatred of Rachel. With these thoughts in mind, she walked down the aisle to exit the church, planning her strategy.

There was still much speculation and gossip concerning the circumstances in the weeks following the blizzard, especially when Cook was overheard at the general store a few days after Mrs. Nettle's ridiculous story at church. Cook told all who were there about how poor Rachel would've died if that nice young man, Jonathan Bailey, hadn't found her. "Mrs. Nettle don't care any that Rachel could've died."

Cook was so angry about Mrs. Nettle's treatment of Rachel that she spent the next two weeks' food allowance money allotted by Mrs. Nettle. Cook bought extras at the butcher's and general store and then lied to Mrs. Nettle, saying the cost for everything she was wanting was more expensive, "'Cause of the blizzard, ya know," and therefore had no money left to return to Mrs. Nettle. "And I'll probably be needin' more for the things on yer list." Cook kept a straight face as she spoke to her employer; but inside, she couldn't help the feeling of triumph for making Mrs. Nettle pay for the problems she had caused for Rachel.

Cook would secretly hide the extra items she bought from the general store with Mrs. Nettle's money. The corner cupboard in the kitchen was a perfect place, as Cook could hide items behind stacks of plates, cups, and saucers. It was, that is, until Mrs. Nettle went snooping one day. Cook, Rachel, and Finney, the horse groom, were taking their brief afternoon tea together in the kitchen that day. The short time from their busyness of work for a cup of freshly steeped tea and bread with homemade jam was something they all three looked forward to. Cook had started this tradition too, after what Mrs. Nettle had done to Rachel.

Mrs. Nettle was usually napping about this time and had no idea her employees were now giving themselves a break of afternoon tea. But Mrs. Nettle was restless that afternoon and had decided to go riding instead. After donning her gray velvet riding habit, she made her way down the stairs and out the side door that led to the stables. When she couldn't find Finney, she stomped back to the house like a spoiled child to ask Cook if she knew where he was. Furious with the discovery of her employees being paid by her while they lolled about, enjoying their tea instead of doing their jobs, she lowered her voice to a menacing tone. "Let's just see what else you're hiding from me."

All three steeled themselves as Mrs. Nettle went through almost every cupboard and closet. The corner cupboard where food and other items for Rachel had been hidden was the only one left. Cook, Rachel, and Finney held their breath, praying Mrs. Nettle wouldn't look in the last cupboard, but she did. Time seemed to stand still as she victoriously made her discovery of flour, dried beans, canned goods, and baked bread. In a rage, Mrs. Nettle smashed every plate, cup, saucer, and bowl on the kitchen floor, demanding to know why the food was hidden behind the plates to begin with. Cook, Finney, and Rachel went about, sweeping up the mess, as Cook thought of an explanation. She stopped her broom for a moment and gave Mrs. Nettle what she hoped was an innocent look.

"Ah, Mrs. Nettle, I completely fergot about them extras from before the blizzard. Must be getting too old ta remember certain things. My mind must be goin.'"

Mrs. Nettle shook with anger at Cook's answer. The bread looked freshly baked, not three weeks old. *But, yes,* Mrs. Nettle thought, *Cook is getting older. Her hair is completely gray, and her face does indeed, have more lines. But she's still sharp as a tack!* Mrs. Nettle knew Cook was lying. She also knew she couldn't do anything about this. Perhaps she was wrong. Feeling helpless to argue with her employee, Mrs. Nettle turned on her heel and walked haughtily out of the kitchen and up the stairs to her bedroom.

From that day forward, Cook and Finney conspired to hide the extra food and other items in the stable behind some bales of hay. They gave Rachel a little at a time for her to take home with her. *Someone has to look out for that little girl,* Cook thought. The butcher and general store owners certainly weren't about to say anything about the extras Cook bought either. Mrs. Nettle had built up a tab in the past and never did pay for it in full. Time they got their money back, they thought. It was a perfect plan.

Cook was happy and relieved to see that Rachel had a new friend in Jonathan. He would meet Rachel and walk with her across his family's field either to or from the Nettle property. He never let her walk home alone. *Jonathan Bailey,* Cook thought, *is becoming Rachel's very own guardian angel. And he comes from such a nice, Christian family too,* she thought as she went about her work one day.

Although the Baileys also heard Mrs. Nettle's version at church that Sunday of what happened the night Rachel almost died, they did not pass judgment on her. Mrs. Nettle had lied to the whole church, they knew, but the judgment was up to God, not them.

Chapter Six

While the ground was left soggy from the too-quickly melting snow and ice of the blizzard, Blue Knob was spared the flooding that occurred in the towns farther down the mountain as the creeks and rivers overflowed.

Jonathan and Rachel were carefully making their way across the wet field, avoiding as many of the soggier spots as they could. The sun was lower but still shining in the late afternoon sky, giving a luminous glow to the yellow of the daffodils as they moved gently in the breeze. Spring on the mountains of Pennsylvania was indeed a beautiful sight to behold. The scent of the fresh, clean mountain air put a little bounce in one's step as the feeling of spring fever took over. Jonathan and Rachel were enjoying the warmth of the sun on their backs as they walked along. Jonathan was walking Rachel home from work. These were becoming times that Jonathan looked forward to each morning and evening, even if it meant he would have to fit in his own chores at different times. For Rachel, the comfort of having someone look out for her like Jonathan did felt very odd at first. But within a few days, Rachel realized that the emptiness and loneliness that she normally felt were gone. Jonathan was her friend. The night of the blizzard had changed everything. She still couldn't remember any details of the blizzard, only leaving to go home that night and then waking up at the Baileys.' When she shared this with Jonathan, he called it a blessing. "Best to forget," he said.

Rachel didn't realize he was telling this to himself as well. When they first started walking together, Jonathan tried to shorten the stride of his long legs so Rachel wouldn't have trouble keeping up with him. They would talk the whole time, never seeming to run out of things to say. Jonathan would talk about work on the farm, the care of the animals, and new crops for the summer. Rachel would share her day's events with Jonathan. But she would never share the bad things that happened in the Nettle home. Rachel never said anything bad about Mrs. Nettle either. Instead, she always found something funny or uplifting to tell him. He found out that her favorite day was baking day. Baking day never felt like a chore to Rachel but something to look forward to.

"See that, Rachel?" Jonathan said. "Baking day is my favorite day too, but obviously for different reasons." Jonathan was looking down at Rachel as she walked beside him. She was smiling up at him. Actually, she was grinning as if she had her own personal joke. "Did you even hear what I said?" Jonathan asked. They stopped for a moment and faced each other. *Why is she grinning?*

"Race you to end of the fence," Rachel said suddenly.

What? She's challenging me to a race? Jonathan started laughing. "I can't race you. You're a girl."

"So what? Are you afraid a *girl* will beat you?"

"Well, no. I just don't think—." Jonathan stopped talking when he heard the sound of snorting behind him. Jonathan and Rachel both turned around to see the Baileys' large black bull facing them. *How did the bull get out of his pen?* Jonathan wondered. This wasn't the first time it had happened. The bull was very temperamental. It was also snorting at Jonathan and Rachel as its large, muscular body lumbered toward them, picking up speed. Uh-oh. Jonathan knew they were in trouble. "Rachel, they say you shouldn't be in back of a horse or in front of a bull. Run!" Jonathan shouted this last part.

Both Jonathan and Rachel sprinted to get away, with the bull following closely behind them, his hooves thundering as they hit the ground so hard they could both feel it. "Run, Rachel! Run!" Jonathan shouted again. Rachel reached the fence line only moments before Jonathan. Quickly climbing up and over, they clumsily dropped to the other side, into the soggy grass. The bull ran past them outside the fence line, snorting in frustration as he made a half circle and headed back toward the farm, slowing down to a trot and still snorting at them as he went past.

Jonathan and Rachel were on their knees, peering out at the bull from inside the fence. They were both out of breath from their sprint to outrun the bull. Rachel plopped down on the soggy ground, not caring that her dress was getting wet. She started laughing. Jonathan looked at Rachel as if she'd lost her senses. "I was afraid you would get hurt. And you're laughing?" Jonathan asked incredulously. Rachel looked at him. His question only made her laugh harder. *Doesn't she realize that she could have been hurt or even killed?* Jonathan opened his mouth to speak again. He wanted to tell her the seriousness of their situation. He wanted to tell her very sternly that the bull could've killed them both. But Rachel's laugh was contagious. And the more Jonathan thought about how she beat him in the race, he started laughing too. In between gulps of air, Jonathan said, "Rachel, you should've seen yourself. I swear your feet were up over your ears trying to get away."

His remark made them collapse into hysterical laughter. They laughed until their sides hurt. When their laughter finally became giggles, Jonathan said, "Well, Rachel, I guess you proved yourself. From now on, it looks like I'll have to keep up with you instead. Let's go." Jonathan stood up and reached out to help Rachel up.

"So, Rachel," Jonathan began after they climbed back over the fence, brushed themselves off, and continued on their way, "what is your next favorite thing besides baking day?"

Rachel smiled as she looked up at him. "Why, outrunning bulls of course."

Jonathan grinned back. "All right, besides baking day and outrunning bulls, what is your favorite thing?"

Rachel answered, "I love to grow things, like flowers and vegetables. And I especially love to grow herbs. Cook showed me how to do it. Did you know you can make tea from herbs like peppermint and spearmint?" Rachel didn't wait for an answer but kept talking excitedly about herbs and their many uses. Jonathan listened intently as they continued their walk.

As they rounded the bend and neared her home, Rachel became very quiet. She looked very serious and very sad. Jonathan noticed this look in her eyes every time they drew closer to the Walters' home. Rachel would stop on the path leading to the front yard. She would never let Jonathan walk any farther with her but would say lightly, "Well, we're here. Thank you for walking me home. I'll see you tomorrow." Rachel's last statement always sounded like a question. It seemed to Jonathan that Rachel wasn't sure if he would want to come back. Jonathan smiled gently at Rachel. "I'll be here first thing in the morning, Rachel," he would say as he turned to walk home, waving goodbye.

Rachel was worried every time she went home because she never knew what to expect. Her stomach hurt. She'd be so ashamed if Jonathan knew the truth about her family. *If Jonathan knew, he wouldn't want to be my friend anymore,* she thought. Rachel remained standing where she was, waiting for Jonathan's usual answer as he walked away. *What would he think?* she wondered.

But Jonathan already knew. "Come on, Rachel. Let me walk you the rest of the way." His tone was caring, soft, and kind. As they drew closer to her house, they stopped for a moment. This was the second time Jonathan saw Rachel's home. The first time was after the blizzard, when he and his Appaloosa, Victor, crossed the snow-drifted field to let Rachel's family know she was at his house. Much of the snow had covered the sad-looking sight that stood before him.

Jonathan worked with his hands and learned to build from his father. He knew good workmanship when he saw it. *But how uncared for it looks,* he thought. Whistling softly under his breath, Jonathan looked up at what must have once been an elegant Victorian home. In Jonathan's eyes, the home seemed saddened by its own neglect, aged before its time, and calling out in desperate need to be taken care of again.

The wide steps leading up to the once-stylish wraparound porch were rotted and broken through. The porch floor itself also had strips of wood rotting through. Even from where Jonathan stood, he could see gaping holes large enough that a small child could fall through and be badly hurt. The posts supporting the porch roof were splitting, with one post completely rotted through. The porch roof sagged dangerously low, especially on one side. Jonathan was surprised it hadn't collapsed during the blizzard. Most of the paint on the porch and the house itself was peeling and, in many places, down to bare wood. Empty whiskey bottles were strewn about, many of them broken as they were carelessly tossed aside. Jonathan had no doubt who those bottles belonged to. He clenched his fists in anger as disgust rose up in his chest. *Poor Rachel and her sisters,* he thought as sadness and concern came over him.

That same sad neglect of the house was also showing in Rachel, although she did her best to hide it. Her clothing was too large for her and frayed from repeated mending in the same places. Her worn boots had holes in the soles. Jonathan knew her feet must've been horribly cold in the blizzard. His heart ached for Rachel as he stood next to her. Jonathan would be very happy when Rachel was all grown up. Rachel would no longer be neglected. She wouldn't have to live this way anymore. Jonathan's thoughts were interrupted as a slight movement caught his eye. He turned his attention to the distraction.

Rachel's little sisters were standing at the open front door. They showed the same neglect as Rachel. Their long hair was tangled and uncombed. Maggie and Jennie stood quietly, watching Rachel and Jonathan. Their feet were bare and dirty. *Where are their shoes?* Jonathan wondered.

Maggie and Jennie were wearing ragged dresses, also dirty, that were too big for them. Rachel, Maggie, and Jennie were still far too thin. Jonathan looked on in disbelief. He felt such an ache in his heart for them that his eyes began to fill. He fought back the hot tears and swallowed hard. His heart felt as if it would break when he saw how they were suffering. *How can this happen?* Jonathan wondered. *It's appalling.*

Rachel tried very hard to take care of Maggie and Jennie. She tried also to take care of her mother, who couldn't seem to cope anymore. But there was no one in her family, it seemed, to care for Rachel. Who did she have? His family took care of Rachel when he found her in the snowdrift the night of the blizzard and the immediate days following. Jonathan shuddered to think of how Maggie and Jennie must also have suffered during that same time. And it wasn't only her home life. Rachel had to go to work every day to help out. Why did no one care?

I care, Jonathan thought, *and so do my parents*. He had heard in town at the general store, through Cook, what was happening at the Nettle home and how Rachel was being treated. No wonder Rachel looked so beaten down at first when she left the Nettles' after work each day. Rachel looked up at Jonathan, embarrassed. *Maybe he won't want to be my friend anymore.* Depressing thoughts flooded Rachel's mind at how Mrs. Nettle treated her since she came back to work and of her life at home.

Mrs. Nettle no longer bothered to talk to Rachel or even acknowledge when Rachel was in her home. With her dark eyes staring straight ahead, she'd walk past Rachel as if she were invisible. *This will be Rachel's punishment*, Mrs. Nettle thought, *for ruining my reputation*.

Rachel felt so guilty each time Mrs. Nettle walked past her, as if she'd done something terribly wrong to deserve this new treatment. Rachel felt as if she didn't exist. So she tried extra hard to do a good job, but it was met with no acknowledgement.

Cook was furious with this backhanded form of punishment to a child, of all things. But Cook had her own way of dealing with Mrs. Nettle. She could cause problems too, and Mrs. Nettle would never know it was intentional either.

"I'm so sorry, Mrs. Nettle. The soup just didn't wanta turn out right tonight. And the bread just doesn't seem ta be bakin' up properly neither. Somethin's wrong with the stove, I think."

This resulted in Mrs. Nettle having to part with her money and buy a new stove for Cook. Cook grinned from ear to ear the day her new Happy Chef stove was delivered to the house.

No need for Mrs. Nettle to know the old stove worked just fine. And this new stove was white and light blue, not black like the old one. Cook also continued insisting that the prices at the general store and butcher's were increasing. And she continued to sneak food to Rachel every day. Between Cook and Finney, Rachel would leave with enough to feed her and her sisters, sometimes even more. But it was done in such a way that Mrs. Nettle never knew. Mrs. Nettle would watch from her bedroom window when Rachel left each day. It seemed odd to her that Rachel would have to go to the stables before leaving for her home. Jonathan never said a word about how full Rachel's satchel looked when she came out of the stables. He had a feeling that Cook and Finney were also helping Rachel, and for this he was very grateful.

Whatever Rachel was given she always shared with Maggie and Jennie. One day after Jonathan dropped Rachel off, she walked into her home only to discover that her stepfather had been drinking again. Usually, he didn't show up until later in the evening, but for some strange reason, he was already home. He noticed that Rachel was carrying a satchel held tightly to her chest. Maggie and Jennie had also been waiting and ran to Rachel as soon as they saw her. They huddled as close as they could to their sister while little Jennie hid her face in the folds of Rachel's worn dress.

Jack stepped toward Rachel before she had time to react and snatched the satchel out of her arms. "It's mine!" Rachel shouted at him as she tried to get the satchel back.

It was as if Jack never heard her. "Les see what ya got here, Rachel," he said drunkenly. Clumsily, he opened the satchel to discover what Rachel was hiding. He reached in and emptied out the satchel. Rachel, Maggie, and Jennie stood, watching helplessly, as Jack ate the entire loaf of bread in front of them. With malicious, drunken pleasure, he tore off chunk after chunk, stuffing the bread into his mouth and chewing loudly before swallowing until it was all gone. Maggie and Jennie started to cry. They hadn't eaten since the day before. Rachel gritted her teeth in anger and frustration. Jack wasn't supposed to be home. She knew better than to show it, but her anger and hatred of him grew deeper every day. She also knew that if she said anything, it would make matters much worse for her and her sisters. Jack had taken a strap more than once to their backs, beating them past the point of black and blue.

From that moment on, Rachel quietly hid any food Cook and Finney gave her under the porch of their home until she knew Jack was asleep. She would tiptoe down the stairs, carefully open the front door, cross the porch and go down the steps. She'd then bend down and reach for the satchel under the porch, carry it inside and sneak it down to the cellar. After this, Rachel would tiptoe upstairs and wake her sisters. Holding her index finger to her lips to let them know not to talk, they would all quietly ease down through the house to the basement. There, Rachel felt they were safe. There, she made sure Maggie and Jennie were fed. They were so thin and hungry all the time that it hurt deeply that she couldn't do more. Many times, Rachel had to turn her head away as tears filled her eyes. When her sisters were done, she would take them back to bed and wait 'till they fell asleep. Then she would sneak down to the basement again to gather whatever was left to give her mother the following morning. Despite having to care for her mother, who, at times, didn't even seem to recognize Rachel anymore, Rachel still loved her. And she loved her sisters too much to ever let them go hungry if she could help it. She vowed she would always care for them, that they'd know she loved them. Maggie was five years old and Jennie only three, so how could they possibly understand why their lives were the way they were? Maggie and Jennie depended on Rachel for everything and would go to her for hugs and warmth. To them, Rachel was their mother. They didn't know or understand why their real mommy was always in bed. Rachel, Maggie, and Jennie lived each day as it came, waiting, always waiting for the day when things would get better for them. Rachel felt beaten down many times in her young life, but this was the first time Rachel felt real hatred well up in her chest. But she knew if she said anything her stepfather would beat her with his belt and perhaps beat her little sisters too. So Rachel remained quiet, counting the days 'till she would be gone from this miserable place. She'd take Maggie and Jennie with her too.

Rachel shook the sad thoughts from her mind and turned to look up at her ally, Jonathan. She drew comfort from the understanding look he gave her as he squeezed her hand in reassurance. "I'll see you tomorrow, Rachel," he said softly.

Rachel nodded and watched as he walked away. When he was out of sight, Rachel tucked her satchel under the porch. Standing up again, she walked up the porch steps and across the porch to Maggie and Jennie, who were still waiting quietly at the door. Rachel knelt down and pulled her sisters close to her.

"I mith you, Rachel," Jennie said. Maggie placed her head on Rachel's shoulder and sighed. They clung to her for several minutes. Rachel listened. It was very quiet. Jack didn't seem to be around anywhere. Rachel hoped he would stay away on his drunken binge overnight, perhaps even a few days, maybe forever she hoped.

Her sisters needed to be bathed and fed. Rachel stood up, taking one of their hands with each of hers. "Let's get you both cleaned up, all right?" Rachel said in a cheerful tone, although she felt far from it. *Yes,* she thought. *I'll heat up some water for their baths and then take them downstairs to eat. It'll be a good night for us if Jack stays away.*

Rachel checked on their mother while Maggie and Jennie were eating. Julianna was sleeping again, in a world of her own, one that seemed better than the life she had, one that Rachel didn't realize Julianna didn't want to come out of.

Chapter Seven

"Rachel. Rachel." Rachel slowly awoke from a deep sleep to hear her name being called repeatedly. In her dream, Mrs. Nettle, upset as usual over something, was calling for her, but Rachel was running away this time. *I won't answer her,* Rachel thought. *I won't!*

The voice was fading softly. "Rachel. Rachel." As the fog lifted from Rachel's dream, she sat up in bed. Confused, she could still hear her name being called. It took a moment to realize it was her mother calling out to her. Julianna's voice was a weak whisper as she called out again, "Rachel."

Rachel could see the first soft light of dawn coming through their bedroom window. Carefully, she slid out of bed while her sisters slept. Placing the thin, worn blanket back over them, she slipped quietly out of the room and padded down the hall to her mother's room. Rachel could hear Julianna's labored breathing even before she entered. It was a sound Rachel had never heard before. It sounded like a rattle. It sent a chill down Rachel's spine. Something was very wrong.

"Rachel," her mother called again.

Rachel's heart pounded in dread and fear as she slowly approached her mother's bed. *Doesn't Jack hear her too?* Rachel wondered. As Rachel moved closer, she saw with relief that Jack wasn't there. Rachel took the last few steps to her mother's side. Looking down at her mother's face, Rachel gasped. Julianna's eyes were glassy and glazed over. They didn't seem to focus on anything, including her daughter. Rachel placed her hand on her mother's forehead and pulled back quickly. Julianna was burning up with a high fever. Her mother had been sick before, but this was different. This wasn't something Rachel could help with. Instead, Rachel stroked her mother's forehead. Julianna needed a doctor right away, but Rachel couldn't leave her alone either. Julianna's breathing sounded more labored. In a panic, Rachel leaned down to speak.

"Mother, I need to go. I need to get the doctor."

Julianna reached her hand out and gripped Rachel's forearm. "No," Julianna said weakly.

For just one brief moment, Julianna's eyes cleared and looked directly into her daughter's eyes. Rachel looked back. The look Julianna gave her daughter this time was different, something Rachel had never seen before. She couldn't understand what it was, but a feeling of warmth enveloped Rachel's whole being. Julianna's voice was raspy as she tried to talk. She struggled to breathe with each word she so desperately wanted to say to Rachel. "I…have always…loved…you," Julianna whispered.

Rachel's eyes filled with tears as the words her mother had never spoken until this moment reached deep into her soul, words Rachel had never realized she needed so desperately to hear all of her young life. She opened her mouth to speak, to tell her mother she loved her too. Rachel's mother never heard her. The words, "I love you, Moth—," hung in midair, suspended for all eternity. Julianna was gone. In sudden shock and grief, Rachel dropped to her knees and placed her head over the silent heart of her mother. Sobbing, Rachel begged her mother not to go.

"Please. Not yet. Don't go. Don't leave us." She broke off, sobbing into the blanket that covered her mother's body. Rachel was too deep in her own grief at first to realize she wasn't alone. The sound of crying behind her caused her to turn. *Maggie and Jennie. I can't let them see me crying like this,* she thought. Turning her head away quickly, Rachel wiped her eyes with the edge of the blanket and turned around again to face her sisters.

Sleep was still in their eyes as they stood at the doorway of their mother's bedroom, watching Rachel. *Why does Rachel have her head on Mommy's chest?* Maggie and Jennie had never heard or seen their sister cry before. It frightened them. Rachel held out her arms as Maggie and Jennie ran to her. She held them closely while they cried on her shoulders. They didn't understand what happened. To Maggie and Jennie, their mother had always been a shadow in their life. She didn't seem to be their mother. Maggie and Jennie were crying for Rachel and clung to her. Rachel knew she had to be strong. She would have to be stronger than she ever was before. Taking a deep, shaky breath, she explained to both of them what happened. They lifted their heads from Rachel's shoulders to look at her.

"Our mommy died?" Jennie asked with wonder. She looked deeply into Rachel's eyes. "Did she go to heaven? Birds go to heaven, don't they?"

Rachel's eyes filled with tears again. Jennie was always so full of questions. Rachel loved her little sisters so much it hurt. She struggled to hold back the sobs and answered her youngest sister. "Yes. Yes, they do, Jennie. And Mommy went to see them. She went to be with them and God." Her voice caught at the end of her sentence, but it went unnoticed.

Maggie and Jennie seemed to be satisfied with her answer. Rachel didn't know what to do next. She was still in shock and disbelief. The ominous creaking sound of the front door opening downstairs sent shivers down Rachel's back. *Please, Lord, not this.*

Maggie and Jennie's eyes went wide with fear. They were terrified of their father. Rachel's heart filled with dread. Jack was thumping clumsily up the staircase, bumping heavily into the walls on either side. As he stopped at the top landing to catch his breath, he let out a loud belch. Rachel could feel disgust rising up in her throat. The girls steeled themselves for the inevitable as they heard him make his way down the hallway. He was coming closer.

Stopping at the entrance to the bedroom, he leaned heavily against the door jamb, taking in the sight of Rachel, Maggie, and Jennie. *What are they doing in here?* Through bleary eyes, he could see they'd been crying. In his confused, inebriated state, he couldn't remember whether he'd just beaten them or not. He looked down at his waist. Yup. He still had his belt on. But the only time he ever saw them cry was when he beat them. *Maybe I put my belt back on but don't remember,* he reasoned drunkenly. Looking past the girls, he could see his wife was still in bed. *Lazy. That's what she is,* he thought. *Just plain old lazy. Shoulda married someone better, even if she was ugly.* His body lurched forward with drunkenness as he took in the scene. The whiskey bottle he held in one hand was just about empty. "Wha's wrong with her?" he asked drunkenly as he pointed a dirty, crusted finger at his wife.

Rachel shuddered in disgust. Maggie and Jennie clung tightly to Rachel on either side, shaking in fear. Bad things always happened when their father was around. The disgust Rachel felt turned to anger, which turned into an even deeper hatred of this man. She hated him more with every passing day. Rachel wanted to scream that his wife, their mother, had just died; that he helped kill her; that she hated him and wished it had been him instead. But Rachel knew that ultimately her sisters would suffer for it. Instead, she took a deep, ragged breath. Rachel said very quietly, "Our mother is dead."

Jack looked at her stupidly for a moment and then looked over at his wife's lifeless body. "Well," he said, "I guess she can wait while you fix us somethin' ta eat."

Rachel took Maggie and Jennie's hands and walked past him with all the dignity she could muster. The stench made all three girls' noses wrinkle. Jack stank.

Chapter Eight

It was the morning of Julianna's funeral. Rachel awoke to a room lit with bright sunshine and warmth. It was the kind of day that Rachel wished so much she could've shared with her mother. In her mind's eye, she pictured the two of them walking arm in arm together along a flowered path, sharing their day, their thoughts, hopes, and dreams. Maybe they could've picked the fragrant blooms and arranged them in vases for each room of their home. Rachel would have loved this. They could've walked and talked like other mothers and daughters. Knowing that her mother loved her made Rachel very happy and filled a deep, aching hole in her heart, but it also left her in confusion. What was she to do with these feelings? Her mother went away just as their relationship should've started. What was she to do with this love she wanted so much to share with her mother? They had only one brief second together in that moment before Julianna died. Rachel had lived so long simply surviving, never knowing of her mother's love. And just when this beautiful gift of the words she needed so badly to hear was handed to her, her mother left forever. Where could Rachel go with this new feeling in her heart? Her throat ached with unspoken words.

Mary Netreba

The cheerful song of robins outside the open window of the bedroom beckoned Rachel, as if to tell her there was no time to waste on this beautiful day. Rachel sat up as she listened to them. The thought came to Rachel that even in her sadness, the world around her still went on. There would be morning and night, sunshine and rain, spring and winter, life and death, grief and joy, with each one to be followed by the other throughout her life and the life of every person around her. She had no idea where this thought came from, but it brought her comfort just the same.

The sound of bees buzzed lazily past the window while a slight breeze brought with it the fragrant aroma of lilacs into the room. Rachel got out of bed quietly. She went downstairs, filled a washbowl with water, and carefully brought it back up. Rachel had learned to hide soap as well as anything else that was given to them by Cook and Finney. After setting the bowl on the wash stand, she tiptoed across the room to the dresser the girls shared in their bedroom. It was made of maple, with intricate leaf designs on the two top drawers. The lower drawers had keyhole locks, all of them broken except for the last drawer. Rachel pulled the key out of her pocket, inserted it into the keyhole, and unlocked it. She placed the key back in her pocket. Sliding open the bottom drawer carefully, she reached back into the far corner and pulled out the special bar of soap. Cook had given it to Rachel. A delighted Rachel had asked her, "Where did you get this?"

Cook answered, "Oh, I found it upstairs one day." Rachel turned at the sound of Maggie and Jennie slipping out of bed. Jennie was wiping the sleep from her eyes. Maggie always looked wide awake and ready for the day.

"We'll have some breakfast after I'm done getting you ready for today."

Jennie walked over to Rachel and hugged her. "Me first, Rachel," Jennie told her. Maggie smiled as she watched and waited for her turn. After washing Maggie and Jennie's hands, feet, and faces, Rachel helped them into the dresses she had ironed the night before, pulling the dresses down over their heads, carefully placing their arms into the sleeves and then lowering each skirt to finish.

"Close your eyes, Jennie," Rachel told her. Jennie didn't like it when the dress covered her face. It scared her when she couldn't see anything. Closing her eyes didn't help either, but she did it because Rachel told her to. The dresses were a little too big, but there were no rips or holes in them. Rachel took extra time with her sisters as she brushed their hair to a shine, then pulled it back in a pretty pink satin ribbon for each of them. Rachel was very quiet as she went about taking care of her sisters, her mind instead on the funeral to be held in a few hours.

"Let's see how we look now, shall we?" Rachel asked her sisters as she walked them over to the dresser.

Attached to the maple dresser was a beveled mirror that could be tilted downward. Rachel tilted the mirror so the girls could see their reflection. She knelt down next to them. The girls seemed surprised at how nice their dresses looked on them. *They also look lost and confused,* Rachel thought.

Maggie and Jennie still didn't understand what happened to their mother. When they walked passed their mother's bedroom only the day before, they expected to see her blanket-covered form. *Where did she go? And why does Rachel look so sad? Is she going away too?*

As they stood in front of the mirror studying Rachel's reflection, Maggie met Rachel's eyes in the mirror. "Rachel, were we bad? Is that why Mommy went away? Is that why you're angry with us?" This last part of Maggie's question ended with a sob, her face twisted with hurt.

Rachel's heart lurched in her chest. Maggie and Jennie turned away from the mirror and faced Rachel. Rachel motioned for them to come closer. She held them tightly to her. Kissing the tops of their heads, she said, "Never ever think for a moment that you were bad or that I'd be angry with you." She stayed down on her knees at eye level and pulled away slightly to look deeply into their eyes. "Mommy died because it was time for her to go be with God and the angels."

Jennie, always inquisitive, looked into Rachel's eyes as she nodded her head slowly and asked sadly, "Then Mommy is allowed to fly?"

The burial service was pitifully small. An almost sober, almost clean-shaven Jack hung back from the other mourners in attendance. He was wearing the one suit he owned, still in good condition since the last time he wore it was on his and Julianna's wedding day. The double-breasted, long black coat hung very loosely, making Jack look even gaunter. He was looking all around him as the preacher started to speak. First, he looked up at the sky with bleary bloodshot eyes and then down at his worn-out shoes. He crossed his arms, uncrossed them, and crossed them again, this time catching a look of irritation from the preacher. Preachers made him uncomfortable. They always did. *They think they're better than anyone else, carrying that Bible around,* Jack thought as he looked away. *Church isn't as bad as a burial service though.*

Seeing how there were more people for the preacher to preach at in a church, he couldn't be singled out so easily. But here at the mountain's only cemetery, with very few people, Jack felt exposed. He sure hoped Preacher Smitty couldn't smell the few sips of liquor on his breath either, which was the other reason he stood back. He then shot a hateful look toward the Baileys.

Those Baileys! Goody two-shoes, that's all they are, Jack thought. *And that boy. What's his name? Jonathan?* Jack's dark eyes narrowed to slits as he watched them. He knew they were giving Rachel things like food and clothing. Jack clenched his fists at his sides. It was frustrating. No matter how hard he tried, he could never seem to find out where Rachel hid anything. *Sneaky. That's what she is. It's no wonder,* he thought. After all, Rachel wasn't really his. What could he expect from an evil seed like her? Jack turned his eyes on Maggie and Jennie.

Hmph! The girls don't look so skinny anymore. They have good dresses on today too, he noticed. *And where did Rachel get those ribbons?* Jack wondered. They each had a pink ribbon in their hair. There was even one on his wife. He saw it just before the pitiful pine casket was closed. *Yes. Those Baileys are certainly up to something,* Jack thought as he glared at them again in hatred. *Rachel should be bringing home what she is given for all of us, especially food. It isn't as if I wouldn't share with my own daughters!*

His hatred was like black, oily smoke choking out and smothering any goodness in its path. It felt evil. It was evil. They could feel his hatred, especially Ellen, who tried not to shudder. Ellen's heart ached for her friend, Julianna, and how she had to live with this awful man. But she would show no response to Jack Walters's hatred. She wouldn't allow him to know the effect he had on her or her husband. Instead, Elias, Ellen, and Jonathan kept their eyes on Preacher Smitty.

This only infuriated Jack further. His mouth twisted with words he wanted to spew at them and everyone in attendance. This was Rachel's fault. *Why does she always have to make trouble for me?*

Rachel was deeply touched to see Cook, Finney, and most of the hired staff of the Nettle home at her mother's funeral. She didn't feel quite so alone in their presence. She didn't know that Cook and Finney had both known her mother long before Jack came along. Those were the days when Julianna was happy and carefree. Those were the days that Cook and Finney wanted to remember, when Julianna was full of fun and joy. As former employees of her parents, they remembered how Julianna had been so kind and gentle to others, always wanting to help and give of herself. The terrible train wreck that tragically took her parents away from her was the final nail in the coffin, so to speak. *And Julianna pregnant by a boy who wouldn't marry her,* Cook thought sadly. Jack Walters had seen her desperation too and had taken full advantage. He had destroyed their dear Julianna.

Cook was watching Jack Walters with burning eyes. Her brows were knitted together in anger. *If there was anyone who ever needed killin,' it was him! He shoulda been the one ta die, not our dear, sweet girl, Julianna,* she thought to herself. Cook's heart thumped heavily in dread at her next thought. *Now Rachel and her young sisters will be all alone with this excuse of a man. Why couldn't it have been him, the no-good, wife-beating, child-beating, drunken son of a—?* Cook stopped herself short. She hung her head in shame. *Dear Lord, I am jus' so sorry for my thoughts…and the soap.*

Rachel, Maggie, and Jennie were tightly huddled together. Jennie was turned in toward Rachel, her head buried in the folds of Rachel's skirt. The little pink ribbon in her hair had fallen out, and she held it tightly in her fist. Jennie was too little to understand as she clung to Rachel, her muffled cries breaking the hearts of everyone around them as they held back their own tears so they wouldn't frighten the little ones—all except for Jack, of course. He couldn't have cared less how Jennie felt.

Jennie wanted to go home. The people at the funeral and burial service scared and confused her. *Why is Mommy in a wooden box?* Jennie saw her mommy in the box. She looked like she was sleeping. Then the box was closed. *Was Mommy still in there, or did she go home? Why is there a big hole in the ground?* It frightened Jennie. She thought Mommy was going to fly away today.

Rachel reached down and picked Jennie up, placing her on one hip as she held her close and kissed her cheek before Jennie, still in tears, buried her head in the crook of Rachel's neck. Maggie reached up to Jennie, placing her hand on Jennie's back. Cook looked on as well as Finney and the others in attendance. Tears filled their eyes and fell down their cheeks. The sight of these three girls was heart wrenching. Cook and Finney especially felt real fear mixed with pity for the girls. They had known of Jack Walters before he married Julianna. It wasn't good. He wasn't good.

Elias and Ellen Bailey, along with their son, Jonathan, were uncomfortably aware that Jack Walters was still watching them. His poisonous hatred for them poured out of his soul. Ellen especially felt that hatred and with good reason too. When they were young girls, Julianna and she were the best of friends. Inseparable since they were five, they shared each other's secrets, hopes, dreams, and descriptions of the boy each of them wanted to marry. They had their future lives figured out by the time they were both thirteen and long before Jack showed up. Ellen's worry and concern of what could happen to Rachel, Maggie, and Jennie was justified. To imagine them all alone with this horrible man made her shudder.

Rachel didn't realize until the moment her mother's casket was lowered into the ground just how much she would miss her. Her own heart ached with pity for the pathetic life her mother was given by a husband who promised to love her and care for her. Instead, hell-bent on destroying her, Jack took everything good that was Julianna until there was nothing left but a shell of a woman, and then he destroyed that too. The only thing left was her physical body. Now Jack would never be able to hurt her again. Rachel vowed she'd never ever allow this to happen to her. She'd never allow any man to do this to her—never!

Jonathan approached Rachel after the burial service. Rachel felt his presence beside her before seeing him. "It'll all turn out, Rachel. I promise you," he said gently.

If there was one thing that Rachel needed more than anything, it was hope, and Jonathan just gave it to her. The tears she had held back during the funeral sprung to Rachel's eyes and threatened to spill over. A sob almost escaped her lips. But she was still holding Jennie. *I can't cry here,* she thought as she fought back another sob.

Rachel looked into Jonathan's eyes questioningly. *But will it? Will it all turn out like you promised?* In the next few moments, she would have to leave, walk away from the tiny cemetery with her little sisters and her stepfather. Her emotions changed quickly at her next thought. Sadness gave way to anger. *How I hate him!* Her stepfather was the vilest, most evil person on the face of the earth. *He is by far worse than even Mrs. Nettle,* Rachel thought. Unexpressed anger and rage turned to deep anguish. Rachel fought to control the sobs that so desperately wanted to escape her lips. She wanted so much to pour out her emotions from her heart. Their mother hadn't been able, really, to protect them when she was alive. So why did Rachel feel that it was going to get even worse?

A heavy blanket of dread seemed to cover both Rachel and Jonathan. Jonathan felt it too, but he couldn't let Rachel know. Instead, Jonathan reached out and squeezed her hand. Rachel squeezed back.

Chapter Nine

Early May 1915

*R*achel kept busy turning over the rich, dark soil in preparation for this season's herb garden. The area she was working on started beside the house and reached all the way to the back. *The combination of sunshine and part shade is perfect,* she thought. Rachel planned to grow some herbs for her own family's use closer to the house.

Rachel stopped her work for a moment, placing one hand over the other on the handle of the shovel and rested her chin on her hands. She gave a deep sigh of contentment. The break felt good. So did the digging. But she knew she would be plenty sore tomorrow morning after all her work today. *I'll rest just a few more minutes,* she thought.

A robin perched on the lower limb of a tree had been watching Rachel turn the soil. As the soil was turned over, it brought up with it many tasty-looking earthworms. The robin, seeing the opportunity for a free meal, swooped down past Rachel's head, startling her as it dove in and carried a worm away in its beak. Rachel chuckled. It had happened every year since she started gardening. The robin would come back for more until it had fed itself and its young brood for the day.

Turning her attention from the robin, Rachel looked up at their home. She had to smile. The fresh coat of yellow paint on the house, with its shutters painted bright white, gave a happy lift to Rachel's spirits. She wondered if this was how their home looked when her mother was growing up in it.

With the help of Jonathan and his father, they had also put on the new front porch roof. That was last year. New posts had been put in place to support the roof and would hold up very well in the inevitable snowstorms the mountain had to bear each winter. Elias Bailey and Jonathan had also taken it upon themselves to repair the areas of the porch where the wood had rotted through. The exterior of the home was no longer the eyesore that Rachel had been so ashamed of for so long. She, Maggie, and Jennie did as much as they could to keep the outside of the home tidy and clean. The biggest challenge had been with Jack himself, both at the time the home was being painted and every day since, as the only change in Jack was that he became worse. He had complained loudly that it was his job to do the work on his home and the Baileys had no right to interfere.

"I was plannin' to get to it this summer," he would say to them. But, true to form, it never did get done. Because he felt angry and insulted that the Baileys had done his job for him, Jack made it a point to make sure he left as many broken liquor bottles on the porch as possible. *They have no respect for me,* Jack thought, *so I will show no respect to them.*

As far as Jack was concerned, the Baileys had always been and always would be his enemies. With every liquor bottle he tossed onto the front porch with malicious glee, Jack found a new way to curse the Baileys. Cleaning up after his bottles and assorted trash was a daily task for Rachel, Maggie, and Jennie. But they were determined their father wouldn't ruin this for them. To them, having a home that looked warm and inviting was most important, even if they did have to clean up after him every day.

Rachel pushed away the distracting thoughts and concentrated on the gardening area where she was digging. *The spearmint and peppermint can grow almost anywhere,* she thought. *But herbs such as basil, dill, and lemon balm prefer the sun.*

Rachel planned to also tuck in more aromatic plants like lavender because she loved its soothing and calming scent as she worked in the garden. Each year, Rachel's herb garden expanded with a larger variety of plants. Some of the herbs would be used for cooking, like basil, oregano, and rosemary. Basil was one of Rachel's favorites, and she used it most often in her homemade soups. Herbs for teas like peppermint, spearmint, and, Rachel's favorites, teaberry, bee balm, and chamomile would make a wonderfully delicious blend. Some of these same herbs, along with feverfew, catnip, hyssop, sage, thyme, and yarrow could be used for medicinal purposes. What had started out as a small patch of yard was growing into several much larger areas for Rachel's herbs. And it would expand even farther since their piece of ground covered several acres. Rachel nodded to herself. *Yes,* she decided. *I'll have myself an herb farm.* With that thought, Rachel went back to work on her garden.

Rachel found a certain peace within herself as she turned the soil. When she was done, Rachel used the hoe to remove the weeds and rocks of various sizes. It was backbreaking work, but Rachel wanted to make sure she pulled out every single weed. The rocks that she pulled out, some of them very heavy, would be used for boundaries and decorating the flower garden. The rocks of every shape and size gave character to her flower beds, depending on how and where they were placed.

After she finished making the rows for the seeds, she dropped to her knees and sat back on her heels for a brief moment of rest. Placing her bare hands into the rich soil, she picked up a handful with each hand and allowed the coolness of the earth to slip between her fingers. Rachel loved the feel of the dirt in her hands. She loved the smell of fresh earth. Closing her eyes, she pictured in her mind how the garden would look at the height of the season. Any herb she needed for her family's use would be right outside their door. The bright reds and purples of the bee balm would bring not only bees to pollinate the gardens, but they would also bring the ruby-throated hummingbirds. These beautiful hummingbirds were always a welcome delight in this area of Pennsylvania, as they only came to visit from the months of April through October.

Rachel was fifteen years old. Jonathan was a young man of nineteen. Rachel was also deeply in love with Jonathan. She imagined she always had been, since she couldn't remember the exact time she fell in love. It seemed as if it was always there, just like there was always a yesterday, and a tomorrow, or spring, summer, winter, and fall. Thinking about Jonathan brought such joy to her that there were times when she thought her heart would burst. Rachel couldn't imagine what she would've done without him. If it weren't for the kindness of people like Jonathan and his parents or Cook and Finny, why, she might not even be in this wonderful garden. Jonathan was the one who had encouraged Rachel to expand her herb and flower gardens. He encouraged her dreams. To Jonathan, Rachel's talent was so easy to see. Rachel remembered the day that Jonathan and she stopped along Wilson creek on their way home from church. They sat on the bank and watched the spring water as it flowed by.

"Rachel, you have a gift. You need to share it with others." He was so emphatic when he spoke that his belief in her went right to Rachel's heart. It was the first time she actually believed in her abilities. Jonathan always lifted her up and encouraged her. He was her almost-constant companion and friend. This too seemed ever present, with no beginning or end.

Maggie and Jennie were very fond of Jonathan and loved him as if he was their older brother. They delighted in his visits to their home which, of course, had to be when Jack Walters wasn't around. Jonathan always paid special attention to the girls. He made sure to spend time with Jennie when she invited him to "high tea."

"Now, Jonathan," she'd say, "you're supposed to be the perfect gentleman, so don't be late, and make sure you wash your hands." Jonathan did both, but he loved to make Jennie laugh too. So as he sat down he would pretend to miss the chair and fall to the floor with a thump. It left them all limp with laughter.

Sometimes he'd even bring little bouquets of flowers for them. With a flourish, he'd present the bouquet hidden behind his back and regally bow to them. Sometimes Maggie and Jennie would hide when they saw him walking up to the house. They loved it when Jonathan had to search for them. Maggie and Jennie were reduced to giggles as Jonathan would

Rosemary for Remembrance

call out with dramatic flair, "Fair maidens, where hast thou gone? Thy flowers will not last forever!" Of course, the sound of their uncontrollable giggling at his voice made it easy for Jonathan to find them. But he played their game every time, even pretending shocked surprise when they jumped out of their hiding place. Jonathan would gasp, drop the bouquet of flowers to the ground, and then clutch his chest as if their surprise was too much for his heart to take. This, of course, made them laugh even harder. And sometimes Maggie and Jennie would be the ones to jump suddenly in surprise when Jonathan snuck up on them.

Rachel was still deep in thought as she looked back over the years since that fateful night of the blizzard. How their lives had changed. A tap on her shoulder made Rachel suddenly jump. She turned her head to see Maggie standing beside her.

"Sorry to interrupt your thoughts, Rachel. I was able to come home early. I thought perhaps I could lend a hand with the garden." She looked around at what Rachel had accomplished so far and smiled. A large area had been dug up and tilled. The rocks Rachel was so fond of were piled high. "Not that it looks as if there is anything much left to do."

Maggie was becoming a young woman, just one month shy of her thirteenth birthday and showing a strong independent streak. Maggie was also the forever optimist and believed that anything was possible. This was especially true when it came to creating a better world for women everywhere. She wasn't planning to work the rest of her life doing odd jobs at the general store for Harold Nelson or getting married too soon. Maggie wanted so much more for her life and for the lives of others.

Jennie, at eleven, wasn't too far behind in age, but hers and Maggie's personalities were completely opposite. Maggie voiced her opinion whether anyone liked it or not. Jennie, however, seemed to consider every situation before she said a word. She was the deep thinker of the three sisters and questioned most everything. Jennie was more delicate, more emotional, and wanted to please those around her, including her father. It worried Rachel and Maggie both. Each of them tried to give Jennie small decisions to make to help with her confidence.

Rachel felt very hopeful for the future. To her it was amazing to think of the many blessings that came about since the night of the terrible blizzard. Even more amazing was how she learned to deal with her mother's death and the deep, unexpressed feelings for months afterward. The impact of knowing that her mother truly had loved her affected Rachel profoundly. Rachel remembered how kind Jonathan's mother was to her the day she went to talk to her.

One day, only weeks after Julianna's death, Rachel felt that she had to talk with someone. Jonathan's mother was the likely choice. Ellen, with her nonjudgmental ways, made Rachel feel like she could tell her anything.

Rachel felt that the weight of the world was on her shoulders that day she went to visit. Ellen Bailey always seemed to have time to talk with others no matter what else she was doing. She would simply set aside whatever task she was working on and give her undivided attention. As Rachel poured out her heart to Ellen that day, tears flowed freely from her eyes. It felt to Rachel as if the dam of pent-up emotions in her heart was set loose all at once. Rachel didn't know what to do with this love she had in her heart for her mother. She'd realized too late that it had been there all along but had been clouded over by the overwhelming, day-to-day desperation of simply surviving as she took of care of Maggie and Jennie and her mother. Rachel voiced to Ellen how there were times when she felt such helpless anger because her mother didn't seem to be there for her. She had even felt hatred at times. This last part Rachel confessed with her head down in shame. She regretted confessing it almost as soon as she spoke the words. *Surely Mrs. Bailey will tell me how awful I am,* Rachel thought. Then an even worse thought seeped into her mind. *Maybe she won't let Jonathan be my friend anymore.* This thought almost made Rachel panic. But Ellen, who listened so caringly, instead gave Rachel the answer she desperately needed.

With kindness and empathy, Ellen put her arms around Rachel's shoulders and simply said, "Rachel, you've been given the rare gift of not only knowing your mother loved you but that you do indeed love her too. Your mother, I'm sure, knows this. But she is home in heaven, and you're still here. That love that you have in your heart can and should be freely given to others. Make each day count because once we leave this earth, we'll no longer be able to share it. And what we share, whether good or bad, will make a difference to someone somewhere." Mrs. Bailey hugged Rachel tightly.

Rachel had one more question. "If God has a glorious life planned for us, then why did my mother have to suffer so much?"

Ellen softly answered, "Because God never said which life." It took a few moments, but Rachel's eyes lit up with understanding.

"Oh, I never thought of it that way."

Ellen continued, "Just keep sharing the gifts God gave you Rachel, and he'll take care of the rest."

Rachel realized that this was how Ellen Bailey lived her life. *No wonder she always has time to listen,* Rachel thought as she looked at Ellen with new eyes. She had chosen what was most important. Rachel could see the blessings that God had in store for her in spite of the tragedies along the way. Rachel experienced firsthand God's promise of redemption. How would she have felt if her mother had died without saying "I love you"?

And Rachel reminded herself that their lives all took a turn for the better when Jonathan and his parents entered. Ellen and Elias Bailey were even more concerned with Rachel, Maggie, and Jennie's predicament since their mother was gone. Ellen fretted over what Jack could possibly do to the girls. So, in their own, not-so-obvious way, the Baileys continued to help—some home-canned goods here, a little extra flour for bread there, extra soup that would "just go to waste if someone didn't help them eat it." Rachel knew that she and her sisters were being blessed through many difficult times.

Rachel thankfully no longer had to work for Mrs. Nettle, who, through the years, became even more miserable and nasty with her employees. Instead, Rachel was hired for a job at one of the factories that recently came to the area. The work was hard and the days were long, but Rachel didn't have Mrs. Nettle to contend with anymore either. *That,* Rachel thought, *is worth its weight in gold.* Her job at the factory was a steady income she could count on too. Of course, no one told Jack about the change in Rachel's employment. He would've expected Rachel to take care of everything and share even more of what she earned, and she wasn't about to let that happen. Rachel came to understand that Jack was a very oppressive, miserable human being, the one thing that continued to make parts of her and her sisters' lives unbearable. There were times that Rachel was left reeling over one of Jack's verbal attacks. They made no sense. He constantly told Rachel terrible things about herself that weren't true. He said it with such conviction that there were moments when Rachel almost believed him.

"You're no good. Your mother died because of you. You're evil. That's what you are, Rachel. And you're no help around here." On and on he'd continue, spewing poisonous words that wormed their way deep into her soul. Rachel would actually start to feel dizzy and sick to her stomach. A new understanding came over her one day after one of Jack's most vicious attacks yet. Rachel had run outside to get away from his abusive words. As Rachel hid in the garden, trying desperately to hold back the sobs so Jack wouldn't find her, she understood. *So this is how our mother must have felt,* Rachel thought. Rachel's heart was filled with pity for her mother. No wonder she had become bedridden. Jack had beaten her down so much for so long that Julianna simply shriveled up within herself and died. *No wonder she couldn't show love,* Rachel realized. Jack had completely buried everything Julianna was long before her actual death. Rachel also came to understand that since his wife's death, Jack needed someone else to abuse in the same way. Rachel was the obvious first choice. Jack delighted in telling her she wasn't his child.

Rachel brought her thoughts back to the present. She felt so grateful at this moment. *Thank you, Lord, for taking our mother home. Thank you that Jack can't ever hurt her again.*

Rachel shelved away any other thoughts that seemed to want to play in her head over and over again. Instead, Rachel smiled and said to her sister, "So, Maggie, what else do you think we should do this year?"

Maggie grinned. "Well, first I think we could use a few more roses," she started. "and I was thinking about…"

Rachel's mind started to drift again as she remembered her first herb garden and how it had progressed. Maggie didn't notice at all as she went on and on excitedly about her roses, and how well they went with herbs.

"And did you know, Rachel, that certain herbs are also excellent insect repellents…"

When Rachel first started her herb garden, she was interested in using the herbs for her family and herself. But as her garden grew over the years, so did the interest of the residents of the tiny mountain community.

She invited one and all to pinch a snip of whatever they liked. Soon, neighbors were coming to her for "just a sprig" of whatever herb they were interested in. And word traveled quickly in the community. Rachel smiled at the memory of the previous year's garden.

Rachel had set out several metal buckets one day on a bench near the herb garden in the front. She was planning to use the buckets for transporting smaller plants with their roots still attached to a better location. She hadn't used them yet because she was too busy on the far end of the garden. Every once in a while, she would hear an odd sound but could never determine where it was coming from. Just a periodic *plunk!* as she went about her work. This went on for several days as she worked on opening up another area for more plantings. Once she was done, she could move those smaller plants. But first she would need one of her buckets. Making her way from the back to the front, she heard another *plunk!* She stood still for a moment and watched as a tall, slender, elegant-looking woman dressed all in black walked away. *That's odd,* Rachel thought.

Rachel had told her neighbors to feel free to pinch off a little something if they wanted it, but she didn't recognize this person walking away. She certainly seemed well dressed for an outing to someone's herb garden, however. *The ladies in our community would never be able to dress that fine,* Rachel thought. Rachel continued moving forward. When she reached the bench, Rachel leaned forward and lifted the bucket up by the handle. *I must be tired,* she thought. The bucket felt heavy. And something rattled when she lifted it. Rachel looked down into the bucket, dumbfounded. Pennies, many pennies had been dropped into the bucket. She looked at the front part of the herb garden. There had been a lot of pinching going on lately, she observed. She realized the plunking sound she'd been hearing had been pennies being dropped into the bucket. She was being paid for her herbs, and she didn't even know it! Ellen Bailey's words came back to her at that moment. "Just do what you should be doing, Rachel, and God will always bless it." Rachel set the bucket down as tears filled her eyes. She looked inside the bucket again and giggled to herself. *There is enough money in there for material to make new dresses for Maggie and Jennie.*

That was last year. Rachel would continue to do what she was supposed to be doing. *I wonder,* she thought, *what the blessings will be this year.* Optimistically, Rachel turned her attention to her still-talking sister as she went on about her roses.

"And I think, Rachel, that several white trellises with climbing pink roses would be nice too. Don't you think?"

Mary Netreba

Chapter Ten

Rachel had a two-mile walk to and from her job at the factory every weekday. The two miles downhill were easy, but the two miles uphill were more of a challenge. Despite the distance, Rachel loved to walk and could move quite swiftly, even uphill. It also gave her quiet time to think, to pray, and to shore up the strength she'd need each time she headed home. This evening was no exception. She had to stay an hour longer at work and was quite anxious to get home as soon as possible. She didn't like for her sisters to be home alone with Jack, and she never knew when he'd be there. The cruel verbal abuse he had spewed into Rachel's soul was also used on Maggie and Jennie when Rachel wasn't around.

Without warning, a coldness suddenly pierced Rachel's heart. It felt as if something terrible had or was about to happen. Rachel imagined whatever she found when she arrived home would be much worse than anything she or her sisters had ever faced so far. *Hurry,* she told herself. *Hurry.* Beads of sweat formed on her upper lip and forehead, yet she felt chilled to the bone. Her calves ached as she forced herself to move quickly up the hill to the road home.

Rosemary for Remembrance

"Oh, Lord, please keep them safe. Please let me find my sisters unharmed," she breathed out in prayer.

The crest of the hill behind her, she ran as fast as she could. She was almost there. *Hurry. Hurry,* the voice inside prompted her. Their home was in sight. Rachel sprinted faster than she ever thought she could. She raced up the front porch steps and stopped suddenly at the front door. The door was ajar. Something was terribly wrong.

Usually, Maggie and Jennie would be sitting outside, waiting for her on the top step. They would run down the steps to Rachel for hugs. But Rachel saw no sign of either of them. Empty liquor bottles and other trash littered the porch. Rachel looked down to find several of Jennie's drawings ripped into tiny pieces on the floor inside the door and strewn about all over the porch as well. She cautiously opened the front door wide enough to slide through.

"Maggie, Jennie, I'm home," Rachel said softly so she wouldn't startle them. She listened closely for them to answer. The quiet was so still and eerie that it sent chills down her back. As Rachel moved forward, she slipped. Catching herself, she looked down to find more of Jennie's drawings ripped into tiny pieces and strewn about. Leaving the front door open, Rachel stood in the hallway as she listened for any sign that Maggie and Jennie were in the house.

The sound of soft whimpering reached Rachel's ears. It sounded as if it was coming from the end of the hallway, near the kitchen. Rachel was too far down the hallway to tell if it was Maggie or Jennie. The sound of whimpering came again. This time, Rachel knew it was both Maggie and Jennie. Her heart pounded in dread and fear. Something terrible was happening. Rachel moved quietly from the hallway and crept into the parlor. Crossing the room, she picked up the long poker used for the fireplace and then quietly tiptoed out of the parlor and down the hallway toward the kitchen. The wood floor creaked a little under her feet in several places. Rachel stopped each time to wait and see if the creaks had been noticed but no one seemed to have heard her. Rachel was very light, and for this she was thankful. When Rachel reached the kitchen door, she slowly pushed it open with her shoulder just a crack. Her hand quickly went to her mouth as she forced herself not to scream. Her heart pounded loudly in her chest. Her eyes filled with rage and her hand tightly clutched the fire poker, taking in the horrendous sight in front of her.

Maggie and Jennie were cowering underneath the long, wooden table, squeezing themselves as far back as they could until they were up against the wall. Maggie was trying to cover Jennie's small form with her own. Even from where Rachel stood, she could see the welts and bruises on Maggie's arms and legs. Her hair had come loose from its braid and was a tangled mess around her face.

"Stop it! Please stop it!" she cried out to her father. Jennie was hysterical, her heart-wrenching sobs unheeded by their cruel father. Rachel felt their desperate cries of terror in her heart. Maggie's pleas of, "Please, Daddy, don't. Please," also went unheeded.

Jack was still holding the leather strap he had used on them. Towering over them, he took tremendous pleasure in hearing their cries. Rachel knew only too well how it felt. He was standing close to the kitchen table, his tall form shaking with unbelievable insane rage. With maniacal laughter he continued his torment.

"You're bastards, all three of you. You're not mine. That mother of yours was a whore. I'll teach you. I'll teach the two of you first. Then I'll take care of that bastard half-sister of yours. I'll make all of you pay." Jack's voice reached a high-pitched, shrill shriek.

Maggie and Jennie crouched back, but there was nowhere else to go. They seemed hypnotized with horror as they watched his bulging eyes. His breath came out in a threatening pant.

"You…just wait…you little bi—"

Maggie and Jennie saw Jack's knees buckle, and watched in disbelief as he dropped heavily onto his knees, falling forward with a loud, slapping thud. His head slammed against the floor last. He never knew what hit him. Rachel stood behind him and stared in horror at what she'd just done. Blood poured from Jack's broken nose. The back of his head was also wet with blood from the wound made by the poker in Rachel's hand. Maggie and Jennie became even more hysterical at the sight of their father lying so near them in a widening puddle of blood. Their whimpering turned to screams.

"Maggie! Jennie!" Rachel called to them. Rachel stepped over her stepfather on the floor. Bending down, she crawled under the table to reach her sisters. Rachel wrapped her arms around Maggie, who had her arms wrapped around Jennie. Both of them were crying uncontrollably. "It's all right," Rachel said reassuringly, although her voice was very shaky. "We're going to be all right." Rachel held onto them while she continued to talk softly. "We're safe. Let's get out from under the table. He can't hurt us. He's asleep."

Jennie was frozen in fear. She couldn't take her eyes off her father. She was paralyzed with shock. Both Rachel and Maggie had to pull her out from under the table and carry her up the stairs to their bedroom. They placed her gently on the bed and covered her with the blanket. They sat quietly with her on either side of the bed, holding her hands and waiting. Jennie didn't respond. She stared up at the ceiling in shock. Rachel and Maggie pulled Jennie up to a sitting position for Rachel to hold her. Rachel held back the sobs when she saw the bruises and welts on both her sisters. She felt the anguish of guilt that she hadn't been home for them and shuddered to think of how much worse this would've been had she not come home when she did.

Maggie had taken the brunt of the beating, as she covered her little sister with her own body, just the way Rachel had done for Maggie all the times their father would beat them. But this was by far the worst beating Rachel had ever seen. Even Rachel had never been beaten this badly. Maggie was covered from head to toe with welts and bruises. Rachel knew in her heart that Jack Walters would've killed them both had she not come home when she did. Her feeling of dread and urgency had been a true warning. Rachel closed her eyes. No matter how horrible this beating had been, she was very thankful that her sisters were still alive. Rachel began to hum a soft tune as she held her little sister.

Jennie lifted her head off Rachel's shoulder slowly. Rachel looked at her and breathed a long sigh of relief. Jennie was going to be all right.

Thank you, Lord, Rachel spoke in her heart.

Jennie's sad eyes looked searchingly into Rachel's own. "Did you kill him, Rachel?" Jennie asked. "Is our daddy dead?"

Chapter Eleven

Rachel's heart almost stopped beating in her chest. Time seemed to stand still. Rachel had to look away from Jennie's inquiring eyes. She didn't know what to say to her. Instead, Rachel held Jennie even closer. Jennie, exhausted, soon fell asleep on Rachel's shoulder. She and Maggie gently lay Jennie down, careful not to wake her, and pulled the blanket up over her. They tiptoed out of the bedroom quietly, keeping the door slightly ajar in case Jennie woke up.

Rachel and Maggie silently made their way down the staircase, fearful that their father might have woken up and was lying in wait for them. Perhaps he was only pretending and was hiding somewhere, waiting for another chance to kill them all. They stopped at the bottom of the staircase, straining their ears for any sound that would indicate Jack Walters wasn't where they left him.

Arms linked together for strength, Rachel and Maggie cautiously made their way through the hallway to the kitchen door. Hearts pounding in dread and fear, they quietly opened the door to the kitchen just enough to see if he was still there. He was. Jack lay perfectly still, too still. The pool of blood had grown larger during the time he was left alone. The girls looked at each other, unsure what to do.

Rachel's heart felt as if it would explode in fear. Did she kill him? *God,* she spoke silently, *I didn't mean to kill him. I only wanted him to stop hurting Maggie and Jennie. He had to be stopped.* Rachel couldn't believe it. *I murdered someone. I murdered him! Oh, God, I'm sorry, so sorry. I didn't mean to…I…*

The moan that escaped Jack's lips sounded guttural and rough. Rachel's legs turned to water as she stood shaking, hoping they wouldn't collapse under her. *I didn't kill him,* she thought. *I'm not a murderer. Thank you, God.*

Maggie could barely breathe from the fear. *What if he gets up and beats us all again? What if he beats us all to death?* She couldn't seem to stop her panicked thoughts.

Rachel and Maggie held their breath as they waited in dread to see what would happen next. Other than one small moan, Jack remained motionless. The pool of blood on the floor started to darken and congeal around the edges. The sight of it made both sisters sick to their stomachs. They shuddered, knowing they would have to do something about their father very soon.

"Rachel," Maggie whispered, "I think we need to move him. Maybe we can get him into the parlor." They looked at each other. The thought of even touching Jack, let alone moving him from the kitchen, down the hallway, and into the parlor was appalling. *How in the world would they be able to pick him up?* they both wondered.

It wasn't easy. Jack was a tall, gaunt man, but for two young girls, his dead weight was very heavy indeed. They pulled, pushed, dragged, and grunted to get him into the parlor. By the time they placed him on the worn couch, they were sick not only from seeing so much blood but from the stench of their father's unwashed body mixed with the smell of whiskey. Rachel felt deep hatred welling up inside her heart again at the sight of him. How she wished he was dead. She was relieved she didn't kill him. *But he should still be dead,* she thought, *especially after what he did to Maggie and Jennie.*

It was hard to tear their eyes from the sight of him as they backed out of the parlor and into the hallway. Both girls turned and looked at each other for a moment. They and their clothing were covered in Jack's blood. Saying not a word, they turned and headed down the hallway to the kitchen. Rachel and Maggie still had to clean up all the blood. They had to keep turning their heads away from the sight and smell. It was very late by the time they were finished. Although they scrubbed themselves afterward thoroughly from head to toe and changed into clean clothes, the sickening smell of their father's filthy body remained in their nostrils. They checked on Jennie, who was still in a deep sleep then silently made their way down the stairs again.

Maggie's hands shook as she fixed tea while Rachel went to the basement for her herbs. She knew Maggie needed help for her welts and bruises. Bringing several jars of dried herbs into the kitchen, Rachel made a medicinal paste with hands that also shook with nerves. Maggie noticed it as Rachel dabbed the paste carefully on Maggie's injuries, but said nothing. They were both deeply affected by what had happened.

Maggie jerked every time the paste was applied because it burned at first, but soon she felt the soothing, calming relief as the pain decreased. Maggie sighed.

"There now. All done," Rachel said comfortingly. Their shaking had stopped, much to their relief.

I'm hungry," Jennie said.

Rachel and Maggie turned and looked to see their little sister standing at the doorway of the kitchen. Rachel walked over to Jennie, placing her arms around her for a hug and then, taking her hand, led her to the kitchen table. While Maggie prepared more tea and bread, Rachel washed Jennie's face and hands and then used the medicinal herbal paste on her as well.

The three sisters sat at the table very quietly, sipping their tea and eating their meager rations of stale bread with honey. It was hard to believe that only hours earlier, Maggie and Jennie were actually under this same table as they tried to get away from Jack.

No sound came from the parlor, to Rachel's relief. She hoped Jack would sleep through the night. She hoped he would sleep forever, but she didn't want God to blame her for it.

"Girls, I can take care of the rest of this," Rachel said, indicating the plates and cups. "Why don't the two of you go upstairs and get some sleep?"

Jennie was starting to nod off at the table, her eyelids heavy with exhaustion. She was leaning into Maggie's shoulder. Maggie didn't seem to be doing too much better. Both sisters, with their many patches of medicinal paste, especially on their faces, made Rachel's heart wrench at the sad sight. Maggie was nodding off too. She was too sleepy to even think about how tired Rachel must be.

Maggie pushed her chair back and stood up. Reaching for Jennie's hand, she said, "Come on, Jennie. Let's go to bed." She had to help Jennie out of the chair.

Jennie managed a mumbled, "Night, Rachel. I love you." Rachel watched her sisters leave the room with a lump in her throat. She waited as her sisters went up the stairs and down the hallway to their bedroom. The house became very quiet. Rachel tidied the kitchen, washing the dishes and wiping the table. She decided to scrub the kitchen floor again. Even the thought of walking across it felt dirty to her. The floor would never seem clean to her again. All she could see in her mind was Jack's blood, how it smeared all around them as she and Maggie repeatedly tried to wipe it up.

Blood, so much blood, she thought. Rachel threw the washrag into the bucket and sat back on her heels. The floor would never be clean again after what had happened. Feeling sick to her very soul, she started to shake again with nerves.

I almost killed him, Lord, she thought. *I wanted him to die. He was hurting my sisters, Lord. I don't know what to do. Please help me, Lord. Help us. Please show me what to do.*

Rachel wiped her hands on her apron and placed her hands over her eyes. She lowered her head in despair as the anguish in her soul overwhelmed her. Rachel sobbed her heart out to God as she waited for an answer. She knew she'd have to continue to work at the factory to take care of her sisters. But she couldn't be two places at one time. What could she do to protect the three of them? *There has to be an answer to this,* she thought.

The house began to feel cold again. Rachel shivered, wiped her eyes, and got up from her knees, leaving the bucket of dirty water to sit as she walked out of the kitchen and down the hall. She cautiously peeked around the corner of the parlor. Jack remained in the exact same position she and Maggie had left him. His head was tilted back slightly with his mouth open as he snored, making guttural noises in his throat. Jack was skin and bones. He was unshaven, unkempt, and, even from where Rachel stood, she could smell the stench of him. He looked like he was out for the night.

It could be from his drunkenness or the blow to his head or both. Rachel didn't know which. She tried not to breathe through her nose as she entered the parlor, walking across the room to add more logs to the fire in the fireplace. As she reached for the poker to stir up the fire, her hands began shaking again. Jack's blood and hair still clung to the end of it. Rachel quickly shoved the poker into the fire. When she pulled it out, the blood and hair were gone.

The parlor was warmer. The fire in the fireplace felt good and would help keep the house warm, hopefully 'till morning. Rachel was exhausted from the weight of the day. She walked over to the other large, worn chair and sat down. She was so very sleepy. Leaning back in the chair, Rachel prayed a prayer of desperation. *Please, God, help me. Please show me what to do.* Rachel's prayer was still on her lips when she fell into an exhausted sleep.

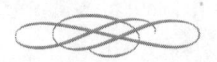

The first thing Jack became aware of was that he felt hot and stuffy. It was as if he was suffocating. He couldn't seem to breathe. He tried to open his eyelids, but they felt as if they'd been glued shut. He tried to think. He had been drinking again. He remembered that. But when did he black out? He couldn't even remember getting drunk. What had happened? His head exploded in pain as he turned his head from side to side. Red flashes stabbed at his closed eyes. An agonized moan came to his lips, but he couldn't make a sound. Why was that? He tried to keep still and ease the pounding in his head. Something happened. There was something else he needed to remember.

He tried to concentrate. What was it? If he could just open his eyes maybe he would remember. The sound of crackling reached his ears, and he recognized the sound of wood burning in the fireplace. That meant he was in the parlor.

But how did I end up here? he wondered as he tried again to open his eyes. *There.* Slowly at first, he opened his left eye and then his right eye. Even that was painful. His vision was blurred, but as it cleared, he found himself looking at the back of someone standing in front of the fireplace. She was stoking the fire. Slowly, the figure turned around to face him. Jack's eyes turned to hateful slits. *Rachel!*

She was holding the fire poker in her hand. Jack nervously noticed the hot, red tip. His eyes widened in fear. Rachel's jaw was tightly set, her lips in a thin, straight line. Her look of dark anger and pure hatred made Jack shrink within himself as she took a threatening step toward him.

"Don't you ever come near my sisters or me again," she hissed. She might as well have screamed it. Her words pierced deeply into his soul, her unfamiliar tone underlining the threat. And Jack Walters remembered. Slowly, he placed his right hand behind his head, flinching as he touched the tender, throbbing lump. Rachel watched him. He looked surprised and something else. For the first time in his miserable life, Jack Walters was the one who felt fear. Looking at him with new eyes, Rachel turned around and tossed the poker from her hand into the fire, watching the sparks suddenly fly upward as if they too were surprised.

Rachel was satisfied. She hit her mark. He wouldn't try anything on Maggie or Jennie again with her around. Rachel realized something else. Jack Walters was nothing but a drunken coward.

Mary Netreba

Chapter Twelve

Jonathan stopped by the next morning to see Rachel before she left for work. Jack had somehow managed to sneak himself out of the house before then, much to Rachel's relief. The look on Rachel's face when she opened the front door told Jonathan something very bad must have happened. She kept looking down at her feet, unable to meet his eyes.

"Rachel, look at me. What happened?"

Rachel opened the door farther to let him in, something she wasn't sure she should do. *What will he think?* she wondered.

Jonathan removed his hat as he stepped into the foyer. Maggie and Jennie sat the bottom of the stairs, looking up at him. Jonathan's breath caught when he saw the girls. They were still in their nightclothes and there was no hiding the ugly, purple bruises and raised welts, especially the ones on their faces. Rachel closed the door. Tearfully, she explained how she came home the evening before to find Jack beating her sisters. She didn't tell Jonathan how she stopped him. Rachel still felt heartsick that she could have killed Jack.

Jonathan was shocked at the sight of their wounds. Rachel told him she had treated the welts with her herbs, otherwise they would be much worse. Jonathan couldn't imagine the welts looking any worse than this. It sickened him to the core. To think that someone would do this to two innocent young girls, his daughters yet; that was beyond comprehension. The whole right side of Maggie's face was swollen so badly that she could barely see out of her eye. Her lower lip was doubled in size and cut from the belt Jack used.

Jennie had lash marks on her legs and arms, and especially her hands as she tried to keep the belt from hitting her face. Anger and rage welled up inside Jonathan; his hands clenched into fists. It was the first time he felt as if he could actually kill someone. Jennie looked up nervously at Jonathan as if he too might hurt her. She saw his hands curl into fists angrily.

Jennie shook. Her lower lip trembled as she leaned back against the step. Rachel suddenly realized that Jennie was reacting to Jonathan's anger because of the anger she'd seen in their father's eyes. Rachel knew she had to calm Jennie immediately. Rachel walked the few steps to where Jennie was sitting and lowered herself to the step beside her. Placing her arms around Jennie's shoulders and holding her closely, she looked up at Jonathan. "Jennie, Jonathan is our friend. He would never hurt us."

Jonathan stepped closer to the girls. He crouched down and looked into Jennie's eyes with compassion. "That's right, Jennie. I would never hurt you. What your father did to you was wrong. But he won't hurt you again. I promise."

Jennie looked at him, wanting to trust him, wanting to not be afraid of him too. She seemed to consider what he was saying and then spoke. "Daddy broke a lot of promises, you know. Do you ever break your promises, Jonathan?" She looked so serious. Suddenly, Jennie didn't seem to be a little girl anymore.

Jonathan smiled. "No, Jennie. I never break a promise."

Feeling reassured, Jennie smiled. Jonathan's heart ached in compassion as he looked at her. Her face was so bruised that her smile seemed completely out of place. Jennie reached up and threw her arms around Jonathan's neck, hugging him tightly for a moment. Jonathan's eyes misted over.

Clearing his throat, he stood up and said. "Girls, I'll be right back. Stay put, all right?"

They nodded in agreement and watched as he left. To Rachel, his steps looked very determined as he walked away. Jonathan crossed the field back to his parents' house as quickly as he could. He told his parents what Jack Walters had done.

Ellen Bailey looked at her husband and said, "Elias, we have to do something. Those poor girls…" She drifted off.

Elias Bailey was fuming over the mistreatment of the Walters girls. He thought for a moment as he clenched and unclenched his fists, *The no-good, drunken bum! Someone ought to beat him so he would know what it felt like.* He nodded in agreement with his wife and son. "Let's go get the girls and bring them here."

Jonathan sighed with deep relief. He didn't realize he'd been holding his breath until he let it out.

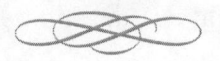

Maggie and Jennie stayed out of school until their injuries healed, which meant they were with the Baileys every day. Jonathan went to the school to get homework for them and return it the next day to the teacher, who knew only that the girls were ill with some unknown sickness. Jonathan lowered his eyes when he spoke to the teacher. It was the first lie he could remember telling. *Lord, forgive me for this. I just want to protect Maggie and Jennie and Rachel. I love her, Lord. Help me protect them. Amen.*

Jack Walters was completely unaware of the changes taking place. He'd show up at his home in the middle of the night in a drunken stupor and pass out across his bed. Other times, he'd be home before the girls but was thankfully passed out on the couch in the parlor.

Maggie and Jennie were given small chores to do around the Bailey farm and in the house with Mrs. Bailey. They were excited to have jobs just like their sister, Rachel, but both expressed deep disappointment when they learned they still had to go back to school. "Learning is important, girls," Mrs. Bailey insisted.

Neither Maggie nor Jennie realized that Jonathan had been the one to help Rachel with reading, writing, and arithmetic through the years. They just thought Rachel always knew. After all, she was their big sister. When Maggie and Jennie's injuries had healed, they continued to go to the Baileys' after school, where they could do their homework and "help" with a few chores.

Rachel walked to the Baileys' from work and picked up her sisters, and Jonathan then walked all of them home. Jack was never around at that time of day, much to everyone's relief. But Jonathan always worried each time he left Rachel and the girls alone there. He couldn't help the feeling of responsibility he had for them. *What if Jack came back in the middle of the night and beat them again?* The thought filled him with anger and fear. Jonathan and his parents prayed every evening for Rachel, Maggie, and Jennie's safety. Each morning Jonathan walked to their house and found them safe, he breathed a grateful sigh of relief and thankfulness to God. His love for Rachel grew with every passing day. Jonathan knew he wanted Rachel to be his wife. He had already talked with his parents about how he felt. They loved Rachel and her sisters. But they also agreed that Jonathan needed to wait awhile.

But deep feelings of dread would come over Jonathan at times. It came from the fear that Rachel, Maggie, and Jennie wouldn't make it out of their home alive—not as long as Jack Walters lived there. Every day, the feeling of dread grew stronger and more insistent.

Chapter Thirteen

Rachel had to work a little later one evening while Maggie and Jennie waited at the Baileys.' They had already finished their homework and chores. The late afternoon was still very warm. Maggie and Jennie had asked Mrs. Bailey after supper if they could stay outside and sit at the picnic table to enjoy the weather. Two chubby robins swooped down and landed on the picnic table close to the girls. The birds studied a delighted Maggie and Jennie for a few moments before flying off again. Both girls started to laugh.

"What's that sound?" Jennie asked Maggie. Jennie stopped laughing. "Don't you hear that, Maggie? It's coming from the bushes over there," she said to her sister as she pointed in the direction of the noise. Both Maggie and Jennie were straining their ears to hear the sound again. Instead, the lower part of the bushes moved slightly as if something were brushing up against them. The girls stood up, ready to run into the house if they needed to.

"Mew, mew, mew."

Both Maggie and Jennie laughed in surprise. "It's a kitten," they both cried excitedly at the same time. The tiny kitten came closer as it mewed pathetically. It was an orange-

and white-striped tabby. As it sauntered closer, they could see that it had white paws on the front legs while the back legs looked like little white boots. The fur on the kitten's chest was also white. Above its mouth was a little white fur mustache. It had beautiful green eyes. The kitten seemed to sense that Maggie and Jennie wouldn't harm it and continued toward them, mewing sadly. Stopping at Jennie's ankles, it wrapped itself around her, purring loudly.

"Can you believe how noisy she is?" Jennie asked.

"She is awfully pretty, isn't she?" Maggie asked back.

Jennie bent down to pick her up. She could feel the poor, little kitten's bony ribs. "Oh, Maggie, she's hungry. She must not have eaten anything for awhile." She glanced over at the bushes where the kitten came from. "Where is the mother, I wonder?"

Rachel had arrived at the Baileys' about five minutes earlier to take Maggie and Jennie home but stopped in her tracks when she saw the kitten come out of the bushes. She stayed back and observed how the kitten went to Maggie and Jennie so trustingly.

"How pretty!" she said as she walked toward the three of them. Rachel reached out to pet the kitten on the head. The kitten rewarded Rachel and the girls with even louder purring.

"Oh, Rachel, please can we keep her? Please, please, please?" Jennie and Maggie both asked.

"Who's going to take care of it?" Rachel asked.

"Oh, Rachel, I will. And it's not an *it*. It's a kitten, a girl. Her name is Katy," Jennie said excitedly. Jennie looked very determined.

Rachel raised her eyebrows. *Jennie's already picked out a name? Well maybe this will be a good way for Jennie to learn about caring for others.* "All right, Jennie, you can keep her, but—."

Rachel couldn't finish her sentence. Jennie hugged her with one arm while holding Katy with her other arm and saying thank you over and over again. "I wasn't done talking, Jennie," Rachel said as she untangled herself from her younger sister. "You can keep her provided you are the one to care for her, feed her, and keep her safe. All right?"

"Oh yes, Rachel. Yes," Jennie answered.

They all smiled as they watched Katy roll onto her back, showing off her white tummy. Jennie's next question made Rachel and Maggie both laugh. "Do you think we can get some milk for Katy? She's very hungry."

With Jonathan walking close to Rachel, she and the girls all headed home with their new, furry, somewhat straggly addition to the family. The kitten especially seemed to take to Jennie and Jonathan.

"Ouch!"

Jonathan had been holding the kitten against his shirt as he carried her. Katy decided to jump down, her back claws digging sharply into Jonathan's chest as she jumped to the ground.

"Mew, mew, mew."

Katy was standing firmly in one place, her tail straight up, paws firmly planted on the ground, refusing to budge. Jonathan tried to pick her back up. But there wasn't a chance. She swatted his hand with a sharp front claw.

"Ouch," he said again.

Rachel couldn't help but smile. "It looks to me as if you might be using that word in your vocabulary more often."

Maggie and Jennie both started to laugh.

"Ouch." This time, it came from Maggie as she tried to pick Katy up.

Rachel tried next. "Ouch!"

They all three turned and looked at Jennie. "Come on, Katy," she said to the kitten, which obediently followed her. Jennie looked back at the three of them as she and Katy continued walking in front. "She doesn't want to be held. She just wants attention." Jonathan, Rachel, and Maggie stood speechless for a moment before continuing their walk home.

Jonathan's feeling of dread and anxiety returned as they came around the bend. Rachel had no idea that the nearer they drew to the house the more worried Jonathan became. As the house came into view, Jonathan's heart dropped. There stood Jack, or rather swayed Jack, as he drunkenly held onto his whiskey bottle with one hand and steadied himself precariously with his other hand on the porch railing. Maggie and Jennie both drew in their breath sharply. Katy the kitten could sense their fear and mewed to be picked up. Jennie bent down quickly to scoop her new kitten into her arms and held her close.

Their father looked even worse than the last time they saw him. His tall frame was gaunt and his shabby clothes hung on him. His eyes were sunken in their sockets, with blue shadows underneath. Jack's salt and pepper hair was greasy and unkempt. The stubble across his lower face was also gray and dirty. Even from where the four of them stood, they could smell the foul stench of Jack's filthy, unwashed body. This, combined with the strong smell of whiskey from his breath, was unbearable. Rachel felt herself becoming nauseated and thought she might be sick any moment. She leaned back slightly into Jonathan to steady herself. Maggie and Jennie, who was still holding Katy, drew themselves in closer to Rachel. Katy mewed unhappily. Looking over Rachel's head at the sight of this filthy, drunken human being on the porch, Jonathan felt a hatred and rage like nothing he ever knew before.

"Well, well, well," Jack said drunkenly. "What have we here?" He looked at Rachel with leering eyes. Turning his attention to Jonathan, Jack pointed at Rachel and said, "Rachel's a bastard, you know. She's not mine." Turning his attention to Rachel, his eyes full of hatred, he accused her, "You're just like your mother, acting all innocent and pure." He belched. "You been sleeping with that boy?" he asked as he nodded in Jonathan's direction. "You gotta a baby growin' in you yet, you little tramp?"

Rachel's cheeks burned with shame. Her heart felt as if it would leap out of her chest. *How could he do this?*

Maggie and Jennie let out a gasp.

"Ya teachin' your sisters too? Never too young, huh." Jack stopped speaking abruptly as a rock that seemed to come out of nowhere hit him soundly on the side of the head.

Maggie had broken away in a panic, picked up the rock from one of Rachel's piles, and threw it at Jack as hard as she could. "Stop it! Stop it! Stop it!" she screamed at him.

Jack looked stunned as he toppled forward over the railing. Sharp thorns tore into his flesh as he fell into the rose bushes below, leaving bloody evidence behind. Maggie's face was contorted in rage and fear as she rushed at her father, not caring or feeling the thorns' sharpness digging into her own flesh. Maggie pummeled him with her fists, but Jack was already unconscious and never felt the blows.

Maggie collapsed onto the ground next to him. "I hate you. I hate you!" Her sobs poured out from deep within her soul.

Rachel was the first one to reach Maggie, followed by Jonathan, Jennie, and the new kitten. Even Katy seemed to feel Maggie's despair and mewed her concern. Rachel dropped to the ground beside her sister and pulled her up to a sitting position. She took Maggie into her arms and rocked her, stroking her hair while Maggie sobbed uncontrollably. Rachel continued to hold Maggie as she poured out her pain and grief until the tears and sobbing subsided. As she accepted the handkerchief Rachel handed to her, Maggie took in a huge gulp of air and breathed it out slowly to calm herself.

"Why is he so mean and horrible to us? What did we do? What did our mother do? He's evil. I wish he was dead!" Fierce anger flashed out of her hazel green eyes.

No one moved or said anything. What could they say? Jack Walters was indeed a drunken, lying, good-for-nothing, evil man.

Jonathan could hardly wait until the day came that he would ask Rachel to marry him. She and Maggie and Jennie and, of course, Katy would be safe at last. *This cannot go on*, he thought to himself.

A low moan caused all of them to look down at Jack again. He was still unconscious. The side of his head where Maggie had hit him with the rock was bruised and very swollen.

"What if he wakes up?" Jennie asked in a whisper. Her eyes were full of fear as she remembered the horror of what Jack Walters did to them the last time he was angry. She held Katy very close to her, drawing comfort from the little kitten.

Jonathan answered reassuringly, "I don't think so, Jennie. He'll more than likely sleep this one off for at least a day or so." Looking directly at Maggie, he continued in a lighter tone of voice, "That was some aim, Maggie. You're a real slugger, you know. Don't you go feeling badly, though. We all understand why you did it. All right?"

Maggie's swollen red eyes filled with tears again as she looked back at him. She could only nod her head, speechless and appalled at what she had done.

Jonathan looked down at Jack. He tried to keep the disgust out of his voice as he spoke. "Let's get him into the house then."

Once again, Rachel and Maggie found themselves having to move the unconscious form of their drunken father. Thankfully, Jonathan was with them and was able to handle most of Jack's dead weight. The stench, however, was a different story. Jack's body odor was so horrible that even Jonathan could feel himself becoming nauseated as he lifted Jack's dead weight up the porch steps, into the house, and up the stairs to the bedroom. None too gently, he, along with Rachel and Maggie, dropped the unconscious man heavily onto the bed. Rachel untied his boots and removed them quickly, holding her breath the entire time. She wasn't about to remove his filthy socks. They left him lying on the bed to sleep off another drunken binge. Each binge was becoming much worse than the previous one. Jack Walters was wasting away a little bit more every day with the help of his whiskey bottle. To Rachel, it couldn't be soon enough as she once again fought back hatred for her stepfather.

Jonathan was very worried for Rachel, Maggie, and Jennie. He knew Rachel would say no to his offer to stay with his family for the night and, of course, he couldn't stay with the girls there. It would be most inappropriate. Jonathan's heart ached as he walked across the field to his home. *Lord, protect Rachel, Maggie, and Jennie and her new kitten. Please, Lord, just a little while longer until Rachel and I can be married*, he prayed.

Rachel stood outside and watched Jonathan from her front porch as he disappeared around the bend. She wanted to call out to him not to leave, not yet. She wanted to grab her sisters, take them with her, and run after him. Fear and anxiety crept into Rachel's heart. *How much longer, Lord?* she asked. *How much longer until we won't have to live in this constant fear?* Rachel walked across the porch and sat down on one of the porch steps, placing her elbows on her knees and her chin into her hands. She let out a deep, sorrowful sigh. She stayed that way until it was almost dark. Rachel shivered. The temperature outside was dropping. She hadn't brought a shawl or coat outside with her. *The house is probably cold too,* she thought. Rachel stood up, turned, and stepped back up onto the porch and walked to the front door. As she entered the house, she felt the warmth of a newly lit fire. Realizing Maggie must have started a fire in the fireplace, she walked the few steps from the foyer to the parlor. The room felt cozy and warm. But her sisters weren't there. Rachel turned and headed down the hallway to the kitchen to make something for the three of them to eat.

Maggie and Jennie were already in the kitchen when Rachel entered. They moved about as quietly as they could so they didn't wake their father. Maggie put more wood into the stove and a pot of water on for tea. Rachel sliced the bread and set out a jar of homemade jam she brought up from the cold basement, as well as the rest of a salty ham Mrs. Bailey had given to them. Jennie's job was to set the table. No matter how meager their meal, they each did their part to make it homey and inviting, a place to simply be together to share their meal. Katy mewed when she smelled the ham, demanding to be given her fair share.

Maggie had brushed her hair and pinned it up again. Except for her red eyes, her freshly washed face looked much better. Maggie was beginning to understand a little more every day just how much Rachel had actually done for them. Looking across the table at a giggling Jennie with her new kitten, she felt such a rush of love and protection for both her sisters. Maggie promised herself she'd never allow them to be hurt again.

Katy had greedily eaten her fill of the ham and was curled up contently on Jennie's lap, licking her paws to wash her face and ears. The soft sound of her contented purrs made them all smile. Jennie placed her hand on Katy's head and softly stroked her.

Keeping their voices low so they didn't disturb Katy or run the risk of waking their father, the girls chatted about their day, carefully avoiding the one part that was most unpleasant. Rachel had made it her habit long ago to remember the best thing that happened in each day. Maggie and Jennie looked forward to it as well. They each took turns. It gave all three of them hope for their future.

"Who wants to start?" Rachel asked with a smile.

Jennie's free hand went up immediately. "Me first! Me first!" Rachel and Maggie smiled at their little sister and waited. "The best thing that happened today was our new kitten."

As if on cue, Katy awoke at the sound of Jennie's voice, stood up on all fours, and meowed her agreement, sending the three girls into helpless giggles. Katy looked at them as if they had lost their minds. Jennie petted Katy's head.

"Oh, Katy, I'm so glad you're mine." Katy curled up again on Jennie's lap and purred contently.

Jennie reached for the jar of strawberry jam, using her spoon, and placed a dollop of it on her slice of homemade bread. She took a large bite. Jennie loved bread and jam. After she ate it, she sipped her tea and rubbed Katy's head. Katy purred. Jennie looked across the table at Rachel and said, "I remember when we were little you would wake us up and sneak us down to the cellar and give us something to eat. But you never ate, Rachel. Weren't you hungry too?" With this question, Jennie reached for another slice of bread and waited for Rachel to answer.

The question came as a surprise to her. Rachel felt a deep twist of anguish in her heart. Her throat tightened as she tried to hold back tears at the memory of those nights. Yes, she was also very hungry, but her sisters always came first. If there was something left after they had eaten, Rachel would then eat. Many times, there wasn't. Rachel would never let them know how bad things had been. Her sisters would never know she went hungry so they didn't. She would never allow them to feel badly over something that was over and done with. Getting up from the table, Rachel turned away, swallowing the lump in her throat. Tears threatened to spill over, but she held them back. Pretending to be busy, Rachel answered softly, "No. I suppose I wasn't."

Maggie and Jennie helped Rachel clean up the dishes, tidy the kitchen, and sweep the floor. Katy sat on Jennie's chair, calmly watching them, still purring softly.

"I'm so tired I think I can sleep for a week," Jennie said.

Rachel and Maggie both agreed. It had been a wonderfully busy day for all of them, with the one exception of what their father had done. They were more than willing to pass this over.

Rosemary for Remembrance

"Oh, Rachel," Jennie said happily, "I'm so glad Jonathan was here. He did keep his promise, didn't he?" Looking up at Maggie, she said, "And you protected us too." With that, she stepped forward to hug her sister.

Maggie was as tall for her age as Jennie was short for hers. To Jennie, Maggie reminded her of a tall, strong oak, someone she could depend on.

"Why don't the two of you go to bed? I want to check on the fireplace one more time. I'll be up soon." Actually, Rachel was tired too but felt very keyed up and anxious. She hoped the girls would fall asleep soon. Rachel needed time alone to think and pray.

Maggie and Jennie kissed Rachel good night. With Katy riding on Jennie's shoulder, they made their way up the stairs and down the hall to their bedroom. The house was completely quiet. Rachel left the kitchen and walked down the hall to the parlor. She sat down on the chair closest to the fireplace for warmth. Rachel felt chilled to the bone.

An oppressive sense of loneliness fell upon Rachel, surrounding her, enveloping her in its suffocating grip. She felt herself going under in a tide of dark emotions. Despair and hopelessness filled her soul. *If only Jonathan was here,* she thought. *Oh, God, I feel so alone in this. When will this be over?* The questions she asked left her with the feeling that she was under a dark blanket of oppression. *When? What if?* The questions swirled around her mind. Rachel did the only thing she could do. She bowed her head and prayed.

The weight of despair seemed to lift from Rachel's heavy heart. *Yes,* she thought. *No matter what happens, Jesus will always be with me, Maggie, and Jennie.* Rachel let out a sigh. *Thank you, Lord,* was all she could whisper in her mind.

Rachel stood up and checked on the fireplace then stepped back to watch the flames. She thought about Jonathan and how grateful she was to have him in her life. *What would have happened today if Jonathan hadn't been here?* Jack Walters might not have accused her of what he did earlier, but he would've found something horrible to say. He always did. Rachel shivered, though this time not from cold. The sense of dread was threatening to take over again. Rachel bowed her head. *Lord, I am scared, but I believe you when you say you'll take care of us. Please protect us. Keep us safe, Lord.*

Rachel reminded herself that God had a purpose for everything. He had glorious plans for her life and for her sisters' as well. Their whole future was in his hands. *It just can't go on like this forever,* she thought.

Stoking the fire one more time, Rachel placed the poker in the metal bucket beside the fireplace. Padding softly from the parlor through the foyer to the staircase, she carefully tiptoed up the stairs so she wouldn't wake her sisters or Jack. On the way down the long hallway, Rachel stopped for a moment at her stepfather's bedroom. She could smell him before she saw him. She peeked her head around the corner of the door jamb to see Jack's still form. He hadn't moved. Relieved, she felt reassured that he'd remain that way until after she, Maggie, and Jennie left in the morning.

Entering the bedroom she shared with her sisters, Rachel crossed the room and stood at the side of the bed. Jennie and Katy were sleeping in the middle.

Rachel knelt beside the bed and bowed her head again. *Why can't I shake the feeling of dread and fear?* Again, she prayed for their safety. With that, Rachel stood, slid into bed under the tattered blanket, and fell into a restless sleep. Maggie, Jennie, and Katy never stirred.

Chapter Fourteen

Jack's head was pounding loudly in his ears. It felt twice its normal size as he struggled to wake up from another one of his drunken stupors. His mind was lost in a thick, black fog. Why couldn't he open his eyes? It felt as if they had been glued shut.

And where am I? he wondered. Jack stretched out his right hand and felt the material of the blanket. He was in his own bed. *How?* He suddenly felt as if he was going to vomit. Rolling clumsily over onto his side, he retched, hearing it hit the floor as the odor reached his nostrils, making him even sicker. With a low groan, Jack rolled onto his back again as he wiped his mouth with his hand, almost retching again at the smell. Feeling around on the bed, he wondered where his wife was. Slowly he opened his eyes. *Julianna went away. She died on me. When did she die?*

His head hurt, especially on one side of his forehead. Reaching up, he gingerly touched the painful area. Just touching it almost made him retch again. It also made him remember. He'd been on the porch, saying something to Rachel and that no-good Bailey boy, Jonathan. Maggie and Jennie were there too. Jack remembered seeing Maggie out of the corner of his eye as she bent down and picked something up. *That was it,* he realized. Maggie threw something at him. It was something hard. *A rock? But why? It couldn't be,* he thought. Maggie would never hurt him. *Why would she have done that unless Rachel told her to do it?* His eyes became slits just thinking that Rachel had that much control over his own flesh and blood.

In his memory, he could still see Rachel, turning to face him as she stood near the fireplace, fire poker in hand, a look of sheer hatred on her face. He especially remembered the ice-cold tone in her voice as she warned him to stay away from Maggie and Jennie. Jack hated Rachel. Maggie and Jennie were his daughters. Rachel wasn't. She wasn't his flesh and blood. Rachel came from an evil seed.

She had no idea what he'd done for her by marrying her mother. *How dare she interfere with his real daughters and cause him this trouble?* That was it. This was all her fault. It was her fault that she drove him to drink, her fault that Julianna died, and her fault that Maggie and Jennie listened to her and not him. *Good for nothing. That's what she is. Nothing.*

Jack allowed the fury to build up inside him until he felt as if he would explode. *Well, I'll show her. I'll show her right now.* Still in a drunken stupor, Jack clumsily crawled out of bed, unaware of slipping in his own vomit. Getting up from his hands and knees, he righted himself and staggered toward the door, stopping for only a moment at the doorway before stepping into the hall. *I'll show her,* he thought. *I'll show them all.* Despite his drunkenness, Jack in his sticky, wet-socked feet made very little noise as he made his way down the stairs, across the foyer, and into the parlor. Crossing the room, Jack lurched to the fireplace. He bent down and tossed more logs

Rosemary for Remembrance

onto the fire. Mesmerized by the flames that flew up from the new wood, he tried to remember what he came downstairs for. His eyes settled on the poker. *Yes. The poker. That's it.* He'd teach Rachel a lesson she would never forget. Picking up the poker, he rammed the lower half of it into the fire until it was blazing hot. Jack pulled it out and held it up. *Yes,* he thought. *This looks like it will do very nicely.*

The evil, leering smirk that came to Jack's dry, cracked lips caused them to split and bleed. He didn't care. Running his tongue across them, he nodded to himself. *Yes. I'll teach those little bastards a lesson they'll never forget. They'll remember it for the rest of their lives.* He laughed inwardly. The rest of their lives would be over tonight.

Jack was about to turn and make his way back out of the parlor when the room tilted suddenly. A sharp wave of dizziness overtook him. As he stumbled forward, darkness closed in on him. The white-hot poker was still tightly gripped in his hand when he lost consciousness, unaware of the flames reaching out for him as a burning log rolled from the fireplace onto the worn carpet.

Rachel felt warm, too warm, as she awoke and started to cough. She sat up. *Why is it hard to breathe?* Fully awake, her heart pounded wildly with fear as the smell of thick heavy smoke reached her nostrils. Frantically, she shook her sisters by the shoulders to wake them. "Girls, get up! Get up quickly! The house is on fire!"

Maggie and Jennie woke to the panicked voice of their sister.

Mary Netreba

"What's wrong, Rachel?" Jennie asked as she yawned, unaware of what was happening.

Maggie had already jumped out of bed and was pulling at Jennie. She could smell the smoke too. "The house is on fire, Jennie! We have to get out!" From somewhere below, they heard glass exploding and the horrible sound of wood popping and crackling as the flames devoured the lower part of the house.

Jennie screamed for her kitten. "Katy! Katy, where are you?" she yelled in panic as tears poured down her cheeks. Maggie checked quickly under the bed. No Katy. "She's not here." Rachel ran out into the hallway. No sign of the kitten. They were running out of time. The fire was beginning to makes its way up the staircase. Their exit was blocked. Rushing back into the bedroom, Rachel shut the door tightly.

Rachel turned to her sisters and told them, "We have to go now! Out the window!"

Jennie screamed, "But Katy! Where is my Katy?"

Rachel and Maggie pulled Jennie to the window as she continued to scream for her kitten. Maggie called out, "We'll find your kitten, Jennie! But we have to get out!"

Rachel yanked open the window. It was a long drop, but they had to do it. There was no other choice. Rachel looked at Maggie and said, "Maggie, you go first. Hang onto the ledge. Then drop to the ground. Let yourself fall."

Maggie was terrified, but she knew that time was too precious to worry about a broken leg. Hoisting herself onto the ledge, Maggie slid herself around so she could hang there before dropping. The popping sounds of the fire grew louder as the fire became more intense. She knew their bedroom would begin to fill with smoke within minutes. Closing her eyes, time stood still as Maggie let go of the ledge and landed with a sound thump. Her ankle hurt terribly, but she forced herself to stand. She looked up. Rachel was looking out the window at her. Thankfully, the underbrush and years of dead leaves helped break Maggie's fall.

Jennie was in a panic and was fighting Rachel for everything it was worth. She kept screaming for Katy.

"We'll find her, Jennie, but we have to get out!" Rachel looked out the window again. "Maggie!" she called, "do your best to break her fall." In one quick swoop, Rachel lifted her younger sister up into her arms, leaned out the window, and, saying a silent prayer, let go.

Jennie was still screaming as she landed on Maggie and the ground, knocking the air out of both of them. But Jennie was safe. "My kitten. My kitten," Jennie whimpered.

Maggie looked up and screamed. Their room was brightly lit with flames, their hot colors dancing toward the open window. *Where is Rachel?* Maggie screamed, "Rachel! Rachel!"

Rachel had lost her balance when she dropped Jennie out the window and fell back onto the floor. Holding onto the windowsill, she pulled herself up. She felt so weak, so sleepy, just like how she felt the night she almost died in the blizzard. The thought of it brought her to new awareness. Rachel forced herself onto the ledge and let herself fall. She sprained her wrist trying to break her fall. But they all made it out alive—all except the kitten.

Jennie screamed desperately for her kitten. "Katy! We have to save Katy!" She sobbed as she begged her sisters to save her kitten. "Please…"

The house moaned heavily as if it had a life of its own. The sound of it sent chills down their spines. It took only a moment for them to realize the screeching noise they thought was the house burning was actually horrific screams coming from inside the house. Rachel, Maggie, and Jennie moved as quickly as they could to get away from the house and the horrible screams. When they were at a safe distance, they reluctantly turned. The sight was unimaginable. Rachel, Maggie, and Jennie stood mesmerized in shocked disbelief as they watched their home fall in on itself. The sounds of the total destruction of their home would be something they would never forget. The fire was too furious and hot to try to save their father. The horrible sound of Jack Walters's screams while he burned to death would never be forgotten as it went deep into their souls. Those last, horrible moments of his life would stay with them forever.

Rachel, Maggie, and Jennie were shaken to the core of their very beings. Rachel couldn't remember telling her sisters to start walking; she only remembered that they turned away from the sight of their home burning to the ground. They walked on with the light of the moon illuminating the darkness. Maggie's ankle hurt too much to go any farther. One sister sobbed her heart out for her precious little Katy, another had a sprained ankle, and the third was devastated as she watched their former life literally go up in flames. They finally stopped to rest at the edge of the Baileys' field. The grass was deep and soft.

We'll have to stay here for the night, Rachel thought. Maggie and Jennie huddled together for warmth. Jennie, her heart completely broken, cried herself to sleep. Rachel's heart ached for Jennie and the kitten. *If only there had been time, perhaps I could have saved her.* Maggie had also fallen into an exhausted asleep.

Rachel, however, stayed awake, her mind numb with the horrible events. *Was it the fireplace?* Rachel was always very careful about the fireplace. *What had happened? Did Jack somehow awake from his drunken stupor and go downstairs? Did he start the fire? But he was so drunk it didn't seem possible he could have even gotten out of bed. If he did, then what was he doing up in the middle of night?* Rachel couldn't help but feel grateful that she and her sisters had made it out of the fire. And out of the life they had with their abusive father. He could never hurt them again. Even though she was thankful, she also felt guilty.

Rachel started to shake with nerves and the chill of the late spring night. She tried to think of something else, but it was impossible. Her thoughts kept returning to the many questions that ran through her mind. *What will we do? Our home is gone forever.* Fear and doubt were mixed with exhaustion as Rachel looked up at the night sky. The full moon beamed down upon the pastures and farmland around them. The stars were bright and beautiful. They were a blur of twinkling lights in Rachel's tear-filled eyes as she thought about what to do next. She remembered Mrs. Bailey once telling her, "When things look down, simply look up." Tears rolled down Rachel's cheeks, but she no longer felt anxiety and dread. Why did she feel God's protection when she had wished so much for her stepfather to die?

Right then, Rachel heard the tiny sound of something coming closer.

"Mew."

The sound of mewing was very weak and pathetic, but there she was. Making her way wearily through the tall grass was Katy the kitten. Rachel couldn't believe her eyes. A very dirty, very frightened, and very determined Katy had escaped the fire. Rachel stood up quickly, walking the last few steps toward Katy, and reached down to pick her up. Cuddling her close, Rachel sobbed into Katy's singed fur. Katy mewed and purred, thankful to be with her family. Rachel couldn't believe it. *How in the world did Katy make it out of that fire alive? Thank you, God. Thank you so much for Katy, for saving us all from dying in the fire.* Rachel carried Katy in her arms back to where her sisters were sleeping. She settled onto her side in the soft grass, holding Katy. Katy clung to Rachel.

Maggie and Jennie slept on exhaustedly, unaware that Katy was all right. Breathing another prayer of thanks, Rachel knew that somehow everything would work out for good.

Things are going to be all right, she thought as she drifted off to sleep with Katy's soft purrs rumbling against her chest.

Katy, content to have found her family all together, placed one tiny paw over Rachel's hand and went to sleep.

Chapter Fifteen

Rachel awoke the next morning to Jennie's soft giggles. Opening her eyes, Rachel sat up and watched as Katy went about, running in circles around Jennie's ankles in the early morning sun.

Jennie bent down and picked her up. Hugging her close, Jennie said, "Oh, Katy, I thought I lost you. Where were you, you naughty kitty?" Katy looked up at Jennie with her big green eyes and gave a "Meow." Jennie hugged her. Noticing that Rachel was awake, Jennie said plainly, "I'm hungry, and so is Katy."

Rachel looked up at Jennie. Jennie's hair was a tangled mess. Her nightclothes were dirty and torn in spots, probably from her jump out the window and sleeping on the ground. Rachel could smell the heavy smoke on Jennie's clothes but then realized they probably all smelled like smoke. It was a miracle to Rachel that they all survived, not just Katy.

Maggie stirred slightly in her sleep. Rachel, not really wanting to wake her, knew they had to get to the Baileys' for help. "Maggie. Maggie." Rachel shook her sister gently. Maggie opened her eyes, sat up, and looked at her Rachel. Just like Jennie, Maggie was dirty and disheveled. Rachel realized she probably looked just as bad.

Tears filled Maggie's eyes as she asked, "It really happened, didn't it, Rachel? I can't believe it really happened. The kitten? And our father?"

Rachel was surprised at how raspy Maggie's voice sounded. *It must be from the smoke,* she thought. Rachel looked at her sister with kindness and sympathy.

It must be true, Maggie thought. Rachel nodded her head. She then pointed to where Jennie was standing, holding her precious kitten. If there was one ray of hope through the terrible events of the night before, that ray of hope was Katy. Maggie looked at Rachel in amazement. *How did this tiny kitten get out?*

"Can we please go get something to eat, Rachel?" Jennie asked plaintively.

The ragtag threesome, barefoot and dirty, along with their little kitten, Katy, slowly made the rest of their way across the Baileys' field. Maggie's ankle was throbbing, but she was determined to walk on it. The sun was higher, indicating it was at least midmorning.

"I need to stop for just a little bit, you two," Maggie said to her sisters. They sat down in the soft grass, Katy mewing her own unhappy opinion of having to stop. She crawled up onto Jennie's lap, gave one more meow, and settled in.

They were just a little over halfway there. The day was becoming warmer with a slight breeze that brushed lightly across their faces. Looking up at the blue sky with the soft, billowy clouds, Rachel could hardly believe their circumstances. *How could there be such a beautiful day following the ugliness and tragedy of the night before?* It was hard to believe the events of the night before actually happened. Rachel and Maggie both looked over at Jennie. She had Katy up on her hind legs, holding her front paws in each hand, singing a song of made-up words repeated over and over again.

"I love you. You love me too. I love you. You love me too…" Rachel and Maggie looked at each other, the worry for their little sister clearly showing on their faces. Maggie clumsily got to her feet. Gingerly, she placed her foot with the sprained ankle on the ground. Their stopping to rest had helped. Rachel stood beside Maggie and drew Maggie's arm over the back of her neck for support as they continued on.

"Come on, Jennie," Maggie said to her sister softly. "Let's go get some breakfast, all right? And something for Katy too."

Jennie looked up at her and answered matter of factly, "Katy is very hungry, you know." Jennie placed Katy on the ground and stood up. "Come on, Katy. It's time to go." Katy followed close behind. As they started walking again, Jennie asked, "How come the two of you are all dirty?" She leaned into Maggie and sniffed. She made a face, wrinkling up her nose in distaste. "You stink too. You smell like smoke."

The Baileys' home was within sight. Smoke was coming out of both chimneys of the large, two-story, frame home with its welcoming porch. Maggie's ankle was throbbing in pain again.

Rachel asked her, "Maggie, do you want to stop? It would be all right to stop for a bit."

Maggie looked ahead. Determination set Maggie's jaw. "No. I can keep going. It's just a little farther."

Rachel could see the pain etched on Maggie's face and heard it in her voice. But she knew that when Maggie was determined to get something done, it would be done. "All right. Let's go then," replied Rachel.

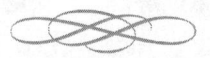

※

Ellen Bailey had been busy in her kitchen since the crack of dawn. Baking days started very early and ended late in the day. She gently placed each newly shaped loaf of unbaked bread into the waiting bread pans, covering them with a light cloth.

Within hours, the wonderful aroma of freshly baked bread, fruit pies with the scent of cinnamon, and light, fluffy cakes would fill her home. Ellen loved baking, but she especially enjoyed the cakes. Frosting them was the best part.

As Ellen put flour, baking powder, salt, sugar, and milk together in a large bowl for her cake recipe, she realized she was short on eggs.

Letting out a brief sigh, she turned away from her work and walked across the kitchen to pick up the basket she used for gathering eggs from the chicken coop. She always kept it on the wooden chair by the door. Picking up the basket, she opened the door with her free hand and gasped in disbelief as her basket dropped to the floor.

There stood Rachel, Maggie, and Jennie, along with the kitten they had adopted the evening before. Ellen was speechless. All she could do was stare. The girls were a mess. All three of them were filthy. Their dirty clothes were shredded in places. There were deep scratches and bruises on their arms, necks, faces, and hands. Maggie was leaning on Rachel for support, with her arm around Rachel's neck. Her foot rested gingerly on the ground. Dark dirt and soot streaked their faces. They were covered with black soot all the way down to their bare feet. Ellen stood aghast. The acrid odor of burned wood reached her nostrils. *What happened to these girls?* Their hair was a loose, tangled mess. Jennie's hung over her face.

Jennie was the first to speak. "Good morning, Mrs. Bailey. Can we have something to eat, and something for Katy too?" Katy, in Jennie's arms, looked up at Mrs. Bailey with her orange and white fur face also covered with soot. Her whiskers were singed. Katy gave a plaintive mew.

Unable to find the right words, or any words for that matter, Ellen Bailey stepped aside as Rachel, Maggie, and Jennie shuffled across the kitchen floor. All three sat down wearily at the large oak table. Asking no questions but allowing herself some time to think, Ellen told them she would be right back and went out to the chicken coop for eggs. Ellen returned to the house and entered through the kitchen. The girls hadn't moved. Rachel and Maggie looked…Ellen's brows knit together. They looked devastated. *But something seemed different about Jennie.* Ellen couldn't quite figure it out. Instead, setting her thoughts aside, she started making the girls' breakfast. She poured a small bowl of milk for Katy and set it on the floor. The girls sat quietly and watched as a very hungry, very noisy little Katy slurped up every drop, licking the entire bowl until it was clean. Tummy full, she curled up at Jennie's ankles under the table for a nap, purring contently.

Nothing was said while Mrs. Bailey went about fixing them a meal of bacon, fried eggs, and thick slices of homemade bread with homemade jelly. Rachel and Maggie's eyes had a haunted look, as if they were lost in their own world. Jennie seemed almost happy to be in the Baileys' kitchen as she looked all around her. The girls were so hungry that they ate every bite on their plates, even wiping up the bacon juices with the bread. Full and satisfied, Jennie looked like she could fall asleep. Her eyes were half-closed and she leaned toward Maggie, who remained silent and sat staring at her empty plate. Rachel murmured a "thank you" for all of them and then was silent as well. She didn't know what else to say. There had been no other place for them to go. Rachel felt at a loss. She didn't know what to do next.

Ellen asked Maggie and Jennie if they wanted to take their kitten outside to play. Jennie woke right up to the suggestion and, bending down, scooped up a surprised Katy, who meowed at having her nap interrupted. Maggie was eager to go outside too. Chairs scraped backward as they stood up to go outside. Maggie winced. She had forgotten about her ankle.

Maggie looks desperate to get away, Ellen noticed.

As they turned away, Rachel said, "Wait a moment, girls. Aren't you forgetting something?" Turning back around, they realized they'd forgotten to push their chairs back in. Maggie did so quickly, also taking care of Jennie's chair since Jennie was holding Katy. "Anything else?" Rachel asked.

In unison, both Maggie and Jennie said, "Thank you for breakfast, Mrs. Bailey. It was very good."

Jennie smiled. "And Katy thanks you too."

Ellen waited until both girls were outside, watching them from the kitchen window until they had reached the barn. Maggie was hobbling along after her sister. She sat down on a bale of hay and watched as Jennie and Katy took great delight in chasing the rooster around the barn yard. From where Rachel sat, she could hear Jennie's laughter. It seemed odd and very out of place. A new wave of despair came over Rachel.

She felt as if she was being pulled into a deep, suffocating darkness. Rachel closed her eyes for a moment. *Please, Lord, make it not be true*, she asked. Rachel could hear Ellen Bailey turning around and walking back to the table. Pulling out a chair across from Rachel, she sat down. Ellen wasn't even sure where to begin. Rachel was becoming more nervous as she sat, quietly waiting, her hands fidgeting on her lap under the table. It seemed to take too long for Ellen to ask the obvious question.

"What happened to you and the girls, Rachel?" Rachel wasn't sure if it was the question itself or the kindness she was being shown, but that was all it took for Rachel to completely fall apart. Her head hung low as she placed her face in her hands, sobbing huge sobs that shook her small frame while hot tears fell through her fingers to drop onto the table, creating a small puddle. Ellen had seen Rachel cry before, but never like this. Her sobs carried every ounce of unimaginable hurt from the years of hardship in their lives, the abuse of Jack Walters, and the constant worry for the welfare of Maggie and Jennie. Her sobs carried the devastation of too many losses on shoulders not strong enough to handle what should never have been hers.

Ellen Bailey did the only thing she could do. She sat quietly and waited. Her own heart broke for what Rachel, Maggie, and Jennie had gone through. Tears filled her eyes thinking of the beautiful person their mother had been and how Jack had destroyed her. Julianna, her friend who thought she was in love with a boy and became pregnant by him. When he refused to marry her, she was terrified. In a panic, Julianna took Jack's offer when he said he would marry her, take the child as his own, and take care of them. Ellen tried to talk her out of it, knowing that Jack was no good. But Julianna, frightened by what her parents, especially her father, would do, married Jack anyway. Within a week of their marriage, her parents died in an unfortunate train accident, leaving Julianna well off financially. But Jack, always looking out for himself, spent all of it over time and destroyed Julianna in the process. Ellen sighed in deep sadness. *So much pain and heartbreak,* she thought, *all because of this evil excuse for a man.*

"He…he's…," Rachel's voice was hushed as she tried to get the words out. Ellen had to strain to hear her. The fear of actually saying the words was overwhelming for Rachel. Saying the words would make it real, and the reality was too much for Rachel to bear. Pausing for a moment, Rachel tried to still the panic in her heart. *Say it! Say it!* The voice in her head would not let her alone. Rachel knew she would have to get this out. Steeling herself, she looked directly at Ellen Bailey. "He's dead. I killed him. It's my fault that he's dead. I caused this." With this last statement, Rachel bowed her head again, sobbing hysterically as she pounded her fists on the table. "It's my fault. It's all my fault!"

Ellen quickly got up from her side of the table and came around to sit down beside Rachel. She grabbed hold of Rachel's shoulders and turned Rachel to face her. She said, "Rachel, look at me. Listen to me. Whatever happened, you didn't cause it."

Rachel looked into Ellen's eyes for a moment. All Rachel could see was compassion. With relief, Rachel collapsed into her loving arms. Ellen cradled her while she cried loudly, loudly enough to bring Elias and Jonathan running from the barn. A surprised father and son ran into Maggie and Jennie, who was holding her kitten closely. Stunned by their appearance, the men knew something very bad must have happened. Even the kitten looked sooty, its fur singed in places, and her little white whiskers almost gone.

"Stay here, girls," Jonathan told them. He didn't want them to see Rachel.

Rachel couldn't understand what would have made her stepfather get up in the middle of the night. If the fire woke him up, why couldn't he get out of the house? She must have done something to have caused this. Maybe she could have saved him too.

Elias and Jonathan stepped into the kitchen, forgetting to shut the door behind them as they stopped in their tracks. Rachel looked even worse than her sisters. Her tangled hair was streaked with soot and badly singed in places. Her clothing was torn and covered with soot. Bruises, scratches, and cuts covered her arms and hands. The whole kitchen smelled like the charred remains of a fire. *What happened?*

Rachel's sobs slowed to a soft cry. Unaware that Elias and Jonathan had entered the kitchen, Rachel tearfully told Ellen about waking up to the smell of smoke and realizing the house was on fire. Her voice faltered as she told Ellen about their frightening escape as they dropped from the bedroom window to the ground below. "That's how Maggie sprained her ankle and I sprained my wrist." Her sobs started again when she tried to tell her about the screams of her stepfather in the fire. She told her of the horrible beatings Jack gave them and how Jack took all their food if she didn't hide it from him first. For Ellen, it was difficult to understand what Rachel was saying as she kept tripping over her words in an attempt to get them all out at once.

The sound of Katy meowing caused both Ellen and Rachel to turn and find Maggie, Jennie, the kitten and Elias and Jonathan standing in the kitchen. Ellen gave a slight shake of her head as she looked at her husband, her eyes full of concern.

"Girls," Ellen said to Maggie and Jennie, "will you help me with some of the housework today?"

Very eagerly the girls agreed. Maggie could do some of the things on the list, like peeling and slicing the basket of apples, while sitting down at the table.

Jennie placed Katy gently on a kitchen chair and told her, "Katy, you stay right here while I do my housework. It's very important." Katy looked up at Jennie with big, green eyes, gave a yawn, and curled up for a nap.

Ellen gave Maggie and Jennie a list of small easy tasks to do while she, Elias, Jonathan, and Rachel made their way back across the field. Elias and Jonathan had stopped at the barn first on the way out. Each of them carried a shovel, not knowing if they would need it or what they would find. The sun was higher in the sky and very warm. Bright patches of brilliant violets and Johnny jump-ups were peeking out here and there throughout the fields.

Rachel took a deep breath. Here, the air smelled fresh and clean. Here, there was no danger. Rachel wanted to stop here, where she wouldn't have to face whatever awaited them. But she knew she couldn't.

With difficulty, Rachel repeated her story to Jonathan and Elias about what had happened and the chain of events leading up to the fire. Little pieces of forgotten memory came back to her in patches. She remembered having to pick Jennie up and drop her from the window to Maggie, who was waiting below. Rachel remembered with horror the loud roar of the fire as it devoured the house. She was relieved that this time, as she told her story, she didn't cry. It seemed impossible on this beautiful, bright day that the tragic events of the night before could have actually happened, but they had. As they approached the collapsed home, still smoldering, the smoke drifting lazily upward, the reality of the situation hit Rachel again with overwhelming clarity. Everything tilted in front of Rachel's eyes before righting itself again.

For Elias, Ellen, and Jonathan, who was holding Rachel's hand, what they saw before them filled them with horror and disbelief. Jonathan could feel Rachel stiffen as her eyes took in the nightmare before her. They stopped in their tracks for several minutes before continuing on. The smell from the dying fire was very strong, overwhelming them as they walked closer to what was once a home. Their eyes welled up from the harsh, acrid smoke.

Ellen remembered times in this once-elegant home when she visited with her best friend in their youth. She remembered how beautiful the home looked after it had been built. This once simple, elegant Victorian home was gone. What she saw before her filled her with deep grief and sadness. Her eyes couldn't contain the devastation. Tears rolled unchecked down her cheeks as she cried to herself. She felt grief for her childhood friend, grief for Julianna's daughters, who also had to endure life with Jack Walters, and grief that he had destroyed everything. It was almost more than she could bear. Ellen's grief turned to anger. Jack Walters had destroyed everything he ever touched.

"Stay here," Jonathan said gently to his mother and Rachel. Tears of sorrow and anger continued to flow down Ellen's cheeks unchecked as she remained where she was. From here, they could all see that a large part of the fireplace was still intact, although blackened in soot and ashes. It looked like a silhouette against the light of day.

Rachel stayed close beside Ellen, their arms linked together. Past the point of tears, she looked at the scene in front of her. The dark ugliness of what was left of the burned, wood-frame home and the charred remains of the life she, Maggie and Jennie shared there would always be with her. Strangely, Rachel felt no sense of loss, only a sense of relief, as if somehow this chapter in her life was closing and a new chapter beginning, although she didn't know what the future held in store for any of them.

Jonathan and his father walked farther on. Slowly and carefully, they picked their way through the piles of charred, burned timber, ashes, and the smaller pieces of wood and jagged, broken shards of glass. In many places, they could feel the heat coming up through the soles of their boots from the dying embers underneath. The complete and total devastation of the home was beyond comprehension. Elias looked over at his son. Both of them were thinking the same thing but didn't say it. *How did Rachel, Maggie, Jennie and Katy escape this fire?* As Elias and Jonathan moved closer toward the fireplace, they hesitated, each dreading what they expected to find. It was only a hunch, but since Jack didn't make it out alive, they knew he had to be somewhere in this rubble. Jonathan's foot bumped on a hard object. They stopped suddenly and looked down. A chill ran down their spines. They had found what they were looking for.

Nothing could have prepared either one of them for this sight. Carefully, Jonathan and Elias Bailey began lifting the burned timber and some of the smaller broken pieces of the fireplace. It didn't take long until they found the rest of the charred remains of Jack Walters. The sight was so horrible that Jonathan could feel the bile rising up in his throat. He forced it back, not wanting his mother or Rachel to see him be sick. Elias had seen many terrible things in his life, including the dead bodies of victims in the train wreck that killed Julianna's parents. He still had nightmares about it. But this horrible sight before him was unimaginable. This was by far the worst sight Elias had ever seen. The smell of burned flesh was overwhelming. Gritting his teeth in determination, he bent down over Jack's charred remains. He noticed there was something peeking out from the ashes next to the body. Standing up, he took the edge of his shovel, gently moving the ashes out of the way.

A fire poker lay beside Jack Walters. His charred hand, burned to the bone, appeared to be wrapped around the handle of the poker tightly. There was no way to remove it. Turning to his son, Elias nodded and said, "Looks like this might be the cause of the fire. Jack was probably stoking it, and the fire got out of control."

Jonathan nodded in agreement, although something seemed amiss. What his father said made sense, but it just didn't feel right to Jonathan. Why he felt this way he didn't know. He did know that Jack Walters had been an evil, vile man. Jonathan couldn't picture Jack Walters caring enough to keep a fire burning for anyone. But he let out a deep sigh of relief at his next thought. Jack Walters could never hurt Rachel, Maggie, or Jennie again.

How very thankful Jonathan was at that moment that the girls had made it out alive. *And Katy too,* he thought. As he looked around at the devastating scene, he could barely believe it. Jonathan knew in his heart that this was God intervening on the girls' behalf. God had kept them safe. He kept Rachel safe for him. God had indeed answered his prayer. Jonathan bowed his head in a silent prayer of gratitude and praise for the mercy and love God bestowed on them in this tragedy.

As they turned away from the sickening sight of Jack's charred body, Elias and Jonathan walked back to Ellen and Rachel. The look on their faces told them what they needed to know. From the look in Jonathan eyes, Rachel knew for sure that they had found Jack and he was dead. Elias repeated to his wife and Rachel the same explanation he told Jonathan. "It looks like he was trying to stoke the fire and somehow it got out of control."

Rachel looked at him and then down at the ground and said nothing. Her stepfather would never have gotten up in the middle of the night to stoke a fire, especially when drunk. All his life, Jack Walters cared only for himself. He must have woken up and gone downstairs to the parlor. *But what was he doing with that poker?* In her heart, Rachel already knew. Jack Walters was planning to hurt her and perhaps Maggie and Jennie. And in her heart, she also knew that God had answered her prayers. God had protected her and her sisters from him. *But what will become of us now?*

Chapter Sixteen

The sound of blood-curdling screams woke not only Rachel and Maggie but the entire Bailey household.

"No. No. I promise I'll be good. Please don't hurt me. Please," the crying voice begged.

"Jennie! Jennie! Wake up!" Rachel and Maggie were both trying to wake Jennie up from her nightmare. Frightened by the commotion, Katy leaped off the bed and crawled underneath, cowering in one corner in fear. Jennie awoke to see Rachel and Maggie on either side of her. Tears were running down her cheeks as she sobbed uncontrollably. She turned her head to look at Rachel and then at Maggie.

Jennie cried, "Please don't let him hurt me anymore." Rachel and Maggie looked over Jennie's head at each other. Jennie hadn't seemed to react to the fire or to their father's death. She never questioned why they were living with the Baileys. All she wanted was to play with Katy and talked to her constantly. She didn't want to talk about what happened. Jennie didn't want to talk to anyone except for her sisters and her kitten.

They all three jumped at the sound of pounding on their bedroom door. "Girls! Girls! Are you all right in there?" Maggie quickly got off the bed and crossed the room to open the door. All three Baileys stood in their nightclothes. There was obvious concern on their faces as they looked past Maggie to see Rachel holding a sobbing Jennie.

Rachel looked up at the four of them still standing in the doorway. To the Baileys, she said, "Jennie was having a very bad dream."

"It wasn't a dream!" screamed Jennie as she pulled away from Rachel angrily. "Daddy wants to hurt me. Please don't let him hurt me." She collapsed into tears again, throwing herself against Rachel's chest.

With a shock, they all realized that Jennie didn't remember anything but Katy. She had no recollection of the fire or jumping from the second-story window, spending the night in the field, their father's death, or his terrible screams as he burned. For this last part, Rachel was grateful. The memory of his screams caused Rachel to shudder still. But someone would have to tell Jennie. She couldn't go on believing their father was going to hurt her. Rachel looked up at the Baileys with pleading eyes.

"I'll do it," Jonathan said gently to Rachel. Rachel gave him such a look of gratitude that his heart actually leaped in his chest. He wanted so badly to hold Rachel at that moment. *But this is not the time,* he reminded himself.

Jonathan waited until everyone had left the room, closing the door softly. As he sat down on the rocking chair beside the bed, Katy crawled out from underneath it, mewing pathetically. Jonathan gently picked her up and placed her in Jennie's arms. The kitten seemed to calm down. Watching Jennie closely, Jonathan said, "Jennie, there's something you need to know."

Elias and Ellen, Rachel, and Maggie all made their way down the stairs to the kitchen. Ellen decided to make a large pot of coffee. There was no going back to sleep anymore that night.

Chapter Seventeen

Jonathan had known for a long time that he wanted Rachel to be his wife. He was planning to ask for her hand on her sixteenth birthday. But the events on the night of the tragic fire changed everything. The girls had nothing. They were all living with the Baileys. Jonathan had talked it over with his parents and told them he wanted to ask Rachel to marry him. They gave him their blessing. Elias and Ellen Bailey loved Rachel, Maggie, and Jennie as their own anyway. It was only right that Jonathan and Rachel should marry.

The following Sunday after church, Ellen suggested Jonathan and Rachel take a walk while she, Maggie, and Jennie fixed Sunday dinner. The sun was high and bright in the beautiful, blue sky with only a few clouds drifting gently as they started walking across the fields, stopping occasionally to pick a flower. Rachel did most of the talking while Jonathan listened. But Jonathan was deep in thought, and didn't seem to hear Rachel. His mind was full of scenarios of how he'd ask Rachel for her hand in marriage. *Should I drop to one knee and propose?* he asked himself. *Did any man ever ask for a woman's hand in marriage while they were walking through a field? More than likely not*, he answered himself. *Maybe I should…*

"You're awfully quiet today," Rachel said.

"Hmm?" was Jonathan's only response.

Rachel stopped walking and turned to face him. Jonathan stopped too and nervously turned to face her. She was a little exasperated as she dropped one of the flowers she'd picked. "I said you're very quiet today."

Jonathan almost blurted out, "Will you marry me?" just to get it over with. *What if she says no?* he wondered. Doubt seeped into his soul. *I'm not a prize, really. Maybe Rachel wants something more, maybe some rich fella like those people in New York. Rachel deserves so much than I can give her. Our lives will be simple and maybe even difficult at times. I'll never be able to give her all the things she deserves. How can I ask her to marry Me? What am I thinking? Maybe I…*

Jonathan's rushing thoughts were interrupted by a new concern. *Oh no. It can't be,* he thought. But the snorting approach of the bull told him it was real. This bull was just over two years old and, like his father, a brute of a beast. He liked to charge and butt heads with the cattle and sometimes people too if they didn't get out of his way fast enough. Their last hired hand left after an encounter with the bull and swore he'd never come back as he limped away.

Jonathan and Rachel looked at each other with wide-eyed surprise and then again at the bull. As they sprinted away, they could hear the bull snorting close behind them. "Run, Rachel! Run!" Jonathan screamed.

The fence was just ahead. With one mighty leap, they hauled themselves up over the fence railing to end up inside the fence as the enraged bull ran past them, his hooves thundering so hard it shook the ground beneath them. Relieved that the danger was past, Jonathan started laughing more from nervousness than anything. But this time, Rachel wasn't laughing. In fact, he noticed, she was downright furious. Her eyes burned into his. She clumsily stood up, which only made Jonathan laugh harder. Stomping her foot on the ground, hands on her hips, she gave him a look that clearly let him know how she felt.

Uh-oh, Jonathan thought. He pressed his lips together in an attempt to stop laughing, but as he looked at her, he couldn't keep the smile from his face. Rachel's neatly pinned-up hair had come undone, some of the long strands hanging over her soft, clear eyes. She looked completely winded, her cheeks flushed from the exertion. To Jonathan, Rachel looked beautiful.

"If you'd been listening to me to begin with, we would've spotted that darn bull sooner," Rachel said angrily.

Jonathan was doing his best not to laugh again. But Jonathan knew Rachel so well. He knew what she was really angry about. He had been so deep in thought about how to ask her to marry him that he never even heard most of what she was saying. Rachel kept on talking as she tried to put her hair in place.

"Maybe you don't care about being gouged to death, but I do. I have two sisters to take care of. I have to go to the factory every day. I—."

"Rachel, will you marry me?" Jonathan blurted out and then checked himself. *Darn it,* he said to himself. *This isn't how I planned it. I wanted to—.*

"What?" Rachel asked. She stood perfectly still. She wasn't sure if she heard him correctly or not. Her hands dropped to her sides, unsure what to do.

Jonathan looked down into her eyes and let out a sigh. "Oh, Rachel, this isn't how I planned this moment. I wanted everything to be so right." He let out another sigh, disappointed in himself, knowing he'd probably ruined everything.

Jonathan took a small step toward her. He lightly brushed away a long strand of hair she had missed and tucked it behind her left ear. Rachel held her breath as she looked up into Jonathan's eyes. They were standing very close, too close.

"Will you, Rachel? I love you. Will you marry me?" Jonathan asked. It was his turn to hold his breath.

For Rachel, this was her dream come true. How often had she dreamed of Jonathan saying those very words she longed to hear? And how often had she dreamed of her response, always a yes. *Yes! I'll marry you*, she would say in her mind.

But this was no longer a dream. Jonathan really loved her. He said so. Rachel opened her mouth to speak, but nothing came out. Yes! Her heart was saying, "Yes," but the words wouldn't come. Rachel did the only thing she could do. She suddenly threw her arms around Jonathan's neck, almost knocking him down, and cried.

As Jonathan's shirt grew wet with tears, he kissed her temple, holding her tightly, and gently said, "I guess I can take this as a yes."

Rachel started to giggle. The giggle turned to laughter until Jonathan was laughing too. Without warning, Jonathan leaned down and kissed her on the lips. Their laughter suddenly stopped. Rachel, her cheeks turning pink, looked down at her feet. She felt as if she was flying.

"Rachel, look at me," Jonathan said softly. Rachel stayed in his arms as she looked up into his eyes. *So this is what love looks like*, Rachel thought as she eagerly returned his kiss.

Chapter Eighteen

Rachel was standing on the plot of ground where their home would be built. The land had been cleared of trees and brush and was ready for the foundation to be laid. Elias and Ellen had deeded part of their property to them and set out to build a home for Jonathan and Rachel. Jonathan knew Rachel would want her sisters with her, and he wanted their home big enough for all the children they would have. Rachel's cheeks grew pink when he said it in front of his parents.

Her heart was filled with joy and thankfulness to God. He had answered her prayers far beyond what she could ever have imagined. *Jonathan loves me! He always has.* He told her how he felt about her the night he rescued her in the blizzard. "I knew then, Rachel. I knew I was meant to watch out for you, to care for you. Later, as the years went by, I realized I would eventually marry you."

Jonathan would be with her always. Rachel would wake up each morning and think she was still dreaming. She'd have her own home. She'd have her own family. Maggie and Jennie would come live with them. They would always be safe.

Jack Walters had been buried in a potter's field. There was no funeral. Neither the Baileys nor Rachel, Maggie, or Jennie could bring themselves to visit his grave. The pain he had caused, and how he lived his life to serve only himself was still too fresh. Rachel wouldn't subject her sisters to that. No one, however, knew of the one lone visitor who visited Jack Walters's grave every Sunday.

Until they were married, Rachel continued to work at the factory. She wanted to make sure she was able to contribute to the Bailey household. The Baileys didn't want to accept any money from Rachel, but she insisted. Rachel didn't know the Baileys put the money back for her and Jonathan, knowing there would come a day they would need it. Ellen called it their rainy-day fund.

Maggie and Jennie screamed with delight when they were given the news of their sister's engagement. Both girls were thriving in their new environment. Jennie no longer had nightmares about her father. Jonathan had been so kind in how he told her of Jack Walters's death. As he talked, it all came back to her. She cried when she remembered the sounds of her father's screams and her fear that she would die too. Jonathan knew she had to get the bad feelings out of her heart. As she cried, Katy curled up closely to her as if to protect her. Jennie reached down and petted her fur and held her close. Katy was Jennie's ray of hope through her tears. Jack Walters could never hurt her again.

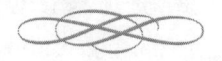

The first person outside of the Bailey family to hear of Rachel's engagement to Jonathan was Cook. Rachel knew if it hadn't been for Cook, she and her sisters might never have survived those terrible years of hunger, harsh winters, and bitter abuse.

Rosemary for Remembrance

Rachel came to visit with Cook one evening after a long day at the factory. Tears fell freely down Cook's chubby, pink cheeks when Rachel told her of her engagement to Jonathan. Alarmed, Rachel started to apologize. "Oh, Cook, I'm so sorry I upset you. I thought you'd be happy."

Cook looked into Rachel's concerned eyes, wiped the tears from her own eyes, and started to chuckle. Her chuckles bubbled over into delighted laughter. Cook laughed so hard her round chubby shoulders shook. "Rachel," she said when she finally was able to catch her breath, "I'm na sad at all. Those were tears o' joy. I only started laughin' when I thought of how Mrs. Nettle will take the news. She'll probably be so upset she won't eat for I don't know how long. That woman has got a vendetta against the world, she does. Each day, she's meaner and more miserable than the day before. And uglier too."

Rachel was trying very hard not to laugh when Cook said this. She opened her mouth to say something, hoping to change the subject of Mrs. Nettle. Rachel didn't get the first word out but stood with her mouth still opened to speak as Cook continued.

"Wouldn't do any good tryin' ta do your best ta please her neither. It's all the same ta her. Something to growl about each and every day. Serve her right if I quit too. Who else would put up with her nonsense? She'd be lost without someone ta fix her fine food. Hoo! This news of your engagement to Jonathan, such a fine young man, just might kill her." Laughter was again threatening to bubble over as Cook continued. "Wouldn't that be somethin,' Rachel? The fine Mrs. Nettle bein' found dead from self-inflicted starvation?" Cook bent over in laughter at her own joke, slapping her hands on her chubby thighs, delighted with her own cleverness.

Rachel closed her mouth and tried to keep a straight face but failed. She couldn't keep from smiling. Cook's laughter was too infectious. Cook's cheeks quivered as she continued to laugh. Rachel couldn't help herself. What started as a giggle turned into full-blown laughter until the kitchen was filled with the sound of the two women laughing so hard their ribs ached.

"It's a good thing Mrs. Nettle's still in town. She'd o' had our heads on a platter by now," Cook said.

Cook has such a good heart, Rachel thought as she looked at her. Rachel was reminded that, had it not been for the blessings of the people God placed in her life, she and her sisters might very well have been the ones to starve to death. Rachel stopped laughing. The thought was a sobering one and made Rachel realize how very blessed she really was. On impulse, Rachel hugged Cook.

Pulling back a little bit to look Rachel in the eyes, Cook's own eyes misted over. "Listen ta me, rambling on and on. You're turnin' into a fine young lady, Rachel. You'll do just fine with Jonathan." Cook continued rather wistfully, "I was married once, early in my life."

Rachel raised her eyebrows in surprise. She'd never have guessed it. Cook nodded her head at Rachel. "Yeah, I sure was. An' I was happy too. But the mister, he got sick an' died. Thomas and me, we never had no children neither." Cook's eyes clouded over in sadness for a brief moment as she remembered the wonderful but short time she'd been given with the only man she'd ever loved in her life. "Ta! Listen ta me goin' on and on." She gave Rachel a smile. "Rachel, I don't think it will be the same fer you, though. I can feel it in my bones. You and Jonathan are goin' ta be very happy indeed, with lots of babies."

Rosemary for Remembrance

Rachel blushed. Cook silently gave a prayer of thankfulness to God that Jonathan and Rachel would be married. Jonathan came from such a fine, Christian family. *Such good people,* she thought. *So unlike that miserable drunk. Poor Rachel and Maggie and Jennie, havin' ta grow up with that.*

Cook remembered one time when she saw bruises on Rachel's face and hands. Her wish had been that when Rachel and her sisters were grown and gone, the house Jack lived in would burn down with him in it. It was just wishful thinking at the time. Cook never believed it could actually happen, but it did. Feeling ashamed of herself, Cook lowered her head. She still couldn't believe it actually happened. *Forgive me, Jesus, for ever wishin' for it.*

Chapter Nineteen

The months flew by in a whirlwind of activity. Rachel was tireless in her wedding preparations. She was thankful to have the help of Ellen, Maggie, and Jennie. *Although,* Rachel thought as she smiled to herself, *Jennie's idea of including Katy in the wedding might be a little too much.* Rachel didn't want to hurt her little sister's feelings and was still trying to find a way to tell Jennie no gently.

Her attention turned to the sound of pounding as workmen hammered nails into place. Several men from the tiny community shouted back and forth to each other over the loud sounds of hammering and sawing as they worked almost nonstop to complete Jonathan and Rachel's new home. Elias and Jonathan were almost done with the front porch floor.

"We need a few more planks to finish," Elias called out to one of the extra hands. A big boy about thirteen years of age easily picked up several of the heavy planks, hoisted them on one shoulder, and brought them to Elias and Jonathan.

"Thank you," they both said to the young man, who gave a nod of his head and walked away.

Rachel had seen the plans for this home advertised in one of Ellen's ladies' magazines. She fell in love with the design.

The spacious two-and-a-half-story home would have oak floors throughout. There were to be five bedrooms, four of which would be on the second floor, along with a large bath and spacious hall to the oak staircase leading down to the first floor. The first floor offered a fifth bedroom, a parlor, a formal living room, dining room, kitchen with pantry, and washroom, and to Rachel's delight, a sun porch. This, she told Jonathan, was where she'd start her seeds for the garden. Jonathan took one look at the happiness in her eyes and knew he had to find a way to make her dream come true. The Baileys were well liked and had helped many in the community over the years. It didn't take long for anyone talented with a hammer and nail to offer their services in return.

What Rachel imagined when she first saw the advertisement and what she was looking at filled her with delight. The porch was so spacious. There would be plenty of room for the swing and rocking chairs and...

Rachel could just picture her and Jonathan sitting on their yellow porch swing in the evenings. The thought brought a delighted smile to her lips. She had already picked out the color without realizing it.

Elias and Ellen had deeded several acres for Jonathan and Rachel as a wedding present. Part of the land that was cleared would be used for Rachel's herb gardens. She couldn't wait to feel her hands in the deep, rich soil again. By then, she'd no longer be working at the factory. Her job would be making a home for Jonathan and her sisters. *And Katy, of course,* she thought with a smile. Rachel could barely contain her happiness. Her heart overflowed each morning when she awoke to thank God for a new day.

Jonathan looked up from his work to see Rachel watching him. Setting his hammer down on the porch floor, he wiped the sweat from his brow, smiled at her, and waved before picking up his hammer again. Rachel's heart gave a little flip. She couldn't wait to be his wife.

Chapter Twenty

The morning of Rachel and Jonathan's wedding day finally arrived. Jonathan awoke shortly before dawn. Staying in bed a few more moments, he pulled the quilt over his shoulders for warmth and closed his eyes. *Rachel.* In his mind's eye, he could see her again the night he rescued her from the blizzard. How light she had felt when he placed her on the saddle, so small and nearly frozen to death. The image of Rachel through the years from young child to young woman was that of great character and inner strength. Her delicate build and gentle manners belied the strength she possessed to face what would have been insurmountable problems for so many others. Jonathan realized that, as much as he thought he'd been the one to help her throughout the years, Rachel had helped him too. She'd shown him a world of hope in the face of pain, heartache, loss, and anguish. Rachel showed him the beauty within despite the harsh life she and her sisters had endured. *Lord, how I love her.* Just when Jonathan didn't think he could love Rachel more, he realized that his love continued to grow. At odd times, like watching her pick up Katy the kitten and hold her close in whispering reassurance, and the way she would brush Jennie's hair away from her eyes with such care and tenderness. To Jonathan, Rachel showed so much love to others although she had done without it so many times in her own life. *How can that be?* Jonathan wondered. But he knew. Rachel had confided to Jonathan once that she felt God's presence and knew a beautiful future was ahead for her. No matter how desperate her circumstances were, Rachel could still look forward to that beautiful future God had planned for her. "So you see, Jonathan," she would say, "it's better to look forward than to look back, unless of course there is a lesson to be learned."

Rachel was indeed wise beyond her years, he realized. The revelation given to Jonathan at this moment could only have come from one source: the almighty God himself.

And on this day, Jonathan's heart overflowed with happiness. Within a few hours, he and Rachel would be married. It seemed to have taken forever for this day to happen. Yet, at this moment, it felt like the years had actually flown by in a second.

His mother had said many times throughout his years of growing up that God was a God not only of miracles but of answers big and small. Jonathan opened his eyes as a new thought came to him. He realized that the years he had with Rachel were not about waiting for her to become a young woman so he could marry her. It was also about becoming the man God intended him to be. He needed to be ready. It was a humbling thought. Jonathan threw back the covers and slid out of bed. He knelt there and bowed his head, hands clasped together in prayer. *Am I ready?* Jonathan wondered. With this question, Jonathan poured out his heart to God on the early, beautiful morning of their wedding day.

Rosemary for Remembrance

Rachel awoke to the sound of her sisters' muffled giggles. *What are those two up to at this hour?* She could hear the sound of their bedroom door being opened and closed and footsteps walking across the floor and over to the bed.

"Rachel, wake up!" Rachel opened her eyes. Jennie and Maggie were standing next to the bed. Jennie was holding a tray loaded down with fried eggs, crisp bacon, homemade bread with jelly, and hot coffee. They were both smiling at her.

"Breakfast in bed, Rachel," Jennie said.

"Yes. This is our wedding present to you," Maggie chimed in.

Rachel brushed a few stray hairs away from her eyes and pushed back the blankets to sit up in bed. "Wait," Maggie said as she took two of the pillows, fluffed them up, and placed them behind Rachel's back. "There," Maggie said as Rachel leaned back on the pillows.

Jennie carefully placed the tray on Rachel's lap. Rachel raised her eyebrows when she saw the amount of food they had cooked for her. She was touched by their thoughtfulness. Both Maggie and Jennie walked around to the other side of the large, four-poster bed and sat down, tucking their legs underneath their nightgowns.

Her wedding day was finally here. She could hardly believe it. Looking at both of her sisters, Rachel was overwhelmed with how God had answered her prayers. She and her sisters had made it out of the terrible childhood they had to endure.

Maggie was a young lady. Tall and angular, she towered over boys her age. Her arms and legs were too long, but Maggie didn't seem to care. Her bright, hazel green eyes were mischievous and full of kind humor. Her curly, red hair was frizzy and never stayed pinned in place. There were times when Rachel and Jennie would be talking to her and watch, mystified, as Maggie's hair would come apart as if it had a life of its own. It was a constant battle for Maggie, who took it all in stride. She didn't care that she wasn't the beauty of the family. She was never jealous of Rachel or Jennie's beauty. Maggie had other gifts, like her wonderful, wholesome, optimistic outlook on life in general. Full of fun and humor, Maggie loved life. These were the traits that everyone who knew her saw. Maggie also knew who she was in Christ and was determined to make a difference in the lives of others, especially for women.

Jennie was in between being a little girl and becoming a young lady. With soft, fine, light brown hair and hazel eyes, she resembled Rachel. Her build was small and delicate like Rachel's. Protected by her sisters all her life, Jennie seemed more cautious, asked more questions, and seemed uncertain of herself. Her only constant companion was her kitten, Katy. Being responsible for another was helping her learn to stand on her own two feet. Jennie emulated both Rachel and Maggie. They were her heroes. She hoped she could grow up to be like both of them.

Rachel ate every bite of the wedding-day breakfast her sisters has so lovingly prepared for her. Her heart was full of gratitude for this day that she'd waited so long for. Within hours, she and Jonathan would be wed, husband and wife; and he would remain her constant lifetime companion.

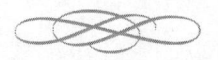

This list of last-minute details has too many last-minute details on it, Ellen thought as she looked over the list while sipping a cup of steaming hot coffee at the kitchen table. Ellen set the cup back down and gave a deep sigh of resignation. This was not intended to be a large wedding. They all agreed.

But news traveled fast on the mountains of Blue Knob. Cook just couldn't contain herself and spilled the beans. When she let out the news of Rachel and Jonathan's engagement at the general store, it didn't take long for word to travel. Suddenly, there seemed to be many "guests" who had no idea they weren't invited to the wedding. Many assumed that if they got the news, they got the invitation too. After all, this was a very big event in their tiny community. The poorer guests were looking forward to the reception afterward, picturing mountains of delicious food on their plates. They weren't going to go hungry at this gathering. Some guests were looking forward to the music and dancing. Many of the men were arguing amongst themselves whether to serenade the newly wedded couple on their wedding night with belling or a shivaree.

Pap Johnson, who looked older than the mountain itself, settled the matter when he said, "Ah, let's just give 'em both." The men cheered and hollered. It sounded like a great idea.

All of the guests, however, even the uninvited ones, wanted to witness the wedding of Jonathan and Rachel—all except one. True to what Cook had said to Rachel on the day she told Cook of her engagement, Mrs. Nettle did indeed lose her appetite. But that lasted only for three days. After planning her revenge, she got her appetite back. Mrs. Nettle showed up in the kitchen and ordered Cook to prepare a meal for her.

Every time Ellen went into town to do her shopping, she'd be approached on all sides. Many a lady's hand would tap her on the shoulder. Ellen would turn to see the bright smiles of ladies she barely knew but wanted to talk about the wedding. Everyone seemed to have her own idea of how the wedding should be planned and offered to help.

Though the Baileys were fairly well known, not everyone knew them personally. Therefore, some folks thought it was necessary to at least talk with Mrs. Bailey. How else could one possibly show up at a wedding and reception otherwise?

Ellen looked up from her list as she heard the kitchen door open. Her husband stepped inside, taking a moment to remove his work hat and hang it on the peg by the door. He turned to face her and took in the look on his wife's face. Ellen never seemed to become frazzled, but right then, there was a look of genuine doubt, as if she wasn't sure she could do everything on the list. *No wonder,* he thought. It was going to be a very busy day. *Thank the Lord Cook will be here later to help.*

Ellen might have looked doubtful, but Elias knew she would see this through and do it well too. She did everything well. Leaving the door open, he walked over to his wife. Placing his hands on her shoulders, he bent down and kissed the top of her head. She smelled like lavender.

"Are all the decorations up, Elias?" Ellen asked.

"Yup. Every one of them," he answered. Ellen still looked a little concerned as her brows knit together. "Come with me," Elias said to his wife as he took her hand. She stood up and faced him. He gave her a smile and leaned in for a quick kiss. Together, they turned and walked to the door and stepped outside. They stopped for a moment. "I have something to show you," her husband said with a smile as he reached to close the door behind them.

Rosemary for Remembrance

Maggie and Jennie carried bucket after bucket of hot water up to the second floor to prepare Rachel's bath. The water had to be heated on the stove first. They also carried a bucket of cold water upstairs in case the tub water was too hot. With the allowance they had earned from doing their chores at the Baileys, Maggie and Jennie bought special rose-scented soaps. After pouring the last bucket of hot water into the tub, they looked at each other and started giggling all over again. They could just picture Rachel's face when she saw the bath and the soaps.

"Should you go get her, or shall I?" Maggie asked Jennie.

"I know. Let's go get Rachel together. Maybe then she won't suspect anything and we can make this a surprise too," Jennie said.

And Rachel was indeed very surprised. The tub of hot, steaming water, fresh towels, a vase of early fall flowers, and fragrant soap awaited her. She turned to her sisters to say, "Thank you," but they had left, closing the door quietly behind them. They would be busy setting out Rachel's wedding dress, veil, shoes, and stockings while Rachel took her bath. This would be yet another surprise for Rachel.

Rachel placed one hand into the water and pulled it out quickly. *Just a little too hot,* she thought. She picked up the bucket of cold water and poured it into the tub. The water was very warm, but Rachel sank down into it, allowing it to flow over her face and hair. As she came back up, she leaned against the back of the tub, eyes still closed. She inhaled the wonderful fragrance of roses as she lathered up the soap. The bath felt heavenly. Rachel was very touched by Maggie and Jennie's thoughtfulness. She knew they must have saved for a long time to buy the special soap. Holding the bar of soap

Mary Netreba

between her hands, she lathered up enough of it to wash her hair.

This was going to be the most important day of her life. As Rachel washed her hair and bathed, she thought about all of the hard years behind her. Looking back, it seemed to have happened very quickly. She knew it was because of Jonathan. He had been her constant friend. If Jonathan hadn't been there, those terrible, heartbreaking years would have seemed endless. She, Maggie, and Jennie might never have survived. Rachel pushed the sad thoughts of the past out of her mind. With a beautiful future ahead of them, it was time to forget the sorrow of the past and leave it behind. Many hard lessons were learned, and while they were very painful, Rachel also recognized that God had been preparing her for the day He would redeem her sorrows. She might not have recognized this if she, Maggie, and Jennie had not gone through the terrible years. Rachel smiled to herself. There was so much to be thankful for.

The Wedding, October 9, 1916

On this beautiful day, the sun shone brightly through the colors of autumn. Leaves of bright orange, gold, red, and yellow gently floated to the ground. Both Jonathan and Rachel agreed that their autumn wedding should take place outside, where the flamboyant colors of the season would surround them and their guests.

To Ellen's relief, Cook had shown up earlier than expected and even brought with her two of the maids from the Nettle home to help out with the reception. Mrs. Nettle's plans to ruin Jonathan and Rachel's wedding were put to a stop when a mysterious illness overcame her.

"I'm not real sure what Mrs. Nettle's got, but maybe she should na' eaten so much of the prune puddin' I made," Cook explained. "But Mrs. Nettle, she loves her prune puddin,' so I made sure to add more prunes to the recipe this time. I guess she loved it so much she had to eat the whole thing." Cook tried to look innocent, but her eyes twinkled with humor. "So since she's gonna be in bed all day anyway, I did na see any harm in bringin' some extra help fer ya today."

Ellen tried hard not to smile. But inside, she was relieved that Mrs. Nettle wouldn't be showing up at the wedding or the reception. Just her presence alone would have been upsetting enough, and one never knew what to expect when she was around. Mrs. Nettle was never invited anywhere. She invited herself and showed up unannounced.

Cook continued, "Now don't ya go worryin' about nothin' there, Mrs. Bailey. We got the whole thing under control. I've had a few weddins' to attend to before myself, ya know, so don't ya go worryin' about a thing." Cook put her arm around Ellen's shoulder to escort her out of the kitchen, talking all the way. "There ya go. Ya get yerself ready fer the weddin.' We'll be takin' care o' the rest. Don't ya worry…"

This time, Ellen did find herself smiling over Cook's somewhat loud, plaintive voice of reassurance. And she was relieved. Ellen felt as if a weight had been lifted from her shoulders.

Many of the guests had already arrived, taking their seats if they'd been assigned. There were many guests, some of whom obviously invited themselves at the last minute. Some sat on benches while others had to stand, straining to see over the shoulders of the person in front of them.

"Coming through. Coming through," a voice called out.

The guests who were standing stepped aside to make room for the wedding party. Elias and Ellen were the first to walk down the aisle to their assigned seats in the front. Ellen smiled again with delight over the surprise that her husband had prepared for the bride and groom. This was going to be a wedding that wouldn't soon be forgotten.

"I'll be back soon," Elias said to his wife as he patted her hand and turned to make his way to the back again.

Jonathan made a handsome groom as he and his father approached the front. He grinned from ear to ear when he saw the surprise his father had made for him and Rachel. Jonathan nervously took his place where he would say his wedding vows. Elias smiled at his son and moved to the back one more time. He himself would be escorting Rachel down the aisle.

There would be no piano player for this outdoor wedding. The town fiddler had been asked by the Baileys to perform the wedding march for Jonathan and Rachel. Heads turned to see Rachel's bridesmaid, Maggie, and her flower girl, Jennie. The guests parted for them to walk down the nature-made aisle. Maggie had convinced Rachel to allow both her and Jennie to wear their hair loose with only a ribbon to keep it away from their faces. It took some convincing, but Rachel agreed when Maggie pointed out that her hair wouldn't stay in place very long during the ceremony anyway.

Jennie went first. The guests turned and smiled as they watched her. She looked quite lovely in her gown of pale pink with a wide, long, pink sash around her waist that ended with a beautiful bow in the back. Holding the basket with her left hand, Jennie slowly walked down the aisle, tossing the rose petals from her basket.

Jonathan looked at her a little closer. *Jennie must've gotten the baskets mixed up,* he thought. It seemed a little difficult for Jennie to reach into the lidded basket for the rose petals, but she was doing all right so far.

Rachel had been the one who came up with the idea of drying the rose petals throughout the summer to save them for the day of the wedding. Cook and her two maids placed the rose petals in water, which then made them look fresh again. The guests could even smell the scent of the roses. Jennie walked the last few steps with a skip as she reached the groom, a bright, happy smile on her face.

"Mew." Katy pushed up the lid of the basket and was peeking out at the wedding guests. Laughter filled the air at the sight of the cat with a pink ribbon tied in a bow around her neck. Indignant, Katy meowed loudly and jumped from the basket and ran down the aisle past the guests and a very surprised Rachel, Maggie, and Elias.

Jennie had taken Rachel quite literally when she had been told, "Jennie, we cannot have you holding Katy in your arms if you want to be the flower girl at our wedding." Rachel, Maggie, and Elias smiled in spite of themselves. And the guests had been delighted with the surprise. But Rachel knew she would have to have a talk with Jennie at some point in the future.

It was Maggie's turn. As Maggie walked down the aisle, the thought never occurred to her how fresh and lovely she looked. Her bridesmaid gown was the soft blue color of a robin's egg. It was designed and made by Ellen. The color of the gown, with its high collar, brought out the green in Maggie's eyes. Maggie found herself blushing with the attention focused on her, which only made her look more becoming. She breathed a sigh of relief as she reached the...*What?* Maggie stopped in her tracks for a moment before continuing. *What had happened to the altar?* she wondered.

Elias turned to his soon-to-be daughter-in-law. "Are you ready, Rachel?" he asked gently. Rachel looked up into his eyes. She imagined Jonathan would look just like him someday.

All of her life, she never felt like she belonged anywhere. Jack Walters had been an angry, abusive stepfather with no love to give. And Julianna, their mother, had been so beaten down in spirit that she finally gave up and died. Working for the unhappy Mrs. Nettle certainly didn't help how she felt either. Rachel felt blamed, accused, and wrong every time she entered that house. Was it really any surprise for Rachel not to know who she was when there was no loving example? But all that changed the night of the blizzard. From that point on, Rachel began to feel something different, something she never had before. Rachel remembered how Ellen nursed her back to health; how Jonathan so caringly fed her when she was too weak to feed herself; the peace that she felt while in their home as she recuperated. The years since that night brought her to people who valued her, demonstrating to her and her sisters that they were cared for. They were valued, loved, and accepted just as they were.

Am I ready? she asked herself. *Oh yes!* Rachel couldn't wait to start her life with Jonathan at her side, as husband and wife. She took a breath, let it out, and nodded her head. Standing side by side, arms linked, Elias Bailey would escort Rachel down the aisle.

Elias gave a nod to the waiting Newton McCaw, who nodded in return. He placed his fiddle, a violin because it was a wedding, under his chin. Lifting his bow, he laid it gently on the strings. The sounds of the wedding march filled the air as the guests stood and turned to watch the bride. They were in awe as they listened. Newton McCaw's fiddle did indeed sound like a violin.

All eyes were on the bride as Rachel, soon-to-be Mrs. Jonathan Bailey, walked down the aisle with her almost father-in-law. Many drew in their breath when they saw her.

Rachel looked exquisite. The ivory-colored gown of lace over satin was unlike anything the ladies in that tiny community had ever seen. The high collar was also edged in lace, as were the cuffs on the puffed sleeves. The wide, satin ribbon tied at the waistline with a large bow in back set off Rachel's tiny waist. Her veil was all lace and simply placed over her head, reaching to her shoulders. Rachel carried a bouquet of dried lavender flowers still attached to the stems, tied together with one long, ivory-colored satin ribbon.

Elias's eyes were shining with unshed tears as he escorted Rachel down the aisle to marry his son. *Yes,* he thought. *Jonathan and Rachel belong together.*

For Rachel, the walk down the aisle seemed to go on forever. She couldn't feel her feet, yet she was drawing closer to Jonathan. *So many people,* she thought. *Why are they all smiling?* Rachel turned her attention toward the front. There her beloved Jonathan stood, tall and handsome and dressed in his Sunday best. Everything and everyone around Rachel faded when she saw him. Before she realized it, she was standing next to him.

For Jonathan, the agony of waiting for Rachel at the altar seemed to last forever. All sorts of thoughts swirled in his head before she reached the altar. *What if Rachel changes her mind? After all, being a wife is not easy. Is she going to be able to love me through the years? What if she thinks she made a mistake? What if...* Relief ran through him. Rachel, his Rachel, would be his wife. She was smiling up at him.

Elias had recreated a smaller version of the fenced corral that Jonathan and Rachel had scrambled over to get away from the Bailey's bull and the same place where Jonathan had proposed to Rachel. The gates of this smaller version of the corral were open wide on each side for the bride and groom to enter. Rachel's heart was touched by the sweet humor of her father-in-law.

There were no dry eyes at this wedding ceremony. The guests had never been to an outdoor wedding before. It was most unusual, they thought, but now that they were here, they understood why Rachel and Jonathan chose the autumn wedding. They witnessed the marriage vows as the colorful autumn leaves gently dropped from the trees and swirled to the ground, surrounding the couple. And the guests smiled in delight as the leaves surrounded them too. Perhaps that was what made this wedding so touching, or maybe it was the beauty of the autumn day. Or maybe it was the wedding march being so gently played by Newton McCaw that took them all by surprise. Or maybe it was just a good wedding to have a good cry at. All of the wedding guests seemed to have a perfectly sensible reason to cry.

Chapter Twenty-one

Rachel had never known happiness like this in her whole life. Everything about her life was so new and exciting. Each morning she awoke with her husband beside her was a day of joy. Thankful that she' longer had to work at the factory, Rachel concentrated on making their house into a home. Even what would seem to be the most mundane chores of cleaning, laundry, and ironing, were, to Rachel, a joy. After all, this was her and Jonathan's home. It was also Maggie and Jennie's home. It was—

"Meow."

Rachel was brought out of her thoughts by the sound of Katy. She jumped up on the chair next to Rachel, who was sitting at the kitchen table with her coffee. Katy looked up at her with big, green eyes. "Mew."

Rachel smiled and scratched her behind the ears the way Katy liked it. "All right, Katy. This is your home too."

Seeming placated, Katy leaped gracefully from the chair to land on the braided oval rug, kneading the fabric until she raised the nap, circled a few times, and curled into a ball, promptly falling asleep. Rachel's thoughts continued. Someday, she knew, their home would be full of all the children the newlywed couple wanted. In her mind, Rachel pictured Jonathan lovingly holding their firstborn. But for now she would enjoy taking care of her husband, her sisters, and their home. With that thought, Rachel got up from the kitchen table to start her day.

Rachel was a natural-born organizer. Her difficult years at the Nettle home as a domestic had paid off. She easily slipped into planning and keeping a schedule that ran her household smoothly. Baking days were her favorites. Wednesday and Saturday, without fail, Rachel was up and about much earlier than any other days of the week. There was a certain peace that came to her as she kneaded the bread dough with her hands. With no other distractions, Rachel did her best thinking while she was baking.

As she punched down the bread dough, she thought about what herbs, vegetables, fruits, and flowers she'd plant in the spring. There was a very large area of fertile ground reserved for Rachel to do with what she wanted. "A garden completes a home," she once said to Jonathan. Jonathan understood this. He remembered the sad state of the dilapidated house that Rachel, Maggie, and Jennie had lived in. If Rachel hadn't planted the flowers and herbs, it would've looked much worse. The beauty of the colorful flowers like petunias, zinnias, and marigolds, brought a sense of cheerfulness to the otherwise sad eyesore called their home. *And Maggie helped too*. Maggie adored her roses. They were her favorite flower, so much so that she learned to propagate them herself. Each year, there had been more rose bushes in different varieties and colors as Maggie continued to work with them. The fragrance of the roses reached a person's nose long before they actually came into view. Rachel would make sure Maggie had many places around the new house and yard to create a masterpiece of fragrant beauty. Jonathan was secretly designing and putting together a special trellis for Maggie as a surprise Christmas present. Rachel smiled, picturing the look she'd see on her sister's face on Christmas morning.

Being married all of three weeks, Rachel felt very optimistic about her and Jonathan's future together. Thankfully, the war wouldn't touch them, although her heart went out to the men who died fighting. Rachel had read stories in the local newspapers of the loss of life and limb, families torn apart, food shortages, and intense suffering and hardship. It was hard to imagine, especially the Battle of the Somme on the Western Front. Thousands died, leaving their already struggling families behind. It was almost too much for Rachel to comprehend. *How horrible to be in a war. And all those innocent people too.* Jonathan and Rachel had discussed how he would cast his vote in the upcoming election. It was a difficult decision to make because both Woodrow Wilson and Charles Evan Hughes, a Supreme Court associate justice, were qualified for the job. But Hughes became labeled as a war candidate. What many voters didn't realize was that Mr. Hughes had many of the same opinions about the war as Woodrow Wilson did. But Wilson's motto, "He kept us out of the war," was convincing. It gave him the advantage over Hughes. Jonathan and Rachel decided together that Jonathan would place his vote with Woodrow Wilson on November 7, 1916, which was only days away. They both felt that it was the right thing to do. Jonathan always considered Rachel in every decision, including this vote for president, especially since women weren't allowed to vote. Most of the wives in the tiny community of Blue Knob, however, were never told anything at all. Their husbands did as they wished. It wasn't even open for discussion. After all, the men reasoned, if their wives couldn't vote, they didn't need to know anything about it either.

Rachel felt very passionately about women not being allowed to vote. Actually, insulted would be more like it. If it took a man and woman to make a baby, why shouldn't that same man and woman have a right to vote? And if their husbands were to be sent off to war, taken from their families, certainly women should have some say in the matter. A woman's vote may have made the difference. It just didn't make any sense. It wasn't fair. While Rachel felt passionately about the subject, she was thankful to have a husband who would openly discuss with her any decision that needed to be made. He understood her frustration. Jonathan would say quite frequently, "Any decision that needs to be made needs to have a woman's viewpoint first."

Maggie, however, felt more than just passion. To her, the unfairness of not being allowed to vote simply because she was a woman was equivalent to not being seen as a real person. Maggie had gone into town several days earlier to purchase flour, yeast, raisins, walnuts, and pecans that Rachel needed for bread-making day. The Smiths, Edward and Anna, were in the general store at the time. The owner of the general store and Edward were having a spirited discussion about casting their votes. Anna tried to join in and was promptly shushed by both her husband and the owner. "Women aren't allowed to vote for a reason. Women are too emotional and can't make a proper decision," her husband said to her. Anna, a sweet, gentle soul, lowered her head and murmured an apology.

Maggie's face turned red as her blood boiled over at their statements and their treatment of Anna. *How dare he act as if being a man meant he knew it all?* Maggie rapped her knuckles on the counter. "Changes will be coming someday soon. And when they do, I'll be right there, casting my first vote." Anna gave Maggie a grateful smile.

Maggie's words were strong, sure, and determined each time she made this statement. Her green eyes would flash with quick anger that any woman should be so insulted. This last visit to the general store was something the town wouldn't forget soon. Word had a way of traveling quickly, and Maggie was someone all the women in the community needed and respected.

Jennie watched Rachel with Jonathan and observed how they seemed to complete one another so well. While her sister was more domestic and loved her role as the homemaker, Jonathan never treated her as anything less than his equal. "Your heart is my heart, Rachel," he often said to her.

Maggie, on the other hand, was strong and didn't care whether she married one day or not. "Plenty to keep me busy," she said to them. "If marriage comes, it will be with the promise that I can be everything I am meant to be. I will *not* be held back, ever. No man is worth that."

Through example, Jennie was learning two very valuable lessons. Never accept anything less than true love, and never allow anyone to make her less of a person. Neither was acceptable.

Chapter Twenty-two

The bitter, high-pitched winds blew across the mountains of Blue Knob in December with a deep, chilling cold. But in the Jonathan and Rachel Bailey household, all were snug and warm. With several fireplaces going on both the first and second floors, along with the stove in the kitchen, the home radiated warmth. Their home had been well built. Very few drafts made their cold presence known. Jonathan was in the barn, taking care of the animals. Rachel, Maggie, and Jennie were in the parlor, enjoying the fire's warmth and sipping hot chocolate from their mugs. And they weren't the only ones enjoying its warmth. Katy, no longer a kitten, curled herself up on the small, braided rug in front of the fireplace, her tail wrapped around her nose, purring contently as she slept. Katy had also turned out to be a very good mouser. Rachel, Maggie, and Jennie all agreed that Katy earned her keep. She deserved the chance to enjoy the warmth from the crackling fire too.

Jennie sipped the rest of her hot chocolate, gave a satisfied sigh, and set the mug down on the floor beside her, legs tucked underneath her as she sat next to Katy in front of the fireplace. She turned slightly to look up at Rachel and Maggie, who were on the couch. Jennie's eyes were bright as she said, "I'm so excited about Christmas." She clasped her hands together close to her heart. This would be the first time in Jennie, Maggie, and Rachel's lives that they would make their own decorations for Christmas. "When do we start, Rachel?" Jennie asked excitedly.

Rachel and Maggie both chuckled. But they knew how she felt. Inside, they felt the same way. It was going to be fun to decorate their new home for Christmas. "Well, Jennie," Rachel answered as she held her now-empty mug in her hands, "we can start tomorrow. We should start with the Christmas wreath for the front door first, though."

Jennie's face fell slightly in disappointment. "Oh," was all she said. She had pictured putting up the Christmas tree first. In her mind, Jennie already had it decorated.

Rachel saw the disappointed look on her youngest sister's face and smiled. Rachel understood. "Jennie," she said, "the reason we start with the Christmas wreath first is because the Christmas wreath is a symbol of faith and of God's unending love and mercy."

Jennie sat up a little straighter. "Oh," she said with some surprise. She looked at the comfortable room around her. "He gave us a very nice home. He must love us very much. I think making the Christmas wreath first is a wonderful idea." This time, her face beamed.

Jennie was so excited about Christmas that she found she couldn't sleep on Christmas Eve. The Bailey household had been very busy for the past couple of weeks. First, there was the holiday house cleaning, as her sister called it. To Jennie's eyes, the house already looked clean, but Rachel insisted there were things to be done. The three sisters scoured, scrubbed, waxed, and polished until the whole house sparkled. Once done, Jennie realized

Rachel was right. By the time the three of them finished, the whole house sparkled with holiday cheer. Jennie also discovered that learning to bake was fun. Rachel was wonderfully patient with Jennie's mistakes, of which there were many. Jennie forgot to add sugar to the sugar cookies, added too much yeast to the bread, and every time she rolled out the pie crust, it stuck to the kitchen table. Rachel took it all in stride. Instead, they made a very sweet icing for the sugarless cookies, cut the bread into small pieces to dry and be used as stuffing for the turkey, and rolled out the pie dough on a floured surface. Rachel wasn't about to let anything go to waste. Rachel would never forget the hollow feeling of hunger from their earlier years. She could make something out of almost nothing. As another cake was removed from the oven, the delicious aromas of vanilla and cinnamon filled the whole house. Rachel set the cake pan down on a thick cloth on the kitchen table to cool. A sigh of contentment left her lips. Rachel decided to see what Katy had been up too. She seemed to have taken a liking to pulling down the garlands from the staircase railings and make off with a ribbon or two.

After putting up their first Christmas wreath on the front door and making sure their home was holiday clean, Rachel, Ellen, Maggie, and Jennie had decorated the home with beautiful green garlands and bright red ribbons that wound their way down the wooden rails of the lovely oak staircase. Smaller versions of the large Christmas wreath that hung on the front door were hung also outside. Between the four of them, they made enough smaller Christmas wreaths for each window in the front of the house; their bright, red bows gave a sense of cheer to any and all who would pay a visit.

"Aha!" Katy froze in her tracks, her paws firmly grounded in place.

Rachel had crept quietly into the hallway and stood at the landing of the staircase. Pieces of garland hung sloppily from the oak railing as Katy stood on the steps. Her eyes were wide with surprise that she'd been caught holding the large, red ribbon in her mouth. She looked so startled to have been caught that Rachel couldn't help but laugh at the sight. Looking insulted, Katy dropped the bow and ran quickly up the stairs. Smiling, Rachel picked up the bow and went about repairing the daily damage. Katy was so precious. *Maybe we'll just give her a red bow as a Christmas present,* Rachel thought as she made her way back to the kitchen. The whole family laughed that evening as Rachel recounted Katy's crime from earlier in the day.

Most exciting for Jennie, though, was decorating the Christmas tree on Christmas Eve. It was tradition for the man of the house to select the tree. Jonathan didn't disappoint. The ladies were delighted with his choice. He proudly presented the Christmas tree as he dragged it into their home, snow dropping onto the floor and rugs from the kitchen to the parlor. No one seemed to mind the mess or cleaning it up. Decorating the tree was going to be so much fun. The strong scent of pine filled the parlor. Hot chocolate was sipped and enjoyed as Rachel, Ellen, Maggie, and Jennie decorated the Christmas tree. Maggie and Jennie had strung popcorn and Rachel wound strand after strand of red, green, and white satin ribbons around the tree from top to bottom and then attached satin bows in the same colors.

The sisters gasped when Ellen brought out her surprise. The large, square box was filled with hand-decorated, blown-glass Christmas ornaments for the tree. They were exquisitely made and looked very delicate. They also looked like they were family heirlooms. Tears sprang to Rachel's eyes. *It must have cost a fortune for them,* she thought.

Ellen looked at the girls with such love. These girls could have been her own daughters. "This is our first Christmas together as a family," she said. "Rachel, Maggie, and Jennie, please choose one of the decorations as your own. Pick out whatever you like. It will be your keepsake to pass down to your own families someday."

They all three were so overwhelmed by Ellen's generosity and thoughtfulness that they stood silent for moment, unsure of who should go first. Maggie and Jennie both looked at Rachel at the same time. "You go first, Rachel," Maggie said.

Rachel was almost afraid to touch the beautiful decorations for fear she'd break one. Very carefully, she picked out an oval-shaped one decorated in what looked like frosted silver tinged with pink. She stepped back, cupping her gift gently in her hands.

Maggie was next. Stepping forward, she reached into the box. A lovely, round, green one had caught her eye earlier. Not as fancy as the rest of the decorations, this one was very simply made in one solid, emerald green color with one small silver star in the center. Very pleased with her gift, she stepped back as well.

Jennie simply couldn't make up her mind. The delicate ornaments were so beautiful and shone with a warm brilliance all their own. She finally selected an oval-shaped one similar to the one Rachel had chosen, only this one was deep blue on the top and bottom with frosted silver in the middle.

All three of them were thrilled with their special gifts. The simple thank you they murmured, as if even the sound of their voices might break the precious ornaments, didn't seem to be enough. But Ellen understood. It was exactly how she felt when this same box had been handed down to her from her mother. "Someday, Ellen," her mother said, "you will hand

Rosemary for Remembrance

them down to your own daughter." Elias and Ellen had been blessed with Jonathan. Ellen now felt as if she had been thrice blessed with daughters as well. Rachel, Maggie, and Jennie were like her own. *And Julianna,* she thought, *would be so happy her girls are with me.*

Hanging their gifts carefully near the top half of the tree, they decorated the Christmas tree with the remaining glass-blown ornaments. When they were finished, they stood back to admire their work. Their sighs of delight filled the room.

This was indeed the most beautiful Christmas tree that Ellen had ever seen. The girls looked very happy. They had never had a Christmas tree in their young lives. Even this had been a distant dream. Yet, as they stood before the decorated Christmas tree with its ribbons, bows, and ornaments, Rachel, Maggie, and Jennie were filled with awe. Jennie was the first to break the silence. "What are we going to do about Katy?"

After a late dinner of chicken, mashed potatoes, peas, and gravy, with Dutch apple pie for dessert, the whole family returned to the parlor to gather 'round the Christmas tree, sing carols, and simply talk and enjoy their first Christmas Eve as a family. Perhaps it was the excitement of being allowed to stay up later than usual or knowing there would be presents under the tree the following morning, but for Jennie, the new life she was living felt as if it had always been this way. The memory of her abusive father seemed as if it had happened to another person. Jennie felt no grief over Jack's death, only a sense of relief that he would never hurt her again. Jennie made a vow to herself that Christmas Eve of 1916. She'd never allow a man to hurt her, not ever.

Chapter Twenty-three

The months from December of 1916 to early March of 1917 on the mountains of Blue Knob seemed to stand still. Winter tightly held its grip with high winds, bitter cold, and snow drifts so high there were days on end where it was impossible to see out through one's windows. All was white.

But the end of March was approaching. The winds grew a little softer, the air a little warmer, and, thankfully, an early thaw had begun. Each day, the high drifts of snow melted a little more, making the ground soft and soggy underfoot. But no one complained. Spring was coming. Funny how one could forget the bitter winters when spring was around the corner. Rachel spotted her first robin just that morning. She had looked out the kitchen window, and there was the robin, searching for a big, juicy worm. It always thrilled her. Each spring, when she least expected it, a robin would appear seemingly out of nowhere.

Rachel had a full day planned. The spring cleaning simply had to be done. Jonathan had kissed her lightly on the cheek before heading out to the barn after breakfast. Rachel was still sitting at the kitchen table, going over her list of chores to do.

Reaching for her coffee, she brought it to her lips. She loved the smell of fresh coffee in the morning. But this morning, the smell overwhelmed her with nausea. Rachel knew she was going to be sick. Putting the cup back down quickly on the table, she got up and rushed to the kitchen sink. Grabbing the pail on the floor next to the sink, she wretched so much her stomach hurt.

Shaking, she walked over to the table and sat down again. *What's wrong with me?* Rachel couldn't remember ever feeling this sick. And she was exhausted too. All she wanted to do was go back to bed and sleep. *Maybe I'm coming down with something,* she thought. *I'll lie down for just a bit.*

By late morning, Rachel felt wonderful. The nap she took really seemed to help. Going downstairs to the kitchen, she made herself another cup of coffee. It smelled and tasted wonderful. Feeling ravenous, Rachel fixed bacon, eggs, and homemade toast. *That's more like it.*

Rachel spent the busy afternoon getting caught up on her morning chores before preparing supper. When Jonathan came home later, Rachel decided not to mention her sickness earlier in the day.

Within a few days, however, Jonathan and Rachel were both very concerned. Jonathan had witnessed Rachel being sick when he came back to the house unexpectedly one morning. Jonathan noticed that dark circles were forming under Rachel's eyes, and she seemed tired all the time. He was worried.

Ellen had stopped by one evening with some extra material she bought at the general store. The fabric was perfect for spring dresses she wanted to make for the girls. She noticed right away that Rachel didn't seem like herself. "Rachel, are you all right?" She reached out and placed the back part of her hand on Rachel's forehead. She didn't have a fever.

"Actually," Rachel started, "I just feel so tired lately. And for the past week I've been sick in the morning."

Ellen looked at her son. "Jonathan, would you mind giving Rachel and me a little time together?"

Jonathan looked confused but nodded his head. "I'll be in the barn."

Ellen asked Rachel several very personal questions. Somewhat embarrassed, Rachel answered.

Why is Ellen smiling? Rachel wondered.

"Rachel, you're going to have a baby."

Rachel's hands went to her mouth. "Oh!" was all she could say. Her surprise turned to excited happiness. Jonathan had just come back in from the barn. Rachel ran to him with a bright smile on her face and threw her arms around his neck. He looked at his mother. She was smiling too.

Rachel was so excited she could hardly contain herself.

"Oh, Jonathan, I'm not sick at all. We're going to have a baby!"

Jonathan was speechless at first. Assurance that his wife wasn't sick would've been enough for him. Knowing Rachel was carrying his baby overwhelmed him with joy. They were going to have a baby! "Do you need to sit down, Rachel?" was all he could think to say.

Maggie and Jennie were beside themselves when Jonathan and Rachel told them about the baby. Jennie especially couldn't contain herself as she jumped up and down with excitement. "I'm going to be an aunt!" This made Jennie feel very grown up. It also made her stop jumping up and down like a child.

Tears of joy filled Elias's eyes when his son told him that he was going to be a grandfather. He couldn't seem to find his voice to say anything and instead hugged his son.

Chapter Twenty-four

The war seemed very far away from the mountains of Blue Knob, as it only touched the people there remotely through newspapers and word of mouth. Both Bailey households were thrilled and excited as they eagerly awaited their new addition to the family due in December.

The early morning sickness left Rachel by mid-April and she didn't feel so tired anymore. Preparing for the baby was her most important thought. It helped keep her mind off the rumors of the war drawing closer to home. According to the local newspaper, the United States declared war on Germany on April 6. The news brought fear and dread to Rachel's heart. This wasn't supposed to happen. *Why?* she wondered.

Wilson had won the election by a narrow margin. "He promised he would keep us out of the war," Rachel said in frustration to Jonathan one evening.

Jonathan didn't know what to say to make her feel better. Instead, he held Rachel close. *She's right,* he thought. *A man is supposed to keep his word, especially if that man is the president of the United States.*

As April closed and early May made its welcome entrance with warmer days, Rachel did her best to keep her anxiety of the war at bay by concentrating on what needed to be done at home. Rachel continued with her plans for her herb and vegetable gardens. She could already feel her hands in the dark, cool soil again. But Jonathan insisted that Rachel do no heavy work. This included digging up the heavy, moist soil with a shovel. Jonathan did that for her. His father used a hoe to break up the soil. Rachel smiled when she saw the piles of rocks her father-in-law set aside for her. They worked in her garden each evening after supper. Within days, the soil was ready for planting. Rachel had started many of the herbs from seeds on the sun porch during the past two months. But she would wait until the end of May before planting just in case there was another frost.

The family's anxiety about the war settled down some when they learned that President Wilson would use volunteers to supply troops that were needed to fight. They breathed a huge sigh of relief, feeling more optimistic as American men signed on for the war effort. Rachel was especially relieved that Jonathan would be with her when their baby was born. She couldn't bear the thought of Jonathan not being there to see their firstborn.

Maggie was itching to get started on her roses. Like Rachel, she also enjoyed the feel of the earth in her hands. Elias and Jonathan had insisted on digging up the soil for her as well. Maggie insisted they didn't. "To create a rose garden from beginning to end requires the person creating it to do all the work. However, I will accept your help, Jonathan, in the placing of the beautiful trellises and arbor you made for me."

Jonathan had designed and made two trellises and a beautiful Victorian arbor with gingerbread trim for her climbing roses. Maggie was so surprised and pleased with her gifts on

Christmas morning it almost brought her to tears. Maggie prided herself on being strong and in control at all times, but she was deeply touched by Jonathan's thoughtfulness.

A trellis would be placed on either side of the house. Maggie and Rachel agreed that the beautiful Victorian arbor should be placed at the entranceway of the path leading up to the front door. But no one had expected it to be so beautiful. As the whole family stood back to see how it looked, the gleaming white arbor seemed to set off the whole front of the home. Maggie was so excited and pleased. She could hardly wait to see her beautiful, climbing pink roses growing up and over the arbor.

The beautiful, warm spring day turned into a beautiful evening. The whole family sat outside at the picnic table after dinner and watched the evening sun slip away behind the mountain ridge. The full moon hung suspended over them, shining brightly across the mountain region as the air cooled in the night. Countless stars sparkled in the dark, velvety sky. Talk around the picnic table was light and happy.

To Rachel, there was something about this night though, something she couldn't quite put her finger on. Something uncomfortably familiar. As she looked up at the twinkling stars in the night sky and felt the coolness of the air on her cheeks, she remembered. Memories flooded through her. It was the anniversary of the night of the fire one year ago, she realized, the night of the horrible fire that caused Jack's death. Rachel shuddered at the memory.

It was also the night that God answered her prayers with his divine protection, bringing her, Maggie, Jennie, and Katy out of the fire and their torturous life with Jack Walters. *Has it really been a year?* As she sat there with her family laughing and talking, she could hardly believe it. So much had happened since that night. Here she was, married to Jonathan, the love of her life. She was expecting their baby in December. They had their own wonderful home. Maggie and Jennie were living in a stable family life without the fear they had known while Jack was alive. How grateful Rachel felt at that moment as her eyes misted over. She thought of her mother. She would've been so happy to see her daughters safe and sound. She would've been so happy that her childhood friend took Rachel, Maggie, and Jennie into her home. And, of course, Rachel couldn't forget the miracle of a little kitten named Katy who somehow made it out of the fire too. Fully grown, Katy was spoiled by all of them.

Jonathan placed his arm around Rachel's shoulder, holding her close to his side. As she looked up into his eyes, he whispered gently, "You seem to be in a world of your own, Rachel. Are you feeling all right?"

For a brief moment, Rachel wondered whether to say anything to him or not. She quickly dismissed the thought. Looking into her husband's eyes, she smiled. The past was dead and gone. God had been good to them. Rachel reasoned with herself for the hundredth time. If God had done this for them, surely he would protect her family from the war too. Surely Jonathan wouldn't have to leave her and fight in the war. With that thought, the anxiety she'd been feeling in her heart quietly faded away. Rachel sighed with a smile for her husband and rested her head on Jonathan's strong shoulder.

Chapter Twenty-five

The mood was a somber one at the train station as the Bailey family: Elias, Ellen, Jonathan, and Rachel, along with Maggie and Jennie, waited for the announcement that the train would soon be boarding. Around them stood many other families whose sons, brothers, or husbands were being shipped off to war as well. Young wives, many with small children, and the mothers of the men drafted to be sent off to the war especially couldn't contain the grief they were feeling. Fathers stood stoically, holding their sobbing wives as they cried. Little did anyone realize the pain they were also feeling. But they had to be strong for their families.

Rachel and the rest of the Bailey family were stunned when Jonathan received his orders. Rachel still couldn't believe that her husband, Jonathan, was one of the first to be drafted into the war after the Selective Service Act went into effect May 18, 1917. Jonathan was to be part of the American Expeditionary Force. Training would take place in the state of Virginia. From Virginia, Jonathan would be shipped out to France for further training before fighting. Just the thought of Jonathan having to fight in this war filled his family with a distress and fear that they'd never known. For his sake, they tried not to show it.

The news had been a devastating blow to the whole family. Elias and Ellen were speechless when Jonathan and Rachel gave them the news. Maggie stood strong after she learned about it and made the decision that she would cry later. Jennie didn't quite understand why Jonathan was leaving for a war, but fear crept into her heart. *Why does he have to go?* she wondered.

Rachel wept openly. Jonathan tried his best to comfort her as he held her tight. He stroked her hair, reassuring her that everything would turn out just fine. "I'll be home sooner than you think, Rachel." But inside, Jonathan's heart was breaking too. To leave his wife at a time when she needed him the most tore him in two. That first night after Jonathan had been given his orders, he stayed awake long after Rachel cried herself to sleep in his arms. With her head still on his chest, Jonathan stared up at the ceiling. He couldn't believe it himself. He was going to fight in a war. Jonathan closed his eyes and prayed with all his might.

Lord, I know I have to do this, but why? Why at a time like this? Rachel needs me. Our baby needs me. What if I don't come back? Please give me the strength to face this. I know I don't have the right to ask this of you, but please let the war end soon. Let me come home to my wife and baby. Let us have more children. Let us grow old together. Please take care of my parents, Lord. Please keep my whole family in your tender, loving care. I will come home, he told himself as he drifted off to sleep. *There's just too much to live for.*

Their thoughts were interrupted as the announcement for the train to begin boarding came too soon. Rachel's heart pounded with dread. She found it difficult to catch her breath. Jonathan turned and hugged his parents first. Ellen silently cried into her handkerchief as she stepped back so that Maggie and Jennie could say goodbye.

Jennie openly sobbed as she hugged Jonathan. "You must come back, Jonathan. Please come back. We all need you so much." Her voice broke with another sob. Jonathan kissed the top of her head. Jennie, not wanting to let go, stepped back reluctantly.

Maggie moved forward and took Jonathan's hands. *It would be best to focus on the future,* Maggie thought. *Yes. Something positive.* She looked directly into Jonathan's eyes. "Jonathan, we'll all be waiting for you at this station when you come home. We'll have a wonderful celebration. And your son or daughter will be waiting for you too." Maggie had no idea the effect her inspiring words meant to those around her, including the other families.

For Jonathan, the words were just what he needed to hear. *Thank you, Lord for Maggie's no-nonsense approach to the war.* Maggie let go of Jonathan's hands and stepped back.

Jonathan turned to Rachel. He couldn't let her see how his heart was breaking. He wanted to hold onto her forever, to remember what could be his last moment with her. The thought was sobering. Jonathan's eyes misted over. *Thank you, Lord, for Rachel. You know how much I love her. Please keep her safe while I'm gone, and please bring me home to her and our baby.*

The train's whistle was a grim reminder that all must board. Jonathan stood back slightly to look at Rachel one more time, his hands still on her shoulders. Her pregnancy was just starting to show; her figure was a little fuller, her sweet face a little rounder. He ached, knowing he wouldn't be with her through the entire pregnancy or for the birth of their child. His eyes grew soft with love as he held her close one more time.

Rachel could feel Jonathan's heart beating strong and steady. It was very reassuring to her. A strange sense of completeness filled her at that moment. Looking up at him, she gently kissed him on the lips. "I love you. We'll be waiting for you, our baby and I."

With that sentence, the last call came out for the remaining passengers to board. Jonathan reluctantly let go of Rachel, said goodbye to his family one more time, turned, and boarded the train, disappearing into its interior.

The ride from the train station and back up the mountains of Blue Knob was very quiet, as each person was lost in his or her own thoughts. Now that they were on their way from the train station, the reality of the situation settled in. Ellen tried to control the thought that she might have seen her son for the last time. All she wanted to do was go home and have a good, long cry. Elias knew he had to be strong for his wife, but his own heart ached that his one and only son might never return home. As he was silently praying, he was reminded that God had given up his one and only son as well. Feeling very humble, Elias asked God for forgiveness and for the faith to keep going.

Rachel and Jennie weren't crying anymore, but their eyes were red and swollen. Maggie tried to involve Rachel in a conversation about her herb garden. "Did you know, Rachel, that I heard somewhere that mints like the peppermint and spearmint you've been growing will help keep certain bugs like aphids off my roses?"

Rachel looked at Maggie in surprise. "No, Maggie, I didn't know that. How does it actually work?" For a short while, everyone's attention was on the conversation between Rachel and Maggie, with Jennie piping in occasionally.

Conversation dropped off as they neared the homestead. For Ellen, the barn, their home, and the fields all looked the same but felt unfamiliar at the same time. Knowing Jonathan wouldn't be there changed everything, even how things looked. Ellen's throat ached with unshed tears. Always the one to keep going, she found that she could barely take the next step.

It was Maggie who suggested that she, Rachel, and Jennie would like to walk the rest of the way home. Elias felt a deep sense of relief. He needed to get his wife into the house as quickly as possible. He gave a very grateful look to Maggie for understanding before taking his wife's arm and turning to walk into the house.

Rachel always felt better when she was doing something. Walking home felt wonderful. It felt normal. For a short while, she, Maggie, and Jennie were able to simply walk and talk about nothing in particular. Mostly, Jennie did the talking, chattering along a mile a minute from one subject to the next. Both Rachel and Maggie saw Jennie growing up just a little bit more every day, but the little girl was still there. Jennie's conversation made them both smile.

"Katy!" Jennie called out suddenly.

"Meow. Meow." Katy was very unhappy to have been left alone all those hours. As she walked toward the girls, she kept up her chorus of meows.

Looking at her, it was hard to believe Katy was ever a helpless, starving kitten. Her beautiful orange and white fur was shiny and soft, even down to her white-booted paws. Katy kept herself clean and groomed at all times. As she continued padding toward the girls, Katy kept her tail straight up in the air. She had grown into a sizable cat, but her tail was unbelievably long. On more than one occasion, Katy's tail had almost been caught in a closing door or the runner of the rocking chair in the parlor. Katy learned quickly never to nap behind the rocking chair and was suspicious of anyone who would sit in such a thing.

Katy stood her ground, her paws firmly planted in place in front of Rachel, Maggie, and Jennie, her eyes looking at them as if wanting to say, "Well, where were you?" The sight was so comical they all three laughed.

Jennie bent down to pick her up. "We're home, Katy," she said reassuringly. "Would you like something to eat?" Jennie turned to look at her sisters, saying, "Katy feels awfully light today, and her purr doesn't seem quite right either."

All three sisters immediately became concerned for Katy. "I know what we can do," said Rachel. "We'll give Katy some catnip tea. That should do the trick." Almost as if Katy understood, she looked over at Rachel and meowed in agreement. They all laughed. Katy was very good at lifting their spirits.

Rachel, Maggie, and Jennie set about preparing a late afternoon meal for themselves. How odd it felt to be without Jonathan. Rachel was in charge of making the tea and slicing homemade bread. Jennie was placing a pretty, flowered tablecloth on the table and arranging the place settings. It felt strange to her to leave an empty space where Jonathan would've sat. Maggie plunked down two jars of homemade blackberry and blueberry jams. After slicing the ham and placing the serving dish on the table, Maggie slipped out the back door. She felt Jonathan's absence too. *Maybe something cheerful to look at would help,* she thought.

When the girls sat down at the table, the aroma of early summer roses in a beautiful glass vase reached their noses. "That's wonderful," Rachel said.

Jennie leaned in to sniff the roses. "They smell really good, Maggie," she said. Maggie beamed. She loved surprising her sisters. And at the moment, they needed their spirits lifted.

Katy jumped into the empty chair that Jonathan always sat in and meowed sadly. All three of the girls looked at her. Katy had never done this before. She meowed again pathetically, looking at them, her eyes wide, questioning. *Where is he?* Rachel's heart ached when she realized Katy was looking for Jonathan. Jonathan's absence didn't affect just the three of them. It affected Katy too.

"Oh, Katy," Jennie said as she reached over to pet her head reassuringly. "Don't you worry. Jonathan will be back very soon." While Jennie was talking, Rachel got up and walked over to the hutch where Katy's catnip tea was cooling in a saucer. Picking up the saucer carefully, Rachel turned and walked back to the table. She gently set it down on Jonathan's chair and then sat in her own chair. Katy slurped up every drop and then groomed herself and curled up in the chair for a nap. The heartache of missing Jonathan washed over Rachel in waves. Both Maggie and Jennie could see and feel the overwhelming sadness in their sister's eyes.

Maggie poured the tea for Rachel and Jennie and then for herself. Always one to try to make someone smile, Maggie decided to do her best imitation of the proper Englishwoman, complete with a nasally accent. "I say. This is a lovely tea party.

I do!" With that remark, Maggie then picked up her tea cup, dramatically stuck her little pinky out, brought the cup to her lips, and slurped loudly. She then placed the cup down loudly on its saucer, only to bring it to her lips again. Her words and actions were so abrupt, so sudden that it took both Rachel and Jennie completely by surprise. Maggie continued slurping noisily she looked over the rim of her cup. Both Rachel and Jennie started to chuckle. As Maggie continued her act of being the proper English lady, it became even funnier. Jennie picked up her tea cup, copying Maggie's imitation. Their chuckles became laughter. They laughed so hard their bellies ached. Tears of laughter rolled down their cheeks at Maggie's outrageous antics.

"Katy is sleeping through this," Rachel said.

"I know," said Maggie.

This only caused them to laugh even more.

Finally, the laughter settled down to chuckles and then giggles. *Thank heaven for Maggie,* Rachel thought. *What would we do without her?* Rachel suddenly felt very hungry.

Actually, they were all hungry as their appetites returned. They ate the ham, bread, and jams, even helping themselves to seconds. Feeling more optimistic, Rachel talked about their future when Jonathan returned.

Good. Maggie nodded to herself. *This is how Rachel should be thinking.*

Chapter Twenty-six

𝒮ummer had produced an abundance of herbs in Rachel's garden. The joy Rachel felt when she saw the bounty God had blessed her with also reminded her that he was truly in control and he would be the one to protect Jonathan. She had received a letter in the post a few days earlier from her husband. Somehow, Rachel couldn't quite get used to the return address on the envelope. The overseas service stamped the words "On Active Service with the American Expeditionary Force" followed by a written "Postal Express Service." Underneath this was the APO number and date. Most envelopes had two American flags with poles that looked like two crisscrossed swords. Below the crossed flags was an emblem. It all seemed so unreal to her.

Rachel still expected her husband to walk through the kitchen door like he did every evening. She would turn toward the door and wait. Jonathan always called her name as if she'd be anywhere other than the kitchen, at that time of day, preparing their meal.

Then the realization would wash over her that Jonathan wouldn't be home that evening. This filled her heart and soul with deep sadness. She ached to see him. Jonathan's letters were so precious to Rachel. They made her feel close to him, but sadly, they were also a reminder of their separation. Rachel missed Jonathan very much. Nighttime turned out to be the worst part. He wasn't there to hold her protectively in his arms. He wasn't there in the middle of the night when Rachel turned to her other side and looked at him before falling back to sleep. Rachel found herself clinging to sweet memories of their closeness. The loneliness overwhelmed her.

Rachel knew she'd have to stay busy. It was the only way she knew how to keep going until Jonathan came home. *And just look what it's produced,* she thought as her eyes looked at row after row of herbs. They looked like a sea of green. As she took a stroll through each row, the leaves gently brushed up against her swishing skirts. The delicious scents of the herbs were heavenly.

Rachel made sure she placed the fragrant lavender at the front entrance of the gardens. Its scent seemed to provide a relaxed, calming atmosphere for potential customers. Within moments of being greeted by the scent of lavender, customers would be smiling, completely at ease as they strolled through her herb garden. And word spread fast.

People from miles around had heard of Rachel's herb garden. It wasn't unusual for families to stop by as part of their outing for the day. It fascinated them that anyone would devote so much time to growing herbs. But when they saw the beautiful herb gardens for the first time, people realized this was much more than just a pastime. Many people looked forward to meeting Rachel as much as seeing the gardens. For the ladies especially, it became the highlight of their outings.

Rachel's father-in-law had even made a decorative sign so potential customers would be able to find the place easier. One sign was placed along the roadside and another was stationed near the Baileys' homestead. The signs simply read "Rachel's Herb Gardens" with a drawing of a lavender, mint, and rose-filled basket. The sign itself looked very inviting and even brought people who weren't planning to make a stop there.

When customers arrived for the first time at Rachel's herb garden, they were taken back by the unbelievable fragrance and beauty of the herbs. And the prices were reasonable too. Because Rachel wanted to make sure almost everyone could enjoy her herbs, she kept her prices very fair. To her, sharing the joy of her herbs was very important. Jennie loved being the cashier and charmed many customers with her gentle smile and easy manner.

Maggie's rose gardens were also gaining attention—so much so that Rachel and she agreed that Maggie should try to sell bouquets of her roses. While many wives were happily strolling through Rachel's herb garden with Ellen or Rachel, Maggie would draw their husband's attention away to her rose gardens. She'd take them on a tour all around the property so they could see the variety of colors and scents of her ever-increasing collection. "Every woman loves roses," she'd say to them. "What is your wife's favorite color?" It was with this answer that Maggie could then convince them with very little effort to purchase a bouquet of roses. "Imagine your wife's surprise when you give her these," she would say as she created a special bouquet while they talked.

And Maggie was right. Every husband who took Maggie's suggestion watched as Maggie cut the roses of his choice to make a bouquet for his wife. And each was delighted with his wife's response. Miss Maggie was right. Many husbands had no idea that a simple bouquet of roses tied together with a pretty satin ribbon was all he needed to do to put that special light back in her eyes. It came as quite a shock, actually. *Imagine that,* they pondered. *Who would've thought that a simple bouquet of roses could do so much?*

Chapter Twenty-seven

Jonathan smiled to himself as he read the latest letter from Rachel. Each time he received a letter from her, he eagerly opened the envelope. Rachel's letters were precious to him. They were his lifeline to her. Her letters made him feel as if he was at home with her each and every time. Rachel always included something in the envelope to remind him of home, something to bring them closer and encourage him that they would be together again, that they still had a future to look forward to. This time, when he had opened her letter, she had included a sprig of lemon verbena and lavender from her herb garden tied together with a small, satin ribbon. He could smell the wonderful scents before he even opened the envelope. To Jonathan, these gifts from Rachel were small, precious treasures he could hold onto until he returned home. They gave him hope.

Jonathan read with delight how well Rachel was doing with her herb garden. *It looks like this venture is turning into a family affair too*, he thought as he smiled to himself. Jonathan had to chuckle when he read how Maggie went about selling her rose bouquets. *It sounds just like Maggie,* he thought to himself, nodding his head. Maggie was turning into an excellent business woman.

Rachel's letter took on a more personal tone. She wrote about how much she missed him. She wrote about her stomach becoming more pronounced as time went on. "Jonathan," she wrote, "I might not be as big as a barn, but I feel like it." Jonathan let out a chuckle at his petite wife's description of herself. Several of the men in his unit turned their heads to see what he was laughing about. Feeling a little sheepish, Jonathan looked at them, shrugged his shoulders, and muttered, "Sorry."

Rachel wrote in her letter that their baby must be very hungry too because she ate often. "It's true," she wrote. "I'm eating for two." Jonathan missed her so much he ached. He missed holding her, breathing in the scent of her hair, and kissing her lips. Closing his eyes, Jonathan smiled as he pictured how Rachel would look with their child.

While he loved receiving letters from his folks, he kept Rachel's letters close to his heart, literally; in his left inside pocket. He wanted to feel his connection with her no matter where he was. Her letters to him were his link to her and their baby. They were his connection to his hope for the future after the war.

How he wished this war would end. Jonathan wanted to come home, hug his parents, hold his wife, and be there with her when their precious baby was born. But he didn't share these thoughts in his letters to her. As Jonathan wrote back to Rachel, he kept his tone warm and light. Rachel didn't need to know how afraid he really was.

Chapter Twenty-eight

Both Bailey households were kept very busy during the summer months, from very early morning to late afternoon. Not one of them had any idea how successful Rachel's herbs and Maggie's roses would be. And Jennie had a surprisingly quick mind when it came to arithmetic. It got so she could tally the exact amount that was due in her head, as well as the exact amount of change.

"I have an idea," Ellen said one evening. They were all sitting down at the picnic table after supper. The day had been another hectic, busy one, and it felt good to simply relax. "Next year, we should include homemade soaps and maybe even candles with the fragrance of roses and lavender and lemon verbena and—." Ellen stopped when she realized that her husband, Rachel, Maggie, and Jennie were staring at her. *What's wrong?* she wondered. Feeling a little doubtful, Ellen thought that perhaps she shouldn't have brought her idea up when everyone was so tired. She was almost ready to apologize when Rachel spoke.

"That's a wonderful idea!" Rachel exclaimed. Suddenly, everyone was talking with enthusiasm about plans for the next summer.

"We could make rose water as well as the soap," Maggie said.

"We could also include some of the herbs, like lavender, in your rose bouquets, Maggie," Rachel said.

"What about something for the men folk?" Elias asked. "We like to smell good too, you know."

They all looked at him in surprise. This remark of his made them burst out laughing. But he did have a point. The thought never occurred to them that they should offer products for men. It seemed odd to them, but Elias was certain his idea was a good one.

"All right. All right," Ellen said as she held her hands up slightly. "Why don't we all have some apple pie together and go over some plans for next year?"

Chapter Twenty-nine

*R*achel moved slower as her pregnancy became more obvious. While she kept saying she felt as big as a barn, she still insisted on doing her own chores, including the cleaning and cooking. But more often, Maggie and Jennie stepped in to help before Rachel had a chance to say anything. To Rachel, it seemed to be more than a coincidence that her sisters were nearby so often. The truth was, however, Rachel was thankful for them as the fatigue of carrying the extra weight of her pregnancy sapped most of her strength. There were also days when Rachel had to fight the overwhelming sadness of missing Jonathan. She spent time in prayer, although not usually on her knees. It was becoming very difficult for her to get back up. The peace God gave her during those times of prayer truly was heaven sent.

One day, Rachel felt especially needful. Leaving the breakfast dishes to be washed later, Rachel went upstairs to her and Jonathan's bedroom. Her need to pray was so great that she knelt with some effort at the bedside. With her hands folded and her head bowed, Rachel humbled herself as she cried, pouring out her heart for God's encouragement. *Please, Lord,* she prayed, *I know I need to move forward, to keep going. But it's so hard. I miss Jonathan. If something happens to him, I don't know how I'll go on. I'm having trouble moving forward in the way you want me to go. Please, Lord. Please show me the reason you want me to go on.* Her last request was barely out of her head when she felt a very hard kick inside her belly. Lifting her head in surprise, Rachel realized that her and Jonathan's baby just kicked her. She'd felt the baby's movement before, but nothing like this. The baby kicked again, almost as a reminder. Rachel, still on her knees, looked up and smiled. *Thank you, Lord, for the biggest reason I need to keep going.*

Rachel felt a renewed strength and peace. Carefully standing up, Rachel turned from the bed and walked across the room to her desk. *Jonathan will be so excited when I tell him about our baby's kick.* Rachel pulled out the desk chair and sat down. Reaching for paper and pen, she wrote a very long letter to her beloved Jonathan.

Chapter Thirty

Rachel sat back on her heels as she took a brief rest and wiped her hands on her gardening apron. When Rachel first began making gardening aprons for herself, everyone in her family, including Jonathan, had chuckled. "Women are supposed to wear aprons in the kitchen," they told her. But Rachel pointed out to them the various pockets she had sewn on the apron and what each pocket was to be used for. There was a pocket for scissors, double-lined for safety, of course, and a large pocket for her trowels and balls of twine. This was more convenient, she pointed out, than misplacing them when they were set down somewhere. Two smaller pockets held seeds for planting. There was even a pocket for a small towel to wipe her face with on hot, humid days when she was tending her garden.

When Rachel made gardening aprons for Ellen, Maggie, and Jennie, they realized with delight that what she'd told them was right. Maggie was particularly impressed. On the evening the family had gotten together to share ideas on soaps and bouquets from the garden for next year's herb season, Maggie said, "I vote that Rachel make gardening aprons too. I know for a fact they will sell." Everyone agreed it was worth a try.

"Maybe you should put a tag on the aprons, Rachel, that says, "Rachel's Herb Gardens," Elias suggested. They all looked at him in surprise.

"What a splendid idea, Elias," Ellen said.

Elias shrugged his shoulders and smiled. "I do come up with something once in a while."

The month of October 1917 was almost at an end. Rachel's Herb Garden was officially closed for the season. Rachel closed her eyelids for a moment. The warmth of the autumn sun on her back felt wonderful. This last crop of herbs would be hung and dried during the coming winter months for her family's own personal use. It seemed to Rachel that the day after she poured out her heart to God, she felt a renewed sense of purpose. Her back no longer ached. She was blessed with more energy, and she could even pray on her knees again. How very much she had to be thankful for!

Rachel inhaled deeply as the scents of lavender, lemon verbena, mint, basil, and oregano, among others, blended together. The oregano had been particularly difficult to harvest. The bees who loved oregano flowers weren't happy to have their last crop of oregano taken from them. As Rachel carefully snipped the oregano stems, more than one bee decided to hang on for the ride. The basket that held the oregano was covered with stubborn bees. Rachel could hear them buzzing as they continued their work, ignoring the fact that they had just been relocated. Opening her eyes, she was amazed at the continued overflow of herbs. *I'm going to need more baskets,* Rachel thought to herself.

"Rachel. Rachel." She heard from a distance the voices of Maggie and Jennie calling.

"Here I am," Rachel answered so they would follow her voice. When Rachel looked up, Maggie, Jennie, and Katy were walking down the path toward her.

Maggie noticed the large amount of herbs Rachel had already harvested. "Oh my. You've been busy, haven't you?" Maggie asked.

"I think we need more baskets, Rachel," Jennie piped in.

Rachel, still sitting back on her heels, smiled up at them. "Yes, I've been busy. And yes, we do need more baskets."

Jennie and Katy stayed with Rachel while Maggie went back to the gardening shed for more baskets.

"Meow," said Katy. Rachel and Jennie smiled.

"Don't worry, Katy," Jennie said as she got down on her knees to help Rachel. "We won't forget your catnip." She reached her hand out to pet Katy on the head. Rachel snipped the catnip stems while Jennie placed them in the baskets. Katy decided to chew on a helping of the catnip and was starting to look very relaxed. Jennie was bored. Maybe this would be a good time to talk with Rachel. "I know how babies are made..." Rachel's head suddenly shot up. Jennie was smiling at her mischievously.

"Jennie," Rachel said, "you shouldn't talk about such a thing."

Jennie sat back on her heels, still smiling. "But why?" she asked her sister.

Rachel stopped snipping the catnip, still holding her scissors, and sighed. She looked at her younger sister directly and said, "Jennie, there is a time for everything. When the time comes, we'll talk. But not right now. All right?"

Jennie hung her head sadly. She didn't mean to upset Rachel. She just wanted to let her sister know how she found out about babies. Kathleen, Jennie's classmate, told Jennie and another girl in their class after school one day as they were walking home that the father planted a seed. "That's how a

Mary Netreba

baby grows," Kathleen said. And Kathleen was the smartest girl in school. Jennie was disappointed because she wanted to share what she knew with Rachel. And she only wanted to ask Rachel what kind of flower seed it was. After all, Jennie reasoned, Rachel was the gardener. Jennie sighed in frustration and hurt feelings. She'd have to wait. Jennie gave in reluctantly, "All right, I'll wait," the tone of her voice indicating that she wouldn't be waiting very long.

"You two look to be in a serious discussion," Maggie said as she walked down the path toward them.

Rachel and Jennie looked up at her. In each of her hands, Maggie was carrying baskets of various sizes. Fortunately, many of them had handles. When Katy was a kitten, she loved being carried in a basket. "I have an idea," Maggie said. She was concerned about what Rachel and Jennie had been talking about. The sad look in Jennie's eyes told Maggie her sister's feelings were hurt over something. Rachel looked like she didn't know what to say. Maggie broke the uncomfortable silence. "Let's take some of the filled baskets back to the house, have something to eat and drink, and then come back to do the rest."

Rachel looked up at her sister with gratitude in her eyes. Maggie always seemed able to read any situation and know how to take care of it right away.

"Jennie," Maggie suggested, "why don't you carry that basket of catnip before Katy eats it all? Maybe Katy should be out of the basket too."

Katy, who had been lazily lying in the basket, lost in the pile of catnip, sat up. "Meow!" Katy, paws deep in the catnip, refused to move.

Jennie stood up and bent down to grasp the handle of the catnip-filled basket with Katy still in it. It took some effort, but she was able to hold the basket just fine. "Katy wants a ride home," Jennie said stubbornly. Jennie was still put out that Rachel didn't want to hear her question.

"All right then," Maggie said. "Katy stays in the basket, but you have to carry her all the way." Maggie emphasized "all the way." She wasn't about to allow Jennie any slack for being so hardheaded.

"Meow." Katy seemed to want to voice her opinion too.

Maggie reached down and held out her hand to help Rachel stand up. Rachel got to her feet rather clumsily and took a moment to balance herself. Maggie handed Rachel two very light baskets, then she bent down, picking up several herb-filled baskets and balanced them on her arms with ease.

The three of them started down the path to their home single file. Rachel, seven months along in her pregnancy, moved slowly and carefully while Maggie, tall and well-coordinated, walked with ease but slowly enough not to get too far ahead of her sister. Jennie brought up the rear, trying hard to keep her balance, pretending as if it was nothing to hold on to her basket of catnip with Katy sitting comfortably inside, her long tail hanging almost to the ground, lazily swishing back and forth.

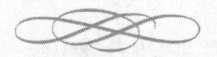

Ellen was waiting for the girls on the front porch of Rachel and Jonathan's home as they approached. By the looks of it, the girls had been very busy. Herbs of spearmint, peppermint, lemon balm, verbena, lavender, and catnip overflowed the baskets. From where Ellen was standing, she could already smell the wonderful, clean scent of lavender. This was by far her favorite herb.

As they neared, Ellen noticed that Rachel looked a little flushed and tired. Maggie looked like she could keep going no matter what. She took long walks every day, even longer when it was raining. Maggie loved the rain. It didn't matter to her how wet she got. She would come home in the best of moods, invigorated from her walk. "That was wonderful," she would say as she came through the door, her hair and clothes completely soaked. No one in either Bailey household could seem to understand how anyone could enjoy a walk in the rain. Maggie never said it out loud, but she carried it in her heart. She felt closest to God at those times. She considered it her own precious, personal time with him.

Ellen almost burst out laughing when she saw Jennie clumsily trailing behind. She cupped her hand over her mouth. Jenny was leaning sideways in the direction of the extra weight she was carrying because of Katy. She looked like she would tumble over any second. With her other hand, she was trying to brush away the hair that kept falling down over her eyes, making it difficult to see. Jennie looked spent. Ellen, Rachel, and Maggie were all waiting together on the porch, watching. Jennie thought she was far enough away so no one could hear her. Muttering under her breath, looking down at Katy, Jennie's words reached their ears. "All I wanted to do was ask a simple question, Katy. Why couldn't Rachel just answer? My arm is really tired too."

Jennie realized too late that she was overheard. As she looked up, she could see their smiles as they made a sincere effort not to laugh. Pulling her shoulders up straight, Jennie stuck out her chin stubbornly and forced herself to walk the last few steps with the heavy weight of Katy still in the basket. She was purring contently and completely relaxed. Jennie didn't have the strength left to place the basket down gently; she let it drop with a plunk on the porch. "Meow!" Katy seemed insulted as she jumped out of the basket and ran into the house, seeking a more comfortable place to nap.

Ellen, Rachel, and Maggie couldn't help themselves anymore. Ellen did feel sympathy for Jennie, but the situation couldn't have been any more comical. The laughter finally escaped from her lips. That was all it took. Rachel and Maggie also tried to keep from laughing, but once Ellen started, they couldn't control themselves either. Bent over in hysterical laughter, it only became funnier as Jennie got angrier.

She didn't like being laughed at. "Stop it! Stop it right now!" Jennie was furious. Stomping her foot down, hands on her hips, Jennie continued. "I mean it! You stop your laughing at me right now! All I wanted was an answer about babies. I don't think this is funny…" Jennie's voice dropped off as she put her head down and started to cry.

Ellen, Rachel, and Maggie immediately stopped laughing. Feeling very bad about hurting Jennie's feelings, they walked the few steps to where the child stood crying. Placing her arms around Jennie's shoulders, Maggie said, "Jennie, I'm so sorry for laughing. I didn't know why you were upset. I shouldn't have laughed." Ellen and Rachel also apologized to Jennie.

Jennie sniffled a few more times. Looking up at Maggie, Jennie asked, "Can we get something to eat now? I'm hungry."

Ellen, Rachel, and Maggie were relieved that Jennie was so quick to forgive and forget. A meal sounded like a good idea to them too. Rachel and Maggie left their baskets of herbs on the porch before turning to walk into the house. The herbs would have to wait.

Chapter Thirty-one

"Oh, Rachel," Ellen said after they sat down at the table to tea, soup, bread, and jam. Ellen pushed her chair back, stood up, and walked across the kitchen to the hutch where she had placed the mail. Picking up the envelope, she came back to the table and handed the letter to Rachel. "This came while you were gone," she said as she sat down again.

The return address of Jonathan's letters from France didn't seem so foreign to Rachel anymore. Each letter Rachel received from her husband was a sign to her that he was alive and safe. She was very thankful to hold each and every one of his precious letters. Many times, Rachel felt as if Jonathan was in the room, talking with her as she read them.

Rachel murmured a "thank you" to her mother-in-law as she took the envelope from her hand. Maggie and Jennie waited expectantly for Rachel to open her letter. Placing the envelope in her apron pocket instead, Rachel just smiled at them and said, "You'll just have to wait this time."

This surprised them. Usually, Rachel opened Jonathan's letters immediately. Rachel couldn't explain it, but this time she wanted to wait until she was all alone before reading his letter. Maggie and Jennie looked at each other and then at

Ellen. They all smiled and shrugged their shoulders. If Rachel wanted to read Jonathan's letter before sharing it with them, that was all right too. They knew she'd share what Jonathan had to say in his letter anyway, so they could wait.

It was late evening by the time the herbs were all harvested, sorted, and hung to dry. Ellen and Maggie had just finished washing and drying the supper dishes. All of them were tired, but it was a good tired. Elias had joined them for supper but left soon after, stating, "I know you women folk have things to do and discuss." After kissing his wife lightly on the top of her head, Elias left through the kitchen door and walked outside. He reached into his pocket for his pipe. Ellen never allowed smoking in their home. He showed the same respect for Rachel, although she never asked. Besides, Elias was used to going outside to smoke and even looked forward to it.

The fragrance of the many herbs that they tied up with string and neatly hung throughout the house was delightful. They all agreed that they'd have plenty to last them until the next season. After harvesting the rest of the herbs, Rachel, her sisters, and Ellen had worked throughout the day into the evening separating, snipping, stringing, and hanging the herbs. When they were finished, they prepared a simple meal of mint tea, homemade bread, bacon, and eggs. Rachel was especially hungry, having seconds of almost everything. Ellen looked across the table at Rachel fondly. Rachel's face was rounder, her cheeks pink with color. Her belly was also growing more.

"I remember how hungry I was when I was going to have Jonathan," Ellen said to all of them. "I couldn't believe how much I enjoyed the food." Rachel smiled at her. It was a relief that someone else knew what it was like to be with child. Rachel knew she had put on weight. Ellen noticed the look of concern in Rachel's eyes. "The funny thing was," Ellen continued, "that after I gave birth to Jonathan, he kept me so busy my figure came right back."

Rachel looked across the table at her mother-in-law thankfully. Sometimes Rachel was so hungry she wondered if she'd ever be able to stop eating. She felt large and clumsy and awkward. To those around her, though, they only saw a petite and very pretty mother-to-be.

Ellen left her daughter-in-law's home soon after the dishes were washed, dried, and put away. Katy meowed persistently at Jennie that it was bedtime. Jennie gave no argument, nor did Maggie. They were both exhausted and soon went upstairs to bed.

The house was completely quiet. Rachel retrieved her letter opener from the bedroom and made her way back downstairs and out the front door. She loved to sit on the top front porch step in the evening. Next to baking day, this was where she did her best thinking. As she carefully sat down with the help of the porch post next to the steps, Rachel felt the night air becoming cool. She breathed in the fresh scent and let out a contented sigh. There was just a hint of winter in the air. She could smell it. Though there would still be some warm days for a short while, the mountaintops of Blue Knob would soon be dressed in fluffy mounds of white.

Rachel reached deep into her left apron pocket and pulled out the envelope that held Jonathan's letter. The moon was full and shining brightly enough that Rachel could read Jonathan's letter easily. *France.* Rachel sighed. France was so far away. Her heart hurt just thinking of the distance between them. The baby gave a quick kick, almost as if to remind Rachel that the letter in her hand was still unread. Rachel took the letter opener and slit the envelope open carefully. As she took out the letter, a small packet fell to the porch floor. Picking it up, she placed it in her apron pocket. Opening the letter, she began to read.

> My darling Rachel, how I miss you. How are you? How is our baby? I wish I could be there to talk to him (or her) too.

Rachel smiled. She had written in one of her letters to him that she talked to their baby. Jonathan was delighted to hear this. *No doubt if he was here,* Rachel thought, *Jonathan would be talking to our unborn baby too.* Rachel read on.

> France is beautiful. There is very pretty scenery. I am sending you some seeds in a packet I wrapped up. I don't know what they are, but perhaps if you plant them you might have a new herb or flower. After this war ends, maybe the two of us can travel here together someday, as I think you would love France.

Jonathan's letter was light as he went on to talk about when he would be home, how much he was looking forward to Rachel's breads and pies, how much he was looking forward to the rest of his life with her and having more babies, of course. Jonathan's letter filled Rachel with such a sense of hope for their future that it was as if he was sitting right beside her, with his arms protectively around her shoulders. "The moon is full tonight," Jonathan wrote. "Isn't it amazing? We are countries apart, but there is still only one moon. It gives me comfort to know that you and I are sharing the same moon. Only God could do that, you know. God is amazing, isn't he? He has it all planned out. He knows when we will be together again. But in the meantime, he gave us the moon."

The words Jonathan wrote on the pages blurred as Rachel's eyes filled with tears. The beauty and simplicity of what Jonathan said in his letter filled her with a sense of completeness. She felt as if they were alone together in spirit at that moment. Rachel sighed and looked up at the sky. The bright moon hung suspended, as if God's invisible hand was holding it in place. Many stars were twinkling, their sparkles breathing life into the night sky. *I'll have to write to Jonathan that we share the stars too,* Rachel whispered to herself. Rachel wiped away the tears that ran down her cheeks. She looked down again at Jonathan's letter and continued to read. "And the stars we share too, my darling." Rachel chuckled. *Of course.*

After reading Jonathan's letter through twice, Rachel was so filled with hope that she believed anything was possible. With that thought, Rachel gently closed Jonathan's letter and placed it back in the envelope and in her apron pocket again. Standing up carefully, Rachel turned and walked across the porch to the front door. Opening the door slowly so she wouldn't wake anyone up, she stepped inside, closed the door, and leaned against it for a moment.

It had been a long, beautiful day. Jonathan's letter had made it complete. Rachel couldn't wait to see her husband again. *In the meantime, I'll have much to write to him about.*

Chapter Thirty-two

Rachel awoke early, feeling very refreshed although she had only had six hours of sleep. Sliding out of bed, Rachel rather clumsily got on her knees to pray. It was easier to get on her knees from the bed rather than from standing. "Thank you, Lord, for today. Thank you for my home, family, and Jonathan's letter. Help me stay in your will today. Please keep Jonathan and all of our men in this war safe. Amen." Rachel usually said the Lord's Prayer every morning. But this morning, it was on her heart to let God know how thankful she felt.

Standing up, Rachel made the bed. She felt so much energy, so much like her old self that she could hardly believe it. With a little extra spunk in her step, Rachel made her way down the stairs, through the hallway, and into the kitchen to start breakfast for her sisters.

When Maggie and Jennie entered the kitchen, they stopped in their tracks and stared at Rachel in disbelief. Rachel had been very busy. She smiled at her sisters. The look of fatigue and sadness in Rachel's eyes since Jonathan had left for war were gone. There was a look of peace on her face too. Rachel's eyes sparkled with enthusiasm. Still smiling, Rachel said, "You're up. Good. I thought it would be best to let you sleep a bit longer this morning since it's Saturday." Maggie and Jennie looked at each other and then back at Rachel. Rachel was moving about the kitchen with ease.

"Hurry up. Sit down while I get your breakfast." Rachel had been busier than they realized. She'd made pancakes, bacon, eggs, homemade syrup, and coffee. A large pan held dough that was rising for bread. The wonderful aroma of chicken soup told them what they'd be having for supper. Rachel had a bowl of milk ready for Katy, who had just entered the kitchen.

"Here, Katy. Come get your milk," Rachel said as she carefully placed the bowl of milk on Jonathan's chair. Katy jumped up and immediately started to slurp her breakfast.

"I do believe that Katy has become just a little too spoiled," Maggie said. "What will you do, Rachel, when Jonathan comes back and wants to sit in his chair?"

Rachel thought about it and smiled. "I suppose Katy will have to sit on Jonathan's lap." Jennie giggled at the thought of Katy on Jonathan's lap while Jonathan held a bowl of milk for her.

"You seem very different this morning, Rachel," Jennie said. "You seem…" Jennie eyes were thoughtful. "You seem very happy."

"I am, Jennie," Rachel said. "There is so much to do to be ready for the baby. Before you know it, he or she will be here, the war will be over, and Jonathan will be home." Rachel said this with so much conviction that it took Maggie and Jennie by surprise. Jennie was the first one to break the silence.

"Rachel, can we read Jonathan's letter? Please?"

Chapter Thirty-three

*E*lias and Ellen received another letter from their son, Jonathan, in November, just one week before Thanksgiving. This one was very different from all his other letters. Usually, Jonathan wrote lightly about his military training and his new friends, one in particular who shared much in common with Jonathan. "Even our names are similar," Jonathan wrote to his parents. "We call him Johnny here," Jonathan wrote, "but his real name is John Dailey, from Arkansas. Can you imagine that? He has a wife back in Arkansas. They're having a baby in December too. Maybe someday both of our families can meet. By the way, do you know they call us Doughboys over here?"

Always, Jonathan's letters had helped keep Ellen's worry from growing. But this letter was different. Elias and Ellen always read Jonathan's letters together and then shared them with Rachel. However, this most recent letter was one they wouldn't be able to share with her.

Dear Mom and Dad,

I'm writing to you from the Allied trenches in the Luneville sector near Nancy, France, where we were assigned October 21. We are officially at war.

Ellen placed her hand over her mouth. Her heart pounded heavily and felt as if it would jump out of her chest. Elias took her other hand and squeezed it reassuringly. She looked at her husband. Elias was trying very hard not to look worried, but his wife knew him too well. Neither one knew what to say. Looking down at the letter on the table again, they continued reading.

> The first shot was fired by an American soldier on October 23 into a German trench about half a mile away from us. This isn't the life we all knew before the war here started. When I first got here, it didn't look to me as if there was really a war going on. But as I write to you, Mom and Dad, the guns are firing again. I felt I had to write this letter and tell you what is in my heart and what I feel you need to know. Our first Americans in this war died near Bathelemont when Germans raided their trenches. There were three soldiers who died. My prayers are for their families to know their boys died for a worthy cause.
>
> I know that God is in control. If it is in his will for me to come home to my family, the thought fills me with joy. I want so much to come home safely to you and Rachel and our baby. But I'm like any other soldier in this war. There aren't any favorites here. Because of this, I feel I should let you know my concerns in the event something does happen to me.

Elias and Ellen stopped reading and looked at each other. Jonathan was their only son, their only child. The thought of losing him was almost too much to bear. But they both knew that many sons were dying, being taken from their families from many different countries. Their hearts filled with grief for the families left behind.

Jonathan wrote about his concerns for Rachel and their baby. In his letter, he gave instructions of what to do in the event that he didn't make it home. Included was a separate piece of paper in which he made out his will. It was at this point that Ellen broke down in sobs. Elias placed his arm around her shoulder, pulling her close to him. Ellen took a deep breath to regain control. They continued to read.

It was the last paragraph in Jonathan's letter that gave some hope to his parents.

> Mom and Dad, please know that I love you both very much. I'm hoping to come home and be with all of you. I can just picture how wonderful it will be. But please also know this, that if I don't return to you or Rachel, I'll still be home with our heavenly Father and I'll be waiting for you.
>
> Love always,
Jonathan
>
> P.S. Please don't tell Rachel of this letter. I don't want her to worry.

Elias and Ellen sat quietly for awhile, not saying anything. With a deep sigh, Ellen folded the letter and Jonathan's will, placing them both back into the envelope. She'd have to make sure that Rachel didn't see this letter. Ellen prayed she'd never have to give Rachel the last will and testament of her husband.

Chapter Thirty-four

*I*t was quiet on Thanksgiving Day in the Baileys' home. Ellen insisted that she prepare Thanksgiving dinner this year. Rachel insisted on baking the breads and desserts.

"And I'll insist on seconds of everything," Elias said, which made both of them smile.

"Me too. Me too." Maggie and Jennie both piped in.

"Meow."

"And you too, Katy," they all said in unison as they laughed.

Although this Thanksgiving wasn't as festive as last year's, with Jonathan being so far away, there was still much to be thankful for. Each time Jonathan's parents or Rachel received a letter from him was another day they knew Jonathan was alive and well. It was their reason for hope.

Rachel had received another letter from Jonathan just two days earlier. In his letter, he talked about their baby and how he already loved him or her.

> I can picture our baby in your arms, Rachel. The thought fills me with so much love for you it takes my breath away. When this war ends, I'll return to you as soon as possible. In my mind, I picture you waiting for me at the door, arms open wide. I'll hold you and never let you go ever again.

Rosemary for Remembrance

Rachel's heart sang with joy. Jonathan would make it. She just knew it. As she, Maggie, and Jennie set the table with Ellen's best china, Rachel talked of Jonathan being with them for the next Thanksgiving. "It feels like forever, but really it's not," Rachel said. "Look how quickly the time has passed since last Thanksgiving."

Jennie piped in, "I know what you're saying, Rachel. Just look at how fast Katy grew up."

Elias and Ellen, who had just entered the dining room, heard Jennie's remark. They, Rachel, and Maggie smiled. *Jennie and her cat.*

Maggie said, "Well, I for one am still looking forward to the day very soon when women have the right to vote. And that will only be the beginning."

Elias looked at Maggie a little doubtfully, not because he didn't agree with her, but because this one simple act would probably never happen. *A woman voting? Not in a million years,* he thought. Out loud, however, Elias gave his own opinion. "Maggie, you're right. Why shouldn't a woman be allowed to vote?" he asked. "Truth be told, women can do anything. They are far more capable than men in many ways. Women seem to care more about what happens to others too."

Ellen always knew she married the right man, but right then, as she looked at him, she felt especially proud and honored to be his wife. No wonder she loved him more with every passing day.

Rachel smiled at her father-in-law. His hair was more gray than brown since Jonathan went off to war. The lines around his eyes were deeper too. But he still carried the twinkle in his eyes, especially around his wife. She was the one who held him together more often than he would like to admit.

Jonathan was a younger version of his father both in appearance and disposition. Elias and Ellen had brought their son up well. *And,* Rachel thought, *Jonathan and I will bring up our children to be everything that God means for them to be.*

"All right, everyone," Ellen called out with a smile. "Let's bring in the food. I don't know about the rest of you, but I'm hungry."

No one needed to be told twice. They all walked single-file to the kitchen to help carry the many delicious dishes Ellen had prepared to the dining room table. There were bowls of mashed potatoes, gravy, peas, and corn on the cob. They carried in cranberry relish, green beans, and muffins with Rachel's recipe of honey butter. Rachel was handed the smaller dishes. In the past few weeks, her belly had grown even more. Rachel was also moving more slowly. Ellen's eyes misted over as she picked up the bowl of candied sweet potatoes, Jonathan's favorite.

"Here. Let me," Maggie said as she took the bowl from Ellen. Giving Ellen a kind, understanding smile, Maggie continued, "When Jonathan comes home, I think one of the first meals he'll want will be turkey with all the fixings, especially these." Maggie lifted the bowl of candied sweet potatoes up slightly as she said it. Ellen gave Maggie a very grateful look.

Elias brought in a baked, twenty-two-pound turkey on a large, heavy plate and set it down at the end of the table closest to him since he'd be the one to carve the turkey. Turning to his wife, Elias smiled and said, "I believe it's my pleasure to help all the ladies to their seats today."

The Bailey family, minus Jonathan, made the most of this Thanksgiving Day. While they missed Jonathan deeply, they were also aware of the many blessings God had given each of them through this time. Each member of the family took his or her turn around the table to express thankfulness to God. Elias went first. "I'm so thankful to wake up each morning to my beloved wife. I'm thankful that our Jonathan is alive and well." His eyes misted over. "I'm thankful for our first grandchild and can't wait to see him or her."

Ellen was thankful for each day God had given her. "This gift," she called it, "is meant to be appreciated and used for the benefit of others. In this way, it also benefits us. This is the next blessing."

Jennie looked confused. Her young mind couldn't understand what Ellen was saying. *How can helping someone else benefit me?* she wondered.

Ellen looked across the table and saw Jennie's look of confusion. She gave Jennie a smile. "Jennie, do you remember the day Katy came to you?"

Jennie smiled brightly. "Of course. Katy was lonely. She was so hungry and dirty and she needed someone to love her."

"That's right, Jennie," Ellen said. Then she asked Jennie, "What did you do about Katy's needs?"

Jennie thought for a moment. "Well, I fed her, cleaned her, carried her everywhere with me, and loved her a lot."

Then Ellen asked, "So, what did Katy give you in return?"

Jennie giggled. "She gave me purrs, and she loves me." It was as if a light went off in Jennie's head. "Oh! I did something nice for Katy, and she loves me. That's the blessing. Now I understand. Well then, I'm thankful for Katy, my sisters, and the two of you," meaning Elias and Ellen. Jennie sat back in her chair, satisfied and happy she'd figured it out.

Maggie spoke next. "I'm thankful for my family and the love and care I've been given and what this family stands for.

I'm thankful for this good food, a wonderful home to live in, a very bright little sister with her cat, Katy, of course, and Mr. and Mrs. Bailey."

Rachel was about to go next. Opening her mouth to speak, she was interrupted by Maggie.

"Just one more thing," Maggie said as she held up her hand and motioned with her index finger. "I'll also be very thankful for the day—."

Almost as if on cue, Elias, Ellen, Rachel, and Jennie finished Maggie's sentence with her. "That women are allowed to vote."

The dining room filled with hysterical laughter. The more they thought about Maggie with her stubborn idea of women voting and Jennie, who seemed to understand things only when Katy was brought into it, made them all laugh even harder. It took awhile before the laughter became giggles and softened to smiles around the table.

Rachel looked at her family with so much love. "This is what Jonathan would like to see if he was here. He'd be so pleased. When he comes home, let's have the biggest celebration this community has ever seen."

Yes. They nodded their agreement. *When* Jonathan came home, not *if*. Worry did no good. God had his eyes on Jonathan. And God would bring him home if it was his will. Both Elias and Ellen felt a huge weight lift off their hearts. God would always do what was best no matter what.

I'm sorry, Lord, for not trusting you in this, Ellen prayed.

Her husband had bowed his head. Her prayer was his prayer.

Chapter Thirty-five

Mid-December 1917

The warmth from the burning logs in the fireplace radiated much-needed heat that bitter, cold December evening. The strong gusts of wind blew with more intensity, creating high drifts of snow against the Jonathan Bailey home. It was likely there would be snow piled up in front of the front door the next morning, making for early morning shoveling. A shovel was kept in the corner of the kitchen pantry just for this reason.

In front of the fireplace, Katy was lying on her side contently, purring loudly as Jennie petted her fur while whispering little silly words. "Katy, my wonder kitty, I love you. You are so pretty..."

Maggie was sitting across from Rachel in one of the matching chairs belonging to the parlor set. The late Victorian-style furniture was given to Jonathan and Rachel as a wedding present from Elias and Ellen. Rachel had been delighted with their gift. The legs and frame of the settee and two armchairs were made of solid walnut. Because the set had been rarely used, it was in very good condition and looked new. The cushioning in the chairs and settee was very comfortable and relaxing. Because this set was upholstered in a soft, muted, pink tone, eating or drinking in the parlor was rarely allowed. There were exceptions, of course: guests and family and holidays such as Thanksgiving, Christmas, and Easter that were special times.

Maggie was also keeping a close watch on Rachel. In the past few weeks, Rachel's pregnancy had become much more obvious. She looked to Maggie as if she could have the baby any second. Rachel's energy had also waned in the past two weeks. She moved more slowly and carefully. Walking up the stairs to bed at night, Rachel would be out of breath from the exertion.

Rachel had been restless all day. She couldn't seem to get comfortable and complained of a backache. Maggie had prepared an evening meal of Rachel's favorites. The fried chicken was crispy with just the right amount of seasonings. The mashed potatoes were put through a ricer, which made them extra fluffy. Just a touch of butter made them especially tasty. The corn, peas, and gravy were done just the way Rachel would have, with a small dash of basil and oregano. There was also a delicious Dutch apple pie with an added touch of cinnamon for dessert. Maggie made sure the topping was extra crunchy just the way Rachel liked it. Jennie had asked for seconds and thirds of the chicken, partly because she was sneaking some of it to Katy, who was under her chair.

Rachel barely touched her food. She did manage a few bites of fried chicken but put her fork down, saying she just wasn't hungry.

Maggie and Jennie helped Rachel to the parlor and into her chair. Maggie added more wood to the fire, which sent a spray of sparks upward as the fire licked at the new logs. Jennie and Katy stayed with Rachel while Maggie returned to the kitchen for cleanup. Jennie turned from playing with Katy and looked up at Rachel.

"You look kinda different, Rachel," Jennie said. "Are you feeling all right? Are you upset with me for giving Katy too much chicken tonight?"

Rachel sighed. She loved Jennie so much her heart ached at Jennie's question. Jennie still had a problem sometimes with thinking she'd done something wrong even when she hadn't. Rachel and Maggie were very careful how Jennie was disciplined when she did do something wrong because Jennie would feel so badly. Rachel knew it was because of what their father had done to her. This time, Rachel decided to face the problem head-on with Jennie. After all, Jennie was now almost a young lady. She'd have to start thinking as an adult soon enough.

"Jennie," Rachel said kindly but firmly, "I'm not upset with you over the chicken you gave Katy. If I was, I would've said so. You're growing up, and it's time that you knew the truth."

Jennie looked confused. *What is Rachel talking about? What truth?*

Rachel continued, "Our father was a very cruel man who tried to make everyone around him feel badly. He never took responsibility for his actions. Never! He blamed our mother first for his drinking and his unhappiness. He hurt her spirit so much she gave up and died." Rachel paused and took a deep breath to catch herself before she started crying. The image of Julianna in those last moments before she died was one Rachel would carry in her heart forever. Rachel continued, "He blamed me too. It became worse after our mother died. He drank even more. When I met Jonathan, my life changed. Jonathan loved me. Because of him, I knew I was valued. Because of him, I learned that God values me too. I knew what our father, Jack, was doing was very wrong. Jack also knew it. He knew I was onto him. He became afraid of me." Rachel paused for a moment.

Jennie had looked surprised. *Our father was afraid of Rachel?*

Rachel decided not to tell her about the threat she made to Jack. Rachel continued. "So our father began hurting you and Maggie even more. That's what cowards do, you know. They hurt the weakest, most innocent ones." Rachel took a moment to allow what she said to Jennie to sink in. "I prayed that God would help us, that he would get Jack out of our lives forever. I prayed that prayer the night Jack died. I never told you this before, Jennie. You should know. Jack was going to kill us that night."

Jennie's eyes opened wide in surprise as she gasped.

"But something—I don't know what—happened. We found his body in the rubble, with the fireplace poker still clutched in his hand. He'd fallen face forward into the fire. Jack was a very evil man. He died a horrible death. God took him out of our lives, thankfully forever.

"Listen carefully, Jennie. You don't ever have to feel like you did anything to make our father unhappy. You don't have to take the blame for who he was. You don't have to feel badly, as if you've done something wrong. His guilt is *not* yours. Don't ever allow anyone to do this to you, ever." Rachel emphasized her last sentence.

Jennie not only heard Rachel's words. She actually felt them. It was as if a very heavy weight had been lifted from her shoulders. Jennie felt free. It was a wonderful feeling. Her heart felt light. She felt happy. Jennie then felt sadness for Rachel and Maggie. Jack had hurt them too. But they were all right. If anything, Rachel and Maggie showed Jennie that it was possible to be anything she wanted to be. Picking up her cat and holding her close, Jennie whispered into her pointed ear, "Just you wait, Katy. Someday, I'm going to take care of cats. And dogs too. In fact, I can take care of a lot of animals. Would you like that, Katy? Would you?"

"Meow," Katy responded while gently touching the pad of her right paw on Jennie's chin.

Rachel smiled. Jennie could move on. She was going to be just fine.

All the while Maggie was washing and drying the supper dishes and putting the kitchen in order, she could hear the wind howling with increasing intensity. There was more of a chill in the kitchen. Maggie added wood to the stove. *That should keep us for the night,* she thought to herself. A swift glance around the kitchen told Maggie everything was in order. It would feel so good to sit down and rest.

When Maggie entered the parlor, she sat down on the chair opposite Rachel's. Rachel looked flushed as beads of perspiration formed on her upper lip. She looked very uncomfortable. Rachel drew her breath in sharply. "Rachel," Maggie asked, "how long have you been having labor pains? How close are they?"

Rachel looked at her sister. Taking a deep breath, she said, "I think we need Doc Greer here as soon as possible."

Jennie, who had been watching and listening, put Katy down and stood up. "Rachel's going to have the baby!" she shouted excitedly as she jumped up and down.

Maggie went right into action. "Jennie, we need to get Rachel upstairs to her room. You keep an eye on her while I go for Mrs. Bailey and Doc Greer. Quickly. Help me get Rachel upstairs."

Maggie and Jennie held onto Rachel's arms as they helped her up the stairs. Rachel had to move slowly, doubling over with another contraction halfway up the steps. By the time they reached the top, they were all out of breath. Walking Rachel down the hallway to her room, Maggie moved Rachel over to the bed while Jennie pulled back the covers. Very gently, they sat Rachel down and helped her into bed. Jennie placed the covers over her sister.

"Keep her warm, Jennie, while I go for Mrs. Bailey and the Doc." Maggie kissed the top of Rachel's head, then swiftly left the bedroom and descended the stairs for her cloak, boots, and hat before exiting out the front door. She carefully made her way down the snow-covered porch steps and headed in the direction of the elder Baileys' home. The wind was thankfully dying down. Maggie looked up. Stars made their appearance as the sky cleared. Maggie made good time to the Baileys,' her long legs handling the deep snow without too much difficulty. Elias sent both his wife and Maggie back to Rachel and he went for Doc Greer.

Another contraction, this one more intense, happened just after Maggie returned with Ellen. As they stepped into her room, Rachel was gritting her teeth, trying hard not to cry out in pain. She didn't want to scare Jennie, who was standing at the foot of the bed, wringing her hands.

Jennie looked at Maggie and Ellen worriedly. "I don't know what to do!"

Ellen took control right away. "Maggie, go downstairs and fill some pots with water and heat them on the stove 'till they boil. Jennie, we'll need clean sheets." Maggie turned and left the room quickly to make her way down the stairs. Jennie headed to the closet in the hallway where Rachel kept all the linens. She loaded her arms with sheets. Their weight felt very heavy in Jennie's small arms. Jennie had no idea how much would be needed.

More is better, just to be on the safe side, she thought as she headed clumsily back down the hall to Rachel's room, her eyes and nose just above the sheets so she could see where she was going and not trip.

Time seemed to hang suspended as the four of them waited for Doc and Elias in Rachel's bedroom. Rachel's contractions were closer together. Her mother-in-law wiped Rachel's forehead with a cloth dipped in water. She prayed the doctor would arrive before the baby was born.

Jennie was becoming distressed to see her sister in so much pain. She felt helpless to do anything about it.

"Come with me, Jennie," Maggie said as she led her out of the room. As they closed the bedroom door behind them, they heard heavy footsteps coming up the stairs. Maggie and Jennie breathed a sigh of relief when they saw a somewhat groggy Doc Greer at the top of the steps. He looked like he'd been woken up from deep sleep, his eyelids still heavy with fatigue as he and Elias made their way down the hall to Rachel's bedroom. Elias stayed in the hall with Maggie and

Jennie. Ellen stayed in the room with Rachel. She stuck her head out long enough to ask Maggie for more water. Several pans of water were brought up and handed to Ellen before the door was closed again.

"Why is this taking so long?" asked Jennie impatiently. Jennie was still wringing her hands and pacing back and forth. Maggie, usually so calm, was also very excited and couldn't wait to see her new nephew or niece. Elias sat on a chair in the hallway quietly, saying nothing, but inside, he felt genuine concern for Rachel. *What if something goes wrong?* He was glad Ellen was with her. He bowed his head and prayed.

"Oh, I just can't stand it!" Jennie said as she headed down the hall to stand in front of the closed door of Rachel's room. She leaned in to place her ear on the door, hoping to hear something. "Psst!" Jennie waved to Elias and Maggie with her hand to come quickly.

Maggie and Elias followed suit. All three were leaning against the door, listening. Tears filled their eyes when they heard the sound of the baby's first wail. Keeping their ears glued to the door, all three practically stumbled into the room when Doc Greer finally opened the door.

He shook his head as he looked at the three of them. Doc Greer didn't look the least bit surprised. *Hmph! They certainly aren't the first family to do this,* he thought. *And they certainly won't be the last.* He neatly sidestepped Maggie, Jennie, and Elias as he walked past them, stating, "You have a very healthy, very loud nephew and grandson. Good night." Donning his hat, he made his way down the stairs and out the front door.

Both Maggie and Jennie took a few steps into the bedroom and stopped. They drew their breath in quickly with surprise and delight.

"Ah. Rachel, he is so beautiful." Maggie said.

And he was beautiful. As they drew closer, they could see that the baby had a full head of dark hair and blue eyes. Elias stayed back some at the entryway while he made an effort to hold back the tears that sprang to his eyes. Feeling a little more in control, he stepped forward. His grandson looked exactly like Jonathan did when he was born, right down to the dark hair. Jonathan had never lost his hair from birth. Elias wondered if it would be the same for his new grandson.

Ellen wept openly as she walked into her husband's arms. "He is so beautiful, isn't he, Elias? Just like Jonathan." The baby was making sweet little cooing noises as he fell asleep in Rachel's arms. Rachel looked exhausted but happy. She smiled at everyone. "His name is Jonathan Bailey Junior, but we'll call him Little Jon."

"Can I touch him, Rachel? Can I hold him?" Jennie asked.

"Of course you can, Jennie. Just be very gentle, though. Babies are very fragile."

Jennie quickly nodded her head in agreement as she walked closer to the bed. Sitting on the edge of the bed, she reached out to touch Little Jon's tiny fingers. "He's so soft," she whispered. "And his fingers are so tiny." Jennie was in awe that any human being could be so little. Jennie leaned in a little closer and whispered to her sleeping nephew, "Just wait 'till you meet Katy. She was little once too."

Chapter Thirty-six

April 1918

The months following Little Jon's birth were hectic and filled both Bailey households with joy and exhaustion. There was always something that needed to be done. The washing of dirty diapers was endless, and Little Jon was hungry almost constantly. Rachel was very thankful to have Ellen, Maggie, and Jennie to help her. Every day, each one of them would center their attention on Little Jon. Little Jon didn't sleep straight through the night for the first three months, leaving both households exhausted. But no one seemed to really mind too much. Little Jon was a joy as well as a reminder to everyone around him that they needed to continue hoping the war would end and Jonathan would come home soon.

Rachel had received another letter from Jonathan earlier in the week. It was Friday. As she held their growing son in the crook of her right arm, she rocked him slowly and read again Jonathan's letter with her free hand. Each word he had written brought his presence closer to her.

My darling Rachel, my wife, I don't know how to express the love I carry in my heart for you and our son. My heart leaps with the knowledge that we have our own baby boy. Little Jon must be growing like a weed. I long to see your sweet face, Rachel, and kiss your lips and watch you with our son. How I long to hear him cooing the way you described it in your last letter. Our Little Jon. Do you talk to him about his daddy? Is he becoming even more spoiled from all the other attention that I know he must be getting from Maggie, Jennie, and, of course, my mother? I'm so very thankful that Little Jon has my father with him too.

My darling Rachel, I can't help but smile as I think of all of you. I can only imagine how life must be there for you. I miss you too, so very much. I pray for you, our son, and our family. It is my wish and dream to be able to come home safely, although I know only our God in heaven holds the true outcome of this war. Rachel, I want you to know, my darling, that I am in his divine hands. We all are. Whatever happens, whatever the outcome is, your sweet, delicate face will be with me always. There's so much to be hopeful for, Rachel. There's so much to look forward to that to dwell on sad things seems to be a waste of time.

As I write this letter, I dream about our home. I close my eyes and see the promise of spring as you plant the seeds I sent to you. You will plant them, won't you? Perhaps we'll know by summer what they are. Perhaps they are an herb you can harvest and sell. And who knows. I might be home by then. If I close my eyes, I can feel the warm breath of spring on my face, and I picture standing beside you happily. I miss the aroma of the freshly baked bread and pies that you so lovingly prepare for us. When I come home, I can assure you that I will want seconds of everything you make. My darling, I must go. Please tell everyone that I love them and miss them. Kiss Little Jon for me. I kiss you in my thoughts. You are in my heart, always. I love you.

Jonathan

Mary Netreba

Rachel held his letter close to her heart and sighed. Little Jon cooed and smiled, reaching up with his tiny hand to touch her face. Rachel took his little hand in hers and held him closely as she rocked him. Little Jon yawned deeply and was sound asleep within minutes.

When Rachel first read Jonathan's letter, she became anxious when he wrote about being in heaven with God. *Does Jonathan think he won't make it home after all?* she wondered. Rachel read his letter again. This time, she felt more reassured.

Little Jon stirred, making a few cooing noises before becoming quiet again. Rachel bent and kissed his forehead. Little Jon had beautiful, long eyelashes so like his father's. A wave of protective love washed over her. How very sad, that this is how her mother must have felt with her daughters but wasn't able to express it.

Jonathan said that God knew the outcome of this war. Rachel believed that, but her mind started to fret again. *What will we do if Jonathan doesn't come home?* She knew that she, Little Jon, and her sisters would be all right and Jonathan's parents would help. But if she lost Jonathan in such a horrible manner, how could she go on, knowing how he died? Tears welled up in her eyes and threatened to spill over. Like a runaway horse, her mind became crowded with more thoughts of worry. The newspapers were filled with reports of the number of gruesome casualties. Just down the road, two farms over, Anna Smith's husband, who was also serving in France, had died. Even worse was how Anna found out. Anna's last letter to her husband came back to her, unopened and marked with the words on the envelope, "Killed in action." The actual telegram of his death arrived the day afterward.

Rachel shivered just thinking about what Farmer Adams had told everyone at the general store. He and his wife were Anna's closest neighbors. He was in the fields plowing that day when Anna received the news. "It was the most horrible, bloodcurdling scream I ever heard. We didn't even know for sure if it was Anna until my wife ran over to the house and found poor Anna, face down on the floor in the kitchen. It was the most awful thing. That poor young woman." He shook his head sadly as he said it.

What scared Rachel most of all was that Anna was the same age as Rachel, much too young for widowhood. The Great War, as it was being called, was coming much too close to home. Rachel felt a flash of anger. *Why do people have to fight?* she wondered.

Little Jon seemed to sense Rachel's anxiety and started to fuss again. Rachel held him close, talking to him softly while rocking him back to sleep. Rachel sighed. There had to be a reason for everything. Jonathan said in his letter that he was in God's care, that all of them were in God's care. It was time, Rachel realized, to put her faith into action. With renewed determination, Rachel prayed with all her might for Jonathan to come safely home.

This last letter from Jonathan was still in her pocket on Saturday morning. Saturday mornings had become a ritual for the Bailey gals, as they called themselves, to gather together for breakfast and a good talk. Rachel, Maggie, and Ellen would take turns cooking, although it usually ended up being all of them plus Jennie each time anyway. Saturday morning's breakfast became an event they all looked forward to.

Today, it was Rachel's turn to cook. But Little Jon had kept her up all night, fussing and restless. Rachel was exhausted.

Ellen, Maggie, and Jennie all pitched in to prepare breakfast while Rachel sat in the rocking chair with Little Jon on her lap.

Little Jon was all toothless smiles this morning. His clear, blue eyes were bright and alert as if he had been sleeping all night. Rachel had given him a sponge bath, drying him gently with a soft towel and then combed his fine baby hair. Rachel kissed him on top of his little head. He smelled like a baby should, clean and sweet. Maggie had warmed up some applesauce for Little Jon. Little Jon loved applesauce and would greedily eat it as fast as he could. Rachel barely had the spoon out of his mouth and Little Jon would be waving his hands in excitement for the next bite.

Outside the kitchen window, the spring sun shone brightly through the budding trees, bringing with it the promise of a warm day as it chased away the early morning chill. It was going to be a beautiful spring day. Jennie had opened one of the kitchen windows to allow some fresh air inside. The melodic songs of the robins could be heard more clearly.

A lone robin, a male, flew in to land on the windowsill and peered in at the Bailey girls. Turning his head to look from one person to another, the robin seemed puzzled by what he saw. Little Jon's eyes opened wide in amazement as he watched the bird strut back and forth on the sill as if to show off his bright, orange chest. The applesauce forgotten, it ran down Little Jon's chin as his hands clasped together in delight. The sounds of his giggles filled the kitchen. It was the first time any of them had heard Little Jon giggle. The robin then flew from the windowsill to land on the table directly in front of Little Jon, who gasped with surprise and chuckled with glee, his hands clapping together in sheer delight. The robin took one more curious look at Little Jon before flying back out the window The scene that Ellen, Rachel, Maggie, and Jennie had just witnessed in the last few minutes with the robin and Little Jon made them all laugh.

"That was amazing!" Ellen said. "I've never seen such a thing in all my life."

"Did you see the way the robin looked at Little Jon? It was almost as if he knew him," Jennie said excitedly. "But it was a good thing Katy was outside," she added.

Rachel and Maggie agreed. Just picturing the commotion Katy would've caused made them all laugh again. Rachel couldn't wait to write to Jonathan to tell him about this morning's blessing and the sound of their baby's first real laugh. The robin's antics were indeed comical. It was just what they all needed. Rachel didn't feel so groggy anymore either. The fatigue of only moments earlier seemed to lift completely.

The mood around the breakfast table was light and happy. All of them ate heartily, including Little Jon, as he waved his little arms for another bite of applesauce.

Ellen, who was sitting closest to Rachel, chuckled and said, "You know, Jonathan was exactly the same way. He loved his food too. I knew which cry was for when he wanted fed. And that, by the way, was the one I heard most often. It got so I knew which cry meant a diaper change and which cry meant he wanted to be held and rocked." Ellen watched as Rachel held Little Jon gently with a rocking motion. Little Jon loved being rocked so much that one rocking chair was kept at the table so Rachel could eat while rocking him. Ellen's heart ached more than a little when she said, "I must say I miss those days very much."

Rachel was now holding Little Jon over her shoulder after feeding him, patting his back until he burped. Unaware she had stopped rocking, Rachel looked at Ellen. She noticed there were new lines beginning to form around her mother-in-law's eyes and between her brows. Though Ellen rarely voiced her concerns, it was clear by looking at her that she was more worried about her son than she let on. Ellen's lovely, soft hair was mixed in with a little more gray. Rachel not only heard the longing in her voice, but she felt it in her heart as well. Rachel also felt a deep pang of guilt. She'd been so busy herself, she missed Jonathan so much, that it didn't occur to her just how much Ellen missed her son. *It's been more difficult for her than I realized, Lord,* Rachel thought. She made a promise right then and there that Ellen would always be a part of Little Jon's life in every way. Ellen had been so good to Rachel, Maggie, and Jennie. How could she ever repay her? Rachel loved her mother-in-law dearly. "Would you like to hold him while we take care of the dishes?" Rachel asked Ellen.

Ellen smiled at her, knowing that Rachel did indeed understand how she felt and how much she missed her son, Jonathan. She reached out to take Little Jon into her arms. Rachel stood up to help with the dishes. Little Jon was happily gurgling in the arms of his grandma.

Now that Rachel didn't feel so tired, she was looking forward to the day. She and Jennie would spend the day in downtown Altoona, shopping, and perhaps stop at a restaurant to get something to eat. Ellen had insisted that Rachel have some time away from the house after Little Jon was born. She knew only too well that time away was needed when taking care of a little one. Rachel was reluctant at first. She worried about leaving Little Jon.

"Rachel," her mother-in-law said, "you need time for yourself to do something you enjoy. Quit worrying about

Rosemary for Remembrance

Little Jon. He'll be fine. You'll come back refreshed and in much better spirits too."

The first time she left Little Jon to go into town, Rachel almost cried. She felt guilty for leaving him for the afternoon with Ellen. But as she and Jennie, and sometimes Maggie too, went into town to shop or have lunch, Rachel found that her mother-in-law was right. Rachel did come home feeling more calm and relaxed. And Little Jon loved being with his grandmother. This would be her fifth time to go into town with Jennie today. Maggie wouldn't be able to go, as she needed to be at work.

Maggie was working as a domestic for a wealthy older couple in one of the more affluent sections of a nearby town. Mrs. Dofford and her husband were very wealthy but never forgot their roots or their poverty from earlier in their lives. They were kind people who treated all their help with dignity and respect, so unlike what Rachel had to bear with Mrs. Nettle. True to what the Bible taught, they believed that the worker deserved her wages. They seemed to take a shine to Maggie, although things certainly got off to a rocky start. When Maggie wasn't yet hired, she expressed her opinions about women's rights so strongly during her interview that she completely shocked the mister. He sat across from her at his desk, his mouth in a large O and speechless. All he had asked her was what she had planned for her future.

She certainly doesn't seem like the type of young woman who would remain a domestic for the rest of her life, he thought. Her answer to him and her outspokenness took Mr. Dofford by surprise. After the initial shock of hearing her answer, he stood up and walked around his desk toward her.

Maggie's heart filled with dread at the look he gave her after she answered him. *Maybe I shouldn't have been so out-*

spoken, she thought. *I really do need this job.* Maggie was just about to apologize to him when she heard him wheezing. It sounded as if he was choking. He was bent forward, leaning on his cane slightly. Alarmed, Maggie stood up to help. "Oh, Mr. Dofford, I am so sorry…I…I just don't know why I had to say what I did…I…"

He looked at her as he straightened up again. He was laughing! He was laughing so hard he could barely catch his breath. It was Maggie's turn to look shocked as she watched him laugh uncontrollably. When he finally calmed down enough to speak, he took his cane and raised it in the air. Maggie sat back down on the edge of her chair.

"Young woman," he said as he pointed the end of his cane at her, causing Maggie to lean back as he spoke. "Young woman, it is a rare thing for any woman to express how they feel about anything the way you just did."

Maggie was getting ready to apologize again, but he stopped her before she could say a word.

Placing the tip of his cane on the floor, pointing the index finger of his other hand at her, he said, "You are the first woman besides my dear wife to say what she really felt. Don't ever apologize for the truth, Maggie. When you do that, you are apologizing for who God meant for you to be." With that, he turned and walked back around his desk and sat down in his chair, placing the cane beside him with a thump. Mr. Dofford doubted that women would ever be allowed to vote, but he knew one thing; Maggie had spunk.

Maggie wasn't sure what to do next as she sat there. Was she hired, or did he just fire her after considering hiring her? Maggie stood up to leave. She turned to walk out of the room but stopped in her tracks as he spoke.

"When can you start?" Mr. Dofford asked. The memory of her rocky start with the Doffords made her smile. Maggie reached down and lifted Little Jon from Ellen's lap for a hug and kiss, holding him closely. He smelled so sweet and clean. Maggie lightly ran her hand over his little head of fine, dark hair. He'd never lost his hair from birth. She loved her nephew so much that she hated leaving him almost as much as Rachel. But the Doffords would be having a special dinner party that evening, and Maggie was asked to come in to help. Maggie loved working for the Doffords. It was a pleasure to help them on a day she normally didn't go in. Mrs. Dofford had even given some beautiful dresses to Maggie that she could no longer use.

"My figure's not what it used to be, Maggie. Since we are both about the same height, the dresses should fit you very nicely indeed." Maggie didn't know what to say. They were so good to her. Her simple thank you didn't seem to be enough.

Placing Little Jon back onto Ellen's lap, Maggie turned her attention to helping with the cleanup of the dishes before she left. "Well, off I go. I must go in early today. Mr. and Mrs. Dofford are giving a dinner party this evening, and I want to make sure the silverware is polished to perfection and the crystal sparkles like diamonds. The dining room must be perfect for the guests." Maggie smiled as she said this last part, but she was serious about her duties at the Doffords.' "They're wonderful people," Maggie said as she walked across the kitchen to the corner stand and picked up her satchel to go. Maggie moved quickly, like she always did, but she never looked like she was rushing. Maggie moved like an elegant dancer, making her grand entrance and exit off the stage.

They all watched from the kitchen window, amused as Maggie continued her long, steady strides to her automobile, watched as she used the crank, hopped into the Ford, started the engine, and took off with a roar, creating a huge cloud of dust that formed behind her as she disappeared. *Heaven help anyone else on the road today,* Rachel thought with a smile.

Though the automobile was older, it was in very good condition and Maggie's first car. Maggie was very excited to have been taught to drive by Elias. Maggie could be spotted easily in her bright red 1909 Touring Model T. Through the winding roads and mountains of Blue Knob, she would cheerily wave to people with one hand as she passed by, her other hand on the steering wheel as she raced down the road to her destination. Many people held their breath when they saw Maggie behind the wheel. She drove too fast, took the turns on the roads too sharply, and would hit the brakes so hard the automobile actually skidded to a stop. If a person didn't see Maggie, he certainly heard her. Maggie became known as the red baroness across the mountains and surrounding towns. Maggie loved the feeling of freedom the open Model T gave her. And turning the crank to start the engine was fun too. To Maggie, this Model T was also special because the red-colored automobile wasn't made anymore. Not that anything was wrong with black. *It's just…so black,* she thought to herself. She didn't care if the automobile was considered too old either. It was well cared for and performed perfectly. And she rather liked being referred to as the red baroness. Besides, how could anyone possibly consider driving an automobile with the steering wheel on the left side? Unthinkable!

Maggie smiled to herself as she sat behind the wheel. *I can't be late,* she thought. Foot pressed to the gas pedal, she roared off, sending clouds of dust flying behind her.

Inside the house, Ellen, Rachel, and Jennie looked at each other. Shrugging their shoulders, they smiled and continued with their work. After the breakfast cleanup and some of the general housework was done, Rachel and Jennie would drive down the mountain into Altoona and do some shopping. *It would be good to get away for awhile today,* Rachel thought.

Sometimes a moving picture would be showing, and Rachel would treat Jennie and herself to one. Of course, they always stopped for ice cream afterward. Jennie hoped that if they went to a moving picture show today, it would be something light and comical. Her happy nature didn't allow much in the way of sad moving pictures. The last one they saw was about a soulful portrait of one woman's sorrow while her husband was at war. It did nothing but make every woman in the audience leave in tears. Jenny shook her head at the memory. Ice cream never tasted good with tears.

When Rachel and Jennie were ready to leave after hugging Little Jon more than enough times, they stepped out of the house and into the perfect, sunny, warm day. The sky was a beautiful shade of spring blue with only a few white clouds. Both Rachel and Jennie looked up at the sky and then at each other for a moment as they stood outside their home. Today seemed somehow familiar. They couldn't quite put their finger on it. But as the soft mountain breeze lightly caressed their faces, it brought with it the memory of another day much like this one.

"Do you remember her, Rachel?" Jennie asked softly in a hushed tone, almost as if she was afraid that this familiar feeling would disappear, this feeling that she wanted to have for awhile longer. Jennie continued, "I think I remember the day our mother was buried, but I don't remember our mother." This last part was said with much sadness and a sense of confusion.

Rachel looked at her sister with compassion and love. Placing her hand on Jennie's shoulder, Rachel answered her sister. "I remember her, Jennie. I remember her very well." They stood in silence for a few more minutes while Rachel collected her thoughts. "Our mother was buried on a day much like this. She would have loved today so," Rachel stated wistfully. Her eyes misted over at the memory and she turned away from Jennie for a moment to collect herself.

"Tell me, Rachel. Please tell me about our mother. What was she like when you knew her?" Jennie asked.

Rachel turned back around to face her sister. Her question took Rachel by surprise. For Rachel, it had been a long time since she really thought about their mother. An idea came to her. Before they left, Rachel asked Jennie to pick some of her favorite flowers. Rachel smiled when Jennie came back with her collection. They were ready to go. "Come along, Jennie," was all she said as she smiled at her sister.

Their drive took them on a long, winding road that ended at the cemetery where their mother had been buried. The bouquet of violets that Jennie held in her hands on the drive to the cemetery were a beautiful, vibrant, deep blue and purple color. As they stood at their mother's graveside, Rachel spoke. She didn't want to mislead her sister in any way but wanted her to have some sense of rightness in a death that made no sense. Rachel started by talking of what Julianna had liked in life.

"She loved violets, just like you, Jennie. And I believe she even had a cat much like our Katy when she was your age. I understand he was quite the mouse catcher too." Rachel let this sink in before saying anything more. Jennie's face lit up with a smile at the thought that she and her mother each had a cat. Rachel continued. "I've been told that our mother had a wonderful sense of humor and loved to play jokes on her friends and family."

Jennie blurted out quickly, "That's what I like to do too."

Rachel grinned at her little sister and said, "Yes. I know." Rachel decided to tell Jennie everything else she could. "Jennie, our mother loved you, Maggie, and me very much. She became very sick and couldn't tell you how she felt. She became lost in her own little world, but God found her and took her home."

A new look of understanding came into Jennie's eyes as she looked upon her mother's grave. Jennie no longer felt confused or sad. Her mother really did love her, she realized. *And I'm just like her*, Jennie thought, pleased. Jennie felt very happy that their mother was with God. Walking alongside Julianna's graveside, Jennie stopped and knelt to place the bouquet of violets on the headstone.

As Rachel watched, the familiar feeling from years earlier came over her when, on the day Julianna died, she found the strength to say her last words that meant so much to Rachel. To know that her mother loved her had made all the difference in Rachel's life. Rachel's own heart had felt renewed with wonder at this beautiful, amazing gift.

Jennie stood up and brushed herself off. She looked at Rachel and said, "I feel different, Rachel. I don't know what it is, but it feels…right." She then added, "Has that ever happened to you, Rachel?"

Rachel smiled. She reached out and took Jennie's hand, and nodding, she said, "I think I know exactly what you mean." Rachel was so glad they had come to their mother's grave. It had been the right thing to do at the right time.

The somewhat long drive down the mountains of Blue Knob seemed to fly as Rachel drove and Jennie talked. Their lighthearted conversation was filled with laughter and fun. For Jennie, it was as if her earlier life had been completely set free. The connection she felt to her mother after all the years of not feeling anything for her was like nothing she'd ever known. It was one that made her realize that although her mother might have been ill, she did love her daughters. Jennie couldn't wait to see Maggie and tell her what they had done.

Downtown Altoona was bustling with activity by the time Rachel and Jennie arrived. Both sides of the main street were lined with automobiles. Rachel slowly drove around the block and found one of two open spots along Eleventh Avenue and parked. Saturday was always the busiest day for downtown Altoona. But this is what Rachel and Jennie loved. The hustle and bustle was a change from the slower pace of living up the mountains. The streetcars that ran down the center of Eleventh Avenue were crowded with people either getting on or exiting when they stopped. Throngs of couples, families, a few church groups, and businessmen filled the sidewalks as they made their way to wherever they were going. There was an air of optimism that only spring could bring to this day. Spring had a way of giving hope even in this time of war. The ladies proudly displayed their new spring dresses and hats as they walked down the sidewalks. Rachel noticed that some men seemed to prefer the military look even though they weren't serving in the war. Other men still wore bowler hats. It never failed to amaze Rachel just how different Altoona was from their tiny, quiet community of Blue Knob.

Rachel and Jennie got out of their automobile and stood for a moment on the sidewalk while they decided where to start first. In front of them was the movie house, which was currently advertising a moving picture about the war and one woman's heartbreak over the tragic loss of her husband—certainly not something Rachel or Jennie wished to see. Theatergoers, mostly women, were exiting the building, wiping tears from their eyes and runny noses with perfumed handkerchiefs as they walked past Rachel and Jennie. Some of the theater's patrons were still sobbing as they made their way down the street. Rachel and Jennie turned around to continue watching the sad procession of women.

"Let's not go see a moving picture today, Rachel. It's much too beautiful a day to stay inside," Jennie said.

Rachel nodded her head. She completely agreed.

Jennie turned to face Rachel. "So, where do you want to start, Rachel?" she asked.

Rachel looked around her. All of the shops were busy today. There was the large department store down on the corner of Twelfth Street that was one of Rachel's favorites. Inside were several floors that offered a large variety of merchandise. The store was well known for carrying many items that couldn't be found anywhere else in the county. In fact, it was said by many that this store was the largest department store in the state of Pennsylvania. Rachel didn't know if this was true or not, but it certainly seemed like it could be. "Hmm. I think we should start there first," Rachel said as she pointed to the store.

Jennie's eyes lit up. She loved going to the department store. Jennie hoped they would start in the basement first since that was where the candy counter was located. Rachel noticed the look of excitement in her younger sister's eyes. "We'll save the candy counter for last, Jennie," she said as she smiled at her.

Jennie couldn't understand it. *How come Rachel always seems to know what I'm thinking?* she wondered. But she was happy they'd be going to this store first anyway. Rachel was rewarded with a big hug. Jennie practically skipped down the sidewalk with excitement. She loved shopping day, not just for the shopping but for the sights and sounds of so much activity around her. Jennie loved to study the expressions on the faces of people as they passed by her. She loved reading their faces because it showed so much of what they were feeling. Young mothers with little ones in tow always seemed so harried, as if there wasn't enough time to simply enjoy the excitement of being downtown. They usually looked anxious and sometimes even annoyed. Young couples walked arm in arm slowly, as if they had all the time in the world. They looked blissful and didn't seem to notice anyone else.

Rachel and Jennie neared the department store. There were large signs in the store's windows advertising a sale on baby items as well as hats and gloves. They pushed open the large glass door and entered the main floor. Rachel reached into her purse for her list. "I think we should start on the third floor. We're going to need some strong cotton material to make the gardening aprons we'll be selling soon. And I need more material for the dress I'm making for you. And some lace would be nice too."

Jennie followed Rachel to the elevator with excitement. This was her other favorite highlight of shopping days, next to going to the candy store and ice cream parlor. Jennie loved to ride the elevator as it took them up or down to the various levels. Rachel didn't say it, but she rather enjoyed it herself and couldn't help but smile at Jennie's enthusiasm.

Rachel and Jennie spent close to an hour on the third-floor level as Rachel carefully considered the wide variety of materials, the colors, and the cost before making their final purchases. Rachel wanted to make sure her gardening aprons were of good quality that would hold up well. For this, she selected a material of heavy cotton. Rachel also made sure the colors she selected were feminine and appealing. Emerald green, sky blue, a lovely, deep pink, and deep yellow were sure to catch the eye and please any lady who loved to garden. When they were finished with their selections for the aprons, Rachel and Jennie turned their attention to what they would need for Jennie's dress. They selected a lightweight cotton in light green. There was also a lovely pastel yellow that caught their eyes. Rachel always tried to stay within a budget, but the look in Jennie's eyes when she saw the pretty yellow cloth changed her mind.

Her delight as she watched the pastel yellow fabric being measured out for her dress was worth stretching the budget. "I believe you should be the one to carry these," Rachel said with a smile as she handed the wrapped package of material to Jennie for her dresses.

Jennie looked very pleased as she held the package closely. "Oh, thank you, Rachel! I just love the colors." Jennie continued, "I can even give up the candy counter if that would help."

Rachel looked at her sister. Raising her eyebrows, she asked, "Would you really?"

Jennie smiled, "Well,"—she paused—"I'd rather not."

Rachel chuckled at her sister's honesty. "Let's go. We've got a lot to do yet."

From the third-floor department, they took the elevator to the second floor, which carried a delightful variety of hats, scarves, and other accessories. Jennie couldn't resist trying on several of them. Rachel smiled at how her sister looked in each one. They didn't really need anything in this department, but Rachel and Jennie loved to look at the latest designs and fashions.

The first floor offered a large variety of furniture and accessories. Although reasonably priced, it was still somewhat out of the Bailey budget, as she and Jonathan would say. Besides, Rachel wanted to wait until Jonathan came home. This would be something they could do together, along with Little Jon.

Pleased with their purchases, they continued on and took the elevator down to the much-anticipated stop at the candy counter. Both Rachel and Jennie had a sweet tooth. They loved peppermint and chocolate, especially if it was together. The wonderful, sweet aromas reached their noses long before they reached the candy counter. Jennie looked up at Rachel. "You know, Rachel, I could find this place without even opening my eyes." Jennie almost skipped the last few steps to the counter.

Rachel and Jennie looked over all the delicious choices before deciding on which candy to take home. They decided on the peppermint candy sticks and the smaller pieces of chocolate wrapped in foil.

As they exited the candy department with Rachel in the lead, Jennie's hand was already in the bag for the second time. Thinking that Rachel didn't see her, Jennie pulled her hand out of the bag with another foil-wrapped chocolate. "One piece is enough, Jennie," Rachel's voice carried back to her.

Jennie dropped the candy back in the bag immediately. *She didn't even look behind her,* Jennie thought.

Rachel and Jennie strolled out of the department store and stepped back onto the busy sidewalk. They were both quite happy they made the decision to pass on going to see that awful moving picture. Taking in the sights, they continued their stroll down the sidewalk. Rachel and Jennie watched as a brand-new Model T drove past them slowly down Eleventh Avenue. The happy beam of pride on the owner's face was brighter than the shiny exterior of his new automobile, as he found any excuse to honk his horn to draw attention to himself and his brand-new Model T. Rachel and Jennie stopped to watch him and then looked at each other and started to laugh. He certainly seemed to be enjoying the attention he was bringing on himself. "I'm tired from walking so much, Rachel," Jennie said. "Could we please stop for something to eat?" Jennie asked with a very hopeful look in her eyes. She knew where she wanted to go and hoped Rachel did too.

Rachel smiled. She was hungry too. They made their way farther down the sidewalk and around the corner to a little place known for its delicious ice cream treats. They entered just as a table became available for them. Rachel realized she felt a little tired too. After they gratefully sat down at the glass-topped table with yellow and white ice cream parlor chairs, they ordered two banana splits with extra nuts and chocolate syrup. When their order arrived, they both dug right in, not stopping until they had completely finished every bite. Neither Rachel or Jennie ever seemed to have a problem finishing everything on their plates. Their earlier life of hunger had a profound effect on them, and they certainly weren't about to waste two delicious banana splits.

Jennie gave a sigh of contentment as she finished the last bite. Placing her spoon down inside the now-empty dish, she asked, "Can we just sit here for awhile, Rachel? I'm enjoying this so much."

Rachel nodded. She didn't want to leave yet either. She had such a sense of peace and contentment that it was quite easy to be optimistic. Rachel sighed happily. *Soon the war will be over and Jonathan will return home to me and our son.* She smiled as she pictured in her mind how Jonathan's face would look the first time he laid his eyes on his own son. *Maybe,* Rachel thought with a blush rising to her cheeks, *we can give Little Jon a baby brother or sister.*

"What are you thinking about, Rachel?" Jennie asked curiously, noticing Rachel's pink cheeks.

"Just never you mind, Jennie. Some thoughts are meant to be private," Rachel responded.

"Oh," Jennie said. "I was just asking. That's all."

Rachel and Jennie sat for awhile longer, each with her own thoughts. As they looked out the windows of the ice cream parlor, they noticed that the sidewalks weren't quite so busy. Some of the shops were closing as late afternoon approached. They also realized that they were the only ones left in the ice cream parlor. The owner was busy sweeping the floor, casting occasional glances at them. He looked tired. Rachel knew they must get home soon. It would be dark in a couple of hours.

As Rachel and Jennie pushed back their chairs and stood up to leave, Jennie stopped for a moment, her hand resting on the back of her chair. "Rachel," she said softly, "I want you to know that I feel so much better about our mother. I feel like I know her."

Rachel smiled at her little sister and nodded in understanding. If only Jennie knew how much talking about their mother had helped Rachel as well. They pushed their chairs in, scraping the floor slightly and turned to leave. The shop owner gave them a tired, relieved smile and went back to sweeping the floor.

The ride back up the mountain was filled with laughter and fun. *This is the best day of my life,* Jennie thought with happiness. It was the first time that Jennie felt completely free of the past.

Chapter Thirty-seven

As Rachel and Jennie approached their home, they saw Elias and Ellen standing on the front porch, waiting for them. It wasn't unusual for them to be on the porch, but usually they were sitting on the front porch swing. This time, they stood at the edge of the porch, near the steps. But it was the anxious look on their faces that gave them away. Rachel's heart started to pound loudly in her chest. Something was very wrong. Rachel stopped the automobile in front of the house, turned off the engine, and got out. She ran quickly up the porch steps with Jennie fast on her heels. *Little Jon!* Rachel thought as panic gripped her heart.

Jennie's heart filled with fear also but for a different reason. Judging by the painful look in Elias and Ellen's eyes, Jennie could only assume that something had happened to Jonathan. *Oh please, God, don't let Jonathan be dead,* Jennie prayed.

As Rachel ran up the front porch steps to Elias and Ellen, the sadness seemed to overflow from their eyes. Ellen's eyes were red from crying, and she looked as if more tears would overflow any moment. "Oh, Lord, please not Little Jon. He's just a baby. Please…" Rachel did not realize she was talking out loud.

"Rachel! Rachel, Little Jon is fine. He's taking a nap," Ellen said as she stepped toward her daughter-in-law, placing her hand on Rachel's shoulder. Rachel felt her knees going weak with relief. Her baby was all right. But she knew something else was terribly wrong. Elias moved to stand next to his wife. Rachel noticed he didn't seem to know what to do with his hands as they hung by his side. Tears began to fill their eyes as Elias and Ellen tried to find the right words to tell Rachel and Jennie what had happened. Jennie, standing beside Rachel, reached out and held Rachel's hand tightly as she steeled herself for what could only be terrible news.

Rachel could barely get the words out, as if there were no air left to breathe. "Is it…Jonathan?" she asked, her voice barely above a whisper. She looked back and forth between the two of them. "Jonathan?" This time, Rachel's question was tinged with a sense of despair.

Elias shook his head no as a sob escaped his lips. He hung his head for a moment. *Oh, God, this is so terrible.* Tears began to flow from their eyes unchecked.

"Please tell us! If it isn't the baby or Jonathan, what could it be?" Rachel asked again as panic overtook her.

Jennie held her breath. *Oh please, God, no. Not this.* But she already knew what was coming.

Elias regained control of his emotions, knowing he'd have to be the strong one. *Ellen, Rachel, and Jennie need me,* he reminded himself. "Rachel, Jennie," Elias spoke, "there's been an accident. Maggie had an accident. We need to leave for the hospital. We need to go now," he added.

Rachel remembered thinking only that morning that Maggie drove her automobile too fast.

"How bad is it?" Rachel breathed out the words to her father-in-law. Ellen had gone into the house to gather Little Jon and a few belongings they would need for the baby as

Elias shepherded Rachel and Jennie to their automobile. Elias didn't answer her.

No one spoke a word all the way down from Blue Knob to Altoona. Each person seemed to be lost in his or her own thoughts. Rachel held Little Jon close to her heart. He had fussed at first but settled down to sleep.

Each one of them was fervently praying for Maggie's safety, not really knowing what to expect when they arrived at the hospital. But Elias and Ellen were told it was very bad. Dread filled their souls at the thought of what they would see.

How Rachel wished Maggie had never learned to drive. But Maggie, so independent, seemed so capable and determined that Rachel gave in. Maggie insisted she knew what she was doing. Guilt overflowed from her heart and washed over Rachel as she realized that it had been a mistake, a terrible mistake to let Maggie drive. Rachel would have gladly taken Maggie to her job. The weight of guilt threatened to pull Rachel under as they arrived at the hospital and entered the building.

Waiting outside Maggie's hospital room were the Doffords and their gardener, Mr. Smitty. Mrs. Dofford had been crying. Her big, round eyes were red, bloodshot, and swollen. When she saw the Bailey family approaching, it was all she could do to keep from completely breaking down. But she knew she had to be strong for them. The Doffords dearly loved Maggie as their own child.

Smitty stepped forward as they approached, his hat in one hand as he extended the other hand wrapped in gauze bandages to Mr. Bailey. Elias carefully shook Smitty's hand, noticing that he also had bandages on his face and neck. Pulling Elias aside, Smitty explained to him the details of what had happened as the rest of the Baileys waited with the Doffords.

Rosemary for Remembrance

Maggie had been helping Sally, one of the domestics in the kitchen, with the baking in between her own duties of preparing the house for the Doffords' guests. No one knew exactly why it happened, Smitty told Mr. Bailey in a hushed tone, only that Maggie had reached into the oven to pull out some freshly baked loaves of bread. Maggie had done this many times before. But somehow, this time, her apron had caught fire. Maggie panicked and ran outside as her clothes became engulfed in flames. Smitty's eyes were threatening to overflow with tears at the image in his mind. Taking in a deep, ragged breath, he continued. He heard someone screaming. Dropping his shovel, he raced around to the other side of the house. The sight of a young woman in flames—her clothes, her hair, and her body—as she tried desperately to outrun the fire that surrounded her was something out of a nightmare. Smitty ran to her. Tears rolled down his cheeks unchecked. "I knocked her to the ground to roll out the flames," he said.

He didn't remember being burned himself or feeling any pain, knowing only that he must save Maggie. Smitty managed to extinguish the flames. He rolled her over to face him. It was a sight he knew he would never forget.

The servants who had been standing in the doorway as they watched in helpless horror stepped outside cautiously. They sucked in their breath when they saw Maggie. Her hair was gone. In its place were blistering red and white patches of skin. Her face and arms were burned almost beyond recognition. Smoke from the extinguished fire rose up and brought with it the smell of burned flesh. But it was the horrible sound of Maggie's moans that caused them to completely break down. Several of the servants turned and ran back into the house, their hands over their ears. The few who remained

Mary Netreba

outside sobbed with grief at the sight of the once-energetic young woman who had always been so kind to them.

The gardener, Smitty, didn't know whether to feel relieved or not when he heard Maggie's moans. As he looked at what had been her face only moments earlier, now with little skin and no lips, it sent a shiver of horror down his spine. *It would have been better for her to have died,* he thought. Surely this must be the worst sort of agony that Maggie was suffering.

Nothing could have prepared Maggie's family for the tragic news. "The burns are too severe," the doctor said. There was nothing more they could do. Nothing could have prepared any of them for what they would find when they entered Maggie's room. The doctor told them to simply talk to Maggie. "Let her know you're there," he told them.

Mr. and Mrs. Dofford and Smitty stayed outside in the hall and waited. When Elias, Ellen, Rachel, Little Jon, and Jennie quietly entered the room, what they saw of Maggie was almost too much to bear. Ellen threw her hands up over her mouth as she tried to hold in the grief-stricken sobs. Elias pulled her tightly to him, his breath shaking at the horror of what Maggie had suffered. Rachel and Jennie stopped in their tracks. Their sister was beyond recognition. They were all shaken to their souls at the sight of their Maggie.

Maggie's face, head, arms, and hands were covered completely with gauze and bandages. A white hospital blanket was pulled up to her chest over her hospital gown. She lay completely still. But she was aware that someone had come into the room. She heard their soft footsteps as they entered.

Maggie could feel their presence, but she couldn't speak. She tried to open her eyes, but she couldn't do that either. *What happened to me?* she wondered. *Why do I hurt so much?*

She remembered driving to get somewhere, but where? *Why can't I move?*

"Maggie. Maggie, we're all here," a disembodied voice spoke.

Who could that be? Maggie wondered. The voice sounded so far away.

"You had an accident, Maggie." The voice became louder and clearer.

Rachel. It's Rachel talking. Why is Rachel here? she wondered. *And where is here?* Maggie knew she was in a bed, but it didn't seem to be her own bed at home. *An accident? What sort of accident?* Maggie tried to speak and found she couldn't. All that came out was a soft whoosh of air through the gauze bandages.

"It's all right, Maggie," Rachel said reassuringly. "You don't have to talk. We're all here: Mom and Dad Bailey, Jennie and I, and, of course, your favorite and only nephew, Little Jon."

As if on cue, little Jon started making cooing noises in his sleep. Maggie could feel herself wanting to smile but couldn't, so instead, she gave another whooshing sound, hoping that her family would understand.

That's when Maggie knew. She was alive, but something was terribly wrong. Her family took turns talking with her, unable to hold her hands they so desperately wanted to reach out for and almost did out of instinct but then pulled back. Maggie was too badly burned and wouldn't have felt their hands anyway.

But the horrendous pain that had been traveling through her body was suddenly leaving. What Maggie was feeling in its place was the tremendous love of her family around her. She felt deep comfort that they were with her.

Mary Netreba

Maggie sensed another presence, the presence of someone whom she knew was taking away the pain, someone who was there to take her home. The warmth of the welcoming love Maggie felt was full and magnificent, encompassing her entire being. She had felt this love in her soul many times in her life, but not like this. In her life, always when she felt this love, it was almost a hint of a promise to come. And here it was. The full, magnificent, pure love was letting Maggie know that she was going home. Her heart grieved for the ones she would leave behind. She loved them so much.

"Come," the voice of pure love said. "It's time, Maggie."

The last whoosh of air that Maggie breathed out carried with it the soft, almost-indistinguishable sound of, "I love you."

With her last breath, they all knew without speaking a word that their precious Maggie had left them. They felt her life leave the badly burned shell that was once her body as it slipped away to her beautiful, final home where there was no longer any pain. In that brief moment of stunned silence, that moment just before the acceptance of Maggie's passing, it was as if everyone in Maggie's room held their breath as one. They could see Maggie's physical body, but the entire beautiful person she'd been was gone.

Rachel completely broke down. As tears ran down her own cheeks, Ellen gently took Little Jon from her arms as he fussed.

All the years of protecting her and it's come to this? Rachel asked herself. *Why?*

Jennie threw her arms around Rachel. Holding onto each other tightly, they sobbed in unimaginable grief and anguish. Elias couldn't stop the hot tears from flowing down his cheeks as he wrapped his arms around his wife and grandson. Each of them knew that Maggie was home with her Lord, and for this, they were very thankful. Maggie had been in so much pain. She would have had no real life in her body that had been so completely consumed by the fire. But the devastating pain of losing their Maggie was profound. Their Maggie was gone.

Chapter Thirty-eight

Unlike their mother's funeral, where the day had been bright with sunshine, blue skies with fluffy clouds, and warm balmy weather, the morning of Maggie's funeral dawned bleak, misty, and gray—a perfect day for walking, Maggie would have said.

There was a cool chill to the air as the funeral-goers held their wraps around them tightly. So many people whose lives had been touched by Maggie came to her funeral to pay their final respects, each with their own thoughts of how she had helped them throughout the years.

Maggie would have so loved this kind of day, Rachel thought. *She said it always brought out the best in her.*

There was nothing Maggie loved more than walking on a day like this. Maggie had said more than once that she loved the feel of the cool mist on her face. She loved the way the wind would brighten her cheeks in the chill. Rachel remembered how Maggie always seemed to have an extra bounce in her step when she returned home after one of her walks. In her mind's eye, Rachel could see Maggie happily walking through the back entrance of their home, calling out a cheery, "Hello. I'm back," as she stood soaking wet, her clothes drenched from the rain. Rachel tried desperately to hold onto that precious vision. The sight of the closed coffin in front of her was almost too much to bear.

Maggie would have been pleased to see so many people at her funeral. They had come from miles around to say their goodbyes. Everyone who had known Maggie shared fond memories of her and had a story to tell, usually something funny, as Maggie had been very good at making people laugh. Others would say that Maggie had been the one to encourage them and sometimes be a shoulder for them to cry on. But what always stood out the most to those who knew Maggie were her kindness, her spirit, and her endless optimism. There would never be another Maggie Walters. There would indeed never be another red baroness.

Rachel held Little Jon in her arms as she, Jennie, Elias, and Ellen stayed at the graveside long after everyone else had left. No one said anything but watched as Jennie walked between the two graves. Bending down to her knees, she placed one fresh bouquet of violets on her mother's grave. Standing, Jennie brushed the fresh earth from her knees and placed the other bouquet on Maggie's coffin then turned and walked back to her family. Looking up at her sister, Jennie said, "The next time I visit, I'll bring roses."

The house felt empty and quiet when the Bailey family returned home from Maggie's funeral. Katy, having sensed something wasn't right, had been hiding under Maggie's bed since she died. She refused to come out. Rachel and Jennie brought her food and water, which she apparently ate and drank while they were asleep. They also left the kitchen window open in case she wanted to go outside. But by morning, she would already be under Maggie's bed again, scooted back in the corner so no one could reach in and pull her out.

Ellen and Elias stayed at Rachel's for a short while but left soon after. They both knew that Rachel and Jennie needed to grieve the loss of Maggie in their own way, as did they. Maggie's death had left a huge hole in their hearts. No longer would they hear the sound of her laughter as she shared something inspirational or funny that she had seen or heard. No longer would they hear the sound of her sweet voice, always off key, as she sang while busily helping with the housework. There would be no more soft, sweet hum of a lullaby as she rocked Little Jon to sleep.

Rachel and Jennie were both reminded of the day Jonathan had left. Their home had that same empty feeling again, only this time it was permanent. Maggie wasn't coming home anymore. *Maggie went home, and we'll see her someday.* This thought filled them with much-needed hope.

Rachel took Little Jon upstairs for his nap as Jennie prepared their afternoon tea. They would still hold to the tradition of afternoon tea. Maggie would have wanted them to keep it that way. Jennie, deep within her own thoughts, realized only after Rachel came back down the stairs and into the kitchen that she had set a place for Maggie simply out of habit. Rachel was walking back into the kitchen and stopped in her tracks. The pain of the loss of Maggie threatened to overtake her again. Jennie, seeing the look on her sister's face, quickly started to remove the place setting for Maggie.

"Oh, Rachel, I'm so sorry. I don't know what I was thinking." Jennie's voice rose to a panic. "It was just such a habit… I…" Jennie placed the cup and saucer back onto the table with shaking hands and dropped heavily into Maggie's chair as tears poured from her eyes and spilled onto her cheeks. Jennie was overwhelmed with grief as she looked at Rachel. "I miss her. Oh, God, I miss her so, so much…" Jennie couldn't stop the deep sobs that escaped her lips.

Rachel walked over to Jennie, tears filling her own eyes as she sat down beside her sister, holding her hand in reassurance. But inside Rachel's heart, she questioned God. *Why, Lord, does life have to be so painful? Why did you take Maggie home? Why did she have to suffer the way she did?*

Rachel had tried so hard to protect her sisters, and God took Maggie anyway. It made no sense. Rachel tried to stop the questions that raced through her mind. She knew God had his reasons and felt ashamed to have doubted him.

Rachel sighed deeply. "Jennie, I miss her too. I think we'll always miss Maggie." Her last few words were choked out as she also broke down in sobs of too-fresh grief.

The sisters held onto each other for a long time as they sobbed their hearts out. Somewhere in the midst of their tears, they also realized that they still had each other. For this, they were very thankful. And Rachel realized something else. This was the first time she understood that no matter how painful, grief was also a gift.

Chapter Thirty-nine

It had been not quite three months since their precious Maggie had passed away. Her memory stayed with Rachel and Jennie every single moment. Maggie could be felt and seen all around them: in a rainy day, in her beloved roses that bloomed so profusely as they scented the summer air with their sweet fragrance. Rachel, Jennie, Ellen, and even Elias had more than one good cry as they stood before the beautiful arbor covered with pink climbing roses. They would share their favorite memory of their beloved Maggie. Sometimes, Rachel and Jennie would even feel Maggie's presence as they took their afternoon tea. The automobile she had loved to drive so much sat in its usual place. It had been returned to them one week after the funeral. Mr. Dofford had driven it back and delivered it personally to Rachel and Jennie. As his wife sat in their automobile to take him back home that day, Mr. Dofford took a moment to talk to Rachel and Jennie about how alike Maggie and his wife were.

"Your sister Maggie,"—he paused before he went on—"she had spunk and determination. Maggie wasn't afraid to speak her mind."

Eventually, Katy decided as well that it was time to come out from underneath Maggie's bed. Jennie woke up one morning to find Katy nuzzled beside her, her head pressed close to her heart while one of her white-tipped paws softly held onto her hand.

While they went about their normal daily routines of life—Jennie with her schooling, Rachel with housework and motherhood, and the Baileys with their farming—it was all done with the knowledge that something was missing. A huge hole had been left in their hearts that seemed impossible to fill. Maggie had truly been one of a kind. Each member of the family missed her deeply in his or her own way. *Will there ever come a day when we'll think of Maggie and not hurt so much?* Even the harsh Mrs. Nettle had shown up for the funeral. It was the first time any of the folks in Blue Knob witnessed Mrs. Nettle showing sympathy. She hadn't really cared for Rachel's family, but the manner in which Maggie died left many people stunned, including Mrs. Nettle.

"How awful for one so young to die in such a tragic way," she said one day to Cook soon after the funeral. Cook had actually dropped the cake pan full of vanilla-flavored batter onto the floor, some of it spattering onto Mrs. Nettle's shoes and the hem of her dress. Cook was shocked to hear such a statement out of Mrs. Nettle's lips.

Well, I'll be darned, Cook thought. *The mean Mrs. Nettle might just have herself a kind heart after all.* Cook bent down to start cleaning up the mess.

"You stupid servant! You splashed that batter onto my shoes!"

Hmph! Cook thought. *If Mrs. Nettle had a heart, it musta just ran off somewhere.*

Mary Netreba

The one thing that did keep the Baileys going was the preparation of Rachel's herb garden—only this year, Maggie would be missing. When the Bailey family opened the business for the season, many customers were surprised and delighted with the new name on the sign: "Rachel's Herbs and Maggie's Rose Bouquets." It was a beautiful tribute and only right that Maggie's name was included on the sign. News had traveled for miles around after Maggie's death. Many of the same customers were also at her funeral. The wives especially wouldn't forget Maggie, who created the most beautiful bouquets for them. Jennie, as it turned out, became quite adept at not only acting as cashier but also in helping to arrange the lovely rose bouquets along with Ellen. The gardening aprons that Rachel had designed and made sold so quickly that Rachel and Jennie had to make several trips back to the department store in Altoona for more material.

All the busyness and hard work was just what the Bailey family needed. It helped ease the pain of their loss. Deep grief slowly but surely lessened a little bit with each passing day.

Rachel hadn't slept well the night before. She hadn't really slept well since Maggie's death. And the stifling heat of what was turning out to be a hot, humid summer, even in the mountains of Blue Knob, showed no signs of letting up this Fourth of July. Farmers especially were becoming concerned about the lack of rain. If it continued, they could lose much of what they had worked for.

Little Jon was cranky and uncomfortable and made sure his displeasure was known to all those around him. Rachel tried to keep him in his diapers only and would fan him as much as she could. He developed a diaper rash, which only added to his discomfort. Everyone in the Bailey family was starting to feel the frustration. Between lack of sleep caused by the heat and humidity, which also sapped a person's strength in no time, and grief over Maggie, it was making for some very short tempers. Rachel was trying to keep tears of frustration at bay as she tended to Little Jon, who was sitting in his highchair, whining from the discomfort of the heat and his diaper rash. He wouldn't take his food but kept spitting it out as he cried in frustration, his little arms thrashing on the table.

Little Jon was such a good baby most of the time. Rachel fanned him some more and was rewarded with a big, toothless smile. Rachel smiled back. She picked him up from his highchair and held him. The love she felt for her baby always made her feel as if her heart would burst. She had never known a love like this. She never knew it was possible. Little Jon looked so much like his daddy that Rachel's heart ached. At almost seven months old, he was already sitting up on his own. Soon, Little Jon would be crawling everywhere around the house and Rachel's life would be even more hectic. Rachel missed Jonathan deeply and longed for him to come home to be with them. His last letter, as usual, was in Rachel's apron pocket. She reached her hand into her pocket and pulled out the letter. Unfolding it, she quietly reread his words that meant so much to her.

Jennie padded into the kitchen quietly, pulled out a chair, and sat down at the table while Rachel read her letter.

> My darling Rachel, how sorry I am that our sweet Maggie has left us for her heavenly home. I wish I could have been there to say goodbye before the angels came and took her away.

Do you remember the day I left to go off to war? Do you remember Maggie's words at the train station? She told me that all of you would be waiting for me when I come home, not *if*. This inspired not only me but many other families who were there that day as they watched their sons or husbands go off to war.

I picture Maggie, whole and perfect, her face aglow with the joy that someday she will see us again and welcome us home to our heavenly kingdom. Perhaps God wanted Maggie there first to help prepare for our arrival. She was always such an organized planner that I don't doubt it.

We will see Maggie again, although her loss on this earth is very painful. But this is in itself also temporary and will be forgotten on the day we see her. Maggie's love will always be with us, my darling.

Jonathan ended his letter with many *I love you*s to Rachel, Little Jon, and Jennie and his parents.

When Rachel finished, she folded the letter again and slid it back into her apron pocket. Just reading Jonathan's letter made Rachel felt a little better. She looked across the table at her sister. *She didn't look as if she slept too well either*, Rachel observed. Jennie, usually so talkative, had spoken very little since the day of Maggie's funeral. But the pain in her eyes gave away everything she was feeling. Katy was meowing from outside, wanting to be let in.

"I'll get her," Rachel said, still holding Little Jon as she got up and walked over to the door, opening it a crack to let her in. Katy made a beeline for Jennie and jumped up on the chair next to hers, which had been Maggie's, and curled up. Jennie reached over and petted her head. She was rewarded with loud, satisfied purrs as she gently went to sleep. Rachel's heart went out to Jennie. She looked so lost. It seemed that the only time she came to life at all was when Katy was around.

Rachel walked back to the kitchen table and sat down again, bouncing Little Jon on her knees. "Jennie, today is July Fourth, Independence Day. I have an idea. Since the herb garden is closed today, why don't we make a day of it? We could go to the amusement park and perhaps have a picnic. There are plenty of picnic tables with lots of trees for shade too. Maybe we can even dip our toes in the lake. It would be better than simply staying here in this stifling heat." Rachel watched Jennie carefully as she spoke. She was hoping Jennie would come around. She waited. Nothing.

Jennie sat still and stared off into space. She didn't want to do anything. She didn't want to have fun. It seemed so wrong to her to have fun without Maggie. Rachel wasn't about to stop. Somehow, she had to get through to her youngest sister.

"Jennie, there's supposed to be an Independence Day celebration later with fireworks and everything. Why don't we go? In fact, let's ask Mom and Dad Bailey to join us. What do you think?" Rachel waited for Jennie's answer.

Jennie reconsidered Rachel's suggestion. She remembered last year how all of them, including Maggie, had gone to the park. They had a wonderful time. Jennie missed Maggie so much, but she knew that Maggie wouldn't have been happy to see either Jennie or Rachel moping around like this.

Jennie gave Rachel the first real smile she had for a long time. "It sounds like a wonderful idea, Rachel. I'll help you pack food for the picnic and also some of Little Jon's things." Jennie hesitated for a moment, unsure of how to say what she wanted to say next. She didn't want to ruin Rachel's offer by saying something sad. "Rachel," Jennie asked carefully, "could we stop by Maggie and Mother's graves today before we go to the park? It would be nice to visit their graves and leave some flowers. Would that be all right with you?"

Rachel's heart melted with compassion for her little sister. She understood how Jennie felt. It was the right thing to do. Nodding in agreement, Rachel said, "Let's go pick some flowers."

It was late morning by the time the Bailey clan was ready to go and on their way. The fragrance of roses filled the automobile with their wonderful scent as they drove to the cemetery first. Maggie had so loved her roses. The memory of her, her arms full of freshly cut roses as she entered the house, with a big smile on her face as she arranged the roses in vases so that all could enjoy them would be with them forever. Maggie had blessed them with much beauty in her short life.

Rachel and Jennie had chosen a large variety of Maggie's roses in soft pink hues, bright cheerful yellows, deep vivid reds, and pure, elegant whites. They also picked long, fresh stems of lavender, lemon verbena, and catnip to complete the two bouquets they arranged and tied together with pink satin ribbons. The drive to the cemetery was somber and hushed. Even Little Jon didn't make a sound, as if he too somehow sensed the need for quiet in this place of solitude. This would be their first visit to Maggie's and Julianna's gravesides since Maggie's death. Up until this point, no one could bear to go, their hearts broken with grief too fresh and deep. It was painful to accept the loss, even more painful for how the loss actually happened.

The tears that were shed this time for Maggie as they stood at her grave were a combination of grief and acceptance. Their Maggie was home in heaven, as was Julianna. With this acceptance came the beginning of the healing they all so desperately needed. Once again, Jennie walked between the two graves. Bending down to her knees, she placed the first bouquet on Julianna's grave and then turned and placed the second bouquet on Maggie's grave. She then stood up, brushed off her knees, and joined her family.

They all remained quiet as they walked back to their automobile, got in, and drove away.

Little Jon was the first to break the silence. They were halfway down the mountains to their next destination when he let out a giggle. Rachel could feel the chuckle from his chubby little body as she held him close to her.

Jennie was sitting beside Rachel. "I'm gonna tickle you," she said as she made her fingers look like a spider crawling toward him. Little Jon's eyes grew wide with surprise as he clapped his hands together and squirmed with delight, giggling this time as Jennie tickled the bottoms of his feet. The sound of the baby's laughter did much to lighten their moods. They found themselves laughing together again.

Jennie felt peace, the same kind of peace she felt the day she and Rachel visited their mother's grave. A brief moment of sadness washed over her. *That day was also the day Maggie died, or rather,* she corrected herself, *Maggie went home to heaven.* Jennie felt peace when she thought of it this way. She could smile at the memory of her beloved sister.

Jennie, still smiling, started to sing loud and slightly off key. " K—K—Katie, beautiful Katie, you're the only g—girl that I adore, when the moon shines over the cowshed. I'll be waiting at the kitchen door..."

This was all the invitation the rest of the family needed as Elias and Ellen, sitting in front, and Rachel in the backseat with Little Jon joined in, "Jimmy was a soldier brave and bold. Katie was a maid with hair of gold…" The interior was filled with the sounds of laughter at the silly, stammering song. Rachel clapped little Jon's hands in time with the tune, and he grinned from ear to ear. The song over, they burst out in laughter again.

"Let's sing another one," Ellen suggested.

"Okay. You pick this time," Jennie answered.

Mom Bailey smiled and looked over at her husband. She started to sing. "Oh how I hate to get up in the morning…"

Elias Bailey glanced over at his wife and smiled. It was wonderful to see his wife happy again. Rachel and Jennie burst out laughing with delight and eagerly joined in. They each took turns choosing a song they wanted to sing and continued singing the most recent popular songs the rest of the way down the mountain. By the time they pulled into the park, their sides ached with laughter. It had been so long since they had laughed together like this.

Rachel sat on the front porch swing, moving back and forth gently as the feeling of contentment stayed with her. It was after midnight, and everyone else was asleep, including Katy. Rachel was wide awake. The night air was cool with a light wind blowing across the mountains. Rachel felt the need to have some time alone. As she thought about their day at the park, it seemed as if it was almost a miracle to her how the Fourth of July started so badly and ended so well. They had stayed until after dark at the amusement park to wait for the firework display to start. Beautiful colors exploded into the night sky as gasps of surprise and delight echoed through the large crowd. Even Little Jon was amazed. The most spectacular display of fireworks always occurred toward the end of the evening's events. The firecrackers exploded high in the clear night sky with glorious colors of red, white, and blue. A large military band played many patriotic songs, but it was the last song, however, that brought tears to the eyes of not only the Baileys but many others in the crowd as they joined in patriotic chorus with the band to sing "Grand Old Flag." The crowd seemed to come together as one.

Rachel sighed. Maggie would have been so proud of her family, to see them move on like this. "Nothing worse than a sour face," she would sometimes say. That was Maggie, though. She was the one who would always see the upside of even the saddest events. "Look for the blessing," she used to say. Rachel did this. The grief of their loss, though painful, was a blessing. The healing of a broken heart was a blessing too. It was a blessing to have a family that loved you. It was a blessing to share a wonderful day with your family and most certainly a blessing to have known Maggie.

With her heart full of hope, Rachel stopped swinging, stood up and headed back into the house. Feeling more optimistic than she had in a long time, her expectations that the war would end soon didn't seem unreasonable to her at all. Anything was possible.

Still feeling wide awake, Rachel decided to write Jonathan a long letter. She would share with him the miracle his family shared today. Rachel smiled at the thought. How encouraged he'd be to know his family, minus Maggie, would be waiting for him when he came home.

Rachel went up the stairs to her and Jonathan's room. She walked across the room, sat down at her desk, opened the top drawer, and pulled out several empty pages of paper. She picked up her pen and, with no hesitation, started to write.

Chapter Forty

October 1918

The seasons progressed, and the hot, muggy days of summer gave way to the fresh, clean, crisp smell of autumn in the air. Next to spring, autumn was Rachel's other favorite season. Many of the herbs that were being harvested for the family's personal use were being done with the help of Ellen, Jennie, and even Elias, although he tried to act somewhat grudgingly at being asked to handle the lavender. The truth was Elias was secretly enjoying his new duty as he took the time to carefully cut back the herbs the way he'd been shown. His wife, Rachel, and Jennie had caught him more than once pressing his nose into an armful of lavender, but they went on as if they didn't notice a thing, trying very hard to keep from laughing. Little Jon sat quietly on his blanket, watching the grown-ups, along with Katy, who was sitting on her haunches, overseeing the harvest of what she considered to be her catnip. It had been a wonderful afternoon, as they took the last of the harvested herbs into the house. Katy as usual rode in the basket of catnip Jennie carried. Little Jon rested on Rachel's hip as she carried a basket of harvested herbs with her other hand.

After working from morning through late afternoon, the herbs were neatly hung to dry. The aroma of the many herbs filled the home with wonderful scents as the family sat down to a dinner of eggs, bacon, homemade bread, and jam. They were exhausted but pleased with what they had accomplished. Elias left first since he still had chores in the barn, and Ellen left soon after she had washed the dishes.

Rachel breathed deeply of the herbs again. The peppermint always reminded her of Christmas and being with her family. Her heart felt the familiar twist of pain in the realization once again that Maggie was gone. This Christmas would be minus Maggie and possibly Jonathan if he didn't come home after the war.

Jennie finished drying the last of the dishes and placed them in the cupboard. "Rachel," Jennie asked, "do you think that Jonathan will be home for Christmas?"

"I hope so, Jennie," Rachel said as she put Little Jon down on the blanket she had placed on the floor. Her arms ached from holding him so long. He was growing so fast. Little Jon was on all fours as he crawled rapidly from the kitchen with a big, wide smile and quickly made his way down the hall. Rachel and Jennie looked at each other and laughed. They knew Little Jon was headed to the parlor again.

Rachel couldn't wait for little Jon to start walking. He was already standing and almost ready to take his first steps. *Perhaps,* Rachel thought to herself, *I'll be able to take small walks with Little Jon in the woods.* She could show him the different woodland flowers. Just then, a picture came to her mind of her and Jonathan walking with Little Jon through the woods together, each holding his hand on either side. *Yes,* she thought. *Perhaps by spring Jonathan will be home.*

But Rachel was starting to feel anxious. She could feel it in her bones that something wasn't quite right. Although they all had a good day with the herb harvest, Rachel caught the look of worry in both Ellen and Elias's eyes. Oh, they tried to hide it, not wanting to concern Rachel and Jennie, but they were worried too. Jonathan had always been prompt in answering his letters to both Rachel and his parents. Their last letters had still to be answered.

A loud, sudden cry from the parlor interrupted Rachel's thoughts. Little Jon must have taken a tumble again. Rachel and Jennie quickly made their way down the hall.

Chapter Forty-one

Late October 1918

Ellen's nature was usually one of peace and optimism. She was, as her husband referred to her, a true Proverbs thirty-one wife. Her heart had known the peace of prayer many times throughout her life and through the most difficult of times. Ellen knew her God and held onto her strong belief that he was always in control. But at that moment, the unrest in her heart and soul filled her with an anxiousness she'd never known before. It robbed her of sleep. It robbed her of peace. Quietly she slid out from under the covers, careful not to wake Elias as she got out of bed.

Ellen got down on bended knees by her bedside and lowered her head as she folded her hands in prayer. The feeling of desperation in her heart was evident in her prayers as sleep continued to elude her. It wasn't quite four o'clock in the morning, but Ellen knew that once again, she would face another day without sleeping the night before.

She was aware of the sound of her husband softly snoring. Elias was able to sleep through just about anything. Ellen loved her husband so much it didn't seem possible to her that her love could grow any deeper and stronger. But it did every day. In all the years they were married, Elias never spoke harshly to her. He never used unkind, careless words. Elias was always thoughtful and caring. He kept his Bible on the stand next to his side of the bed. Each morning when he awoke and after he kissed his wife, he would read the pages from Scripture before he even got out of bed. Every night before going to sleep, he did the same thing. More than once, Elias stated that Jesus was never harsh when it came to women, never. *How fortunate and blessed I am,* Ellen thought to herself, *to have been given such a wonderful, God-fearing man who lives out his faith every single day of our marriage. And we've been blessed with our son, Jonathan.*

The feeling of sadness came over her as her thoughts turned to Rachel's mother and how each of their lives had turned out so differently.

Jack had successfully destroyed everything that had once been Julianna, including her friendships. And yet God found a way to redeem the situation through Jonathan and Rachel's marriage and the birth of their son. Ellen's thoughts returned to the present. *Yes,* she reminded herself, *God does redeem, and he'll redeem this situation too.*

Elias and Ellen hadn't received a letter from their son, Jonathan, for much too long. Each day, when the postman arrived, Ellen's heart pounded with dread and fear that Jonathan may have died in battle. Ellen couldn't help herself. Each morning that she awoke, she wondered if this would be the day they would learn that their precious Jonathan was killed in action. They were deeply worried for him. They were also concerned for Rachel, Little Jon, and Jennie.

The grandfather clock in the downstairs hall chimed, reminding Ellen of all the times she nursed Jonathan in the middle of the night. The soothing sounds of the clock brought some of the same comfort to her.

Where is our son? she wondered. *If only we knew. What if Jonathan is hurt or worse? Has he become a prisoner of war? Is that why he hasn't written back to us?* Ellen knew these thoughts weren't what she should be thinking, but she felt so overwhelmed. Ellen took a deep breath to calm her nerves.

So many men had lost their lives in this horrendous war, leaving behind the people who loved them. Perhaps it was a combination of Maggie's untimely death, too many nights of disturbing bad dreams, and the worry for Rachel, Jennie, and Little Jon. Ellen's brows knit together. Rachel was losing weight from her already-small frame. She tried to put up a good front for the Baileys, but Ellen saw through her forced cheerfulness. *Dear Lord, what has happened to our precious son?*

The tears that Ellen had held in check for so long were too close to the surface to hold back. Her face in her hands, a sob escaped Ellen's lips. The sound awoke her husband. Elias said not a word as he pushed the covers back, got out of bed, and walked around to her side and got down on his knees. He looked into her eyes for a moment, reached for her hand, and then bowed his head in silent prayer. Ellen felt his comfort. Bowing her head once again, she thanked God for the blessing of her kind, gentle, understanding husband. Whatever circumstances they had to face, they would face them together.

Chapter Forty-two

Rachel awoke while it was still dark. She lay still for a few moments as she gathered her thoughts together. Nothing made sense. Wearily she sat up in bed, pushing back the quilts, and got up, hardly noticing the early morning chill. Exhausted, she reached out for the bedpost to steady her before she sat down on the edge of the bed. She looked down and realized she was still holding one of Jonathan's shirts in her other hand from the night before. It still held the smell of Jonathan and she clung to it. Sleeping with it always helped her feel closer to him somehow. But the reality that she woke up with every day broke the spell. Rachel hung her head low in grief as she fought back the tears that threatened to spill over. The aching pain in her heart went so deep that she was afraid she would lose herself forever if she let it out. Her shoulders hunched forward in defeat. How would she get through another day?

The love of her life was gone. In an instant, Rachel's life was changed. The telegram said so. Rachel turned her head to see the telegram on the nightstand. This small piece of paper carried the weight of her whole future. Rachel squeezed her eyes shut, denying the words she'd read. She didn't have to read it again. The words were burned into her soul forever.

The telegram with its somewhat scribbled message was legible enough, and her stomach churned once again with dread at the words, "J. Bailey...killed in action...we regret to inform you...stop."

Just like that, all the years of Jonathan's life had come down to two short sentences. With her hands still clutching Jonathan's shirt, she covered her face with it, her eyes closed against the painful onslaught of bitter reality that hit her daily with such cruel force. Rachel just couldn't understand how this could have happened.

Rachel found herself once again trying to reason with God. She found herself doing this more and more. *Lord, Jonathan had almost made it to the end of the war. If only you kept him alive those last few weeks before he was to be sent home to us. He was so close, Lord, to coming home to me, Little Jon, and the rest of his family.*

Rachel had questioned God many times since the telegram arrived with those few words that changed her life forever. *Why, Lord? Why?* she asked over and over again. *Lord, Jonathan was a good man, a good son, a good husband, and he would've been a good father too. I don't understand, Lord. Why couldn't you have let him live?* Rachel knew her thoughts were wrong, but they flooded her entire being almost every waking moment.

Jonathan had been there for Rachel through so many of the tragedies in her own life. From the moment he'd found her and rescued her from the blizzard, Jonathan was her constant companion. It was as if he'd always been there. The one person who'd been there to share so many heartaches was the most devastating heartache Rachel had ever known. How could she hold out her arms to the emptiness she had when the one person she had clung to gone? How could she go on? Each morning she awoke and she did go on, thankful that another day had passed. Perhaps when she had enough yesterdays behind her she wouldn't cry for Jonathan so much anymore.

Rachel's still-fresh grief would waver from questioning God to becoming determined and stubborn that she would see this through. Sitting up taller and setting Jonathan's shirt aside, Rachel placed her hands firmly on her lap. "Stop your crying," she said to herself. "You have Jonathan's son. You do have someone to hold onto." Rachel could feel the shift in her feelings. How grateful she was to know that part of Jonathan was still with her. She saw Jonathan in their precious son more every day. The tremendous sadness from her loss would be in her heart for a long time. But then again, so were the reminders of how blessed she was to have had the time God gave her with Jonathan. Rachel was reminded that Elias and Ellen had suffered the loss of their son, their only child. She was not alone in her heartbreak and pain. *There were many families who'd also lost their loved ones. I still have much to be thankful for.*

Rachel bowed her head and silently sent a prayer of gratitude to God for the wonderful life she'd been given with Jonathan. *And thank you, Lord, for the love you put in Jonathan's heart for me, for the blessing of having a part of him still with me. Thank you for your unending mercy and in keeping Jonathan in your care until we can all be with you one day. Amen.*

Just as with the heartache of losing Maggie, Rachel knew that this heartache was also in God's hands. She stood up and went about preparing herself for the day. After dressing and pinning her hair up in a soft, simple bun the way Jonathan liked it, Rachel walked over to the nightstand before leaving the room. Picking up the telegram, she placed it in her skirt pocket as she did every morning since it arrived. *I'll hold onto it for a little while longer,* she thought to herself.

Rachel decided she'd bake bread this morning. Jonathan had so loved her freshly baked bread hot from the oven. A small smile came to her face at the memory as she softly opened the bedroom door to see Katy waiting for her in the hallway. She stepped out, closing the door behind her, and padded down the hallway and stairs quietly so she didn't to wake up Jennie or Little Jon. Katy padded down the stairs ahead of Rachel.

Chapter Forty-three

There were no banners or welcome home signs to greet Jonathan as he stepped down from the train. He had been the last passenger. As he stood for a moment on the platform, he looked around him. The train gave a long, lonesome whistle before departing again. Jonathan watched as the train pulled away, watched as it disappeared from sight. Alone, Jonathan turned around. Through tired, bleary eyes, he saw that the wooden building that served as the train depot was dark and empty. Why was there no one to greet him? Loneliness enveloped him in the quiet of the cold night.

Jonathan couldn't understand why Rachel or his parents weren't there to greet him. The journey home had been long and arduous, especially since he was still in such a weakened state from the illness that almost took his life. But his will to get better and be able to come home to his family was what drove him on. His love for Rachel, his son, and his family had kept him going in the darkest moments of those dreadful days.

Jonathan began to wonder if this was another one of his dreams. In his illness, his dreams seemed so real that when he actually awoke he couldn't tell the difference at first. He closed his eyes. Taking a deep breath, he inhaled and exhaled slowly. His first thought was how the cold night air smelled: pure, clean, and crisp. *This couldn't possibly be a dream, could it?* Jonathan opened his eyes and looked up at the full, bright moon and the many twinkling stars in the sky. It certainly felt real enough. *If this is a dream,* he reasoned, *well then, I'm going to savor every moment of it.* The journey home had been a long one, and he wasn't about to stop. It would be dawn by the time he reached his destination. Pulling his worn, military-issue coat around him for warmth, he set off on the final stage of his journey. He could see his breath as he exhaled with each determined step, one tired foot in front of the other. He stopped for a moment to get his bearings. *How far away is the road?* Although things around him looked familiar, it still felt strange, and Jonathan couldn't quite remember where the road was that would take him home. But the full moon would help him see where he was going. *Home,* Jonathan thought. *I'm going home.*

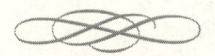

Rachel kneaded the bread dough one more time before shaping it into loaves. As she gently placed the loaves into the bread pans, her brows knit together in concentration. *It's odd,* she thought to herself, *how something so seemingly insignificant like working one's hands through bread dough can bring about a sense of calm and quietness.* Rachel was also becoming aware of the many things she'd taken for granted that were true blessings to help her through her grief.

Jonathan's parents kept close watch on Rachel, Jennie, and Little Jon. They were always nearby to help in any way they could. Many of the customers who visited Rachel's Herb Garden sent cards and notes of sympathy and support. Rachel went through the list in her head. *No,* she realized. *I'm not alone in my grief.*

Rachel placed a large, soft cloth over the loaves of bread until they rose and were ready to go into the oven. Rachel decided that while the dough was rising, she'd work on the pantry. She turned away and started to head toward the pantry and stopped. Dawn streaked across the early morning sky as she looked out the kitchen window. Rachel sighed. A new day had begun. The sudden feeling of loss overwhelmed her again as she quickly made her way to the door instead. Opening it, she stepped out, forgetting to close it behind her. Rachel squeezed her eyes shut and breathed deeply in and out several times to calm herself. These feelings of near-panic still came to Rachel with no warning but thankfully not as frequent. Relieved that the feeling had passed, Rachel opened her eyes again. She let out a shaky breath and watched it crystallize in the early morning cold.

From where she stood, she could see the fields where Jonathan and his father would've been working in the spring, summer, and autumn. Sometimes Jonathan would see her standing at the kitchen door, watching them. Jonathan always took off his hat and waved it to let her know he'd seen her. Sometimes he'd stop what he was doing and walk across the field to their home simply to give her a kiss and hold her closely for a moment before going back to his work. Rachel smiled at the memory. She could still feel the warmth of his body close to her as he held her and smell the scent of masculine sweat from his work in the hot summer sun. It never bothered her. She loved the feel and smell of her hardworking husband as he wrapped his arms around her. The image in Rachel's mind of her Jonathan felt so real it was as if he was actually with her. The image didn't fade as she slowly became aware of someone at a distance walking across the field and coming closer. Rachel's feet were frozen in place as she held her breath. *Am I losing my mind?* she asked herself as she fought back the panic. Her heart was beating so rapidly it felt as if it would jump out of her chest. Rachel closed her eyes, shaking her head. *No. This can't be. I'm seeing things.* She heard once a person could grieve so much she could lose her mind. Slowly, she opened her eyes. The image of Jonathan came closer still. *It seems so real,* she thought in the back of her mind. Rachel could actually see his breath in the cold morning air as he continued toward her until he was standing directly in front of her.

Too many thoughts swirled in Rachel's mind as she stood in disbelief at the sight of Jonathan standing so close to her. But this wasn't the Jonathan she remembered on the day he left for war. This Jonathan was much thinner. His face looked weary and gaunt. His military coat hung loosely on him like a worn-out blanket. Up close, Rachel could see he was shaking. He looked so tired. Tears welled up in his eyes at the sight of his Rachel. How he had longed for this moment. How he had lived for this moment. She was more beautiful to him than she had ever been. She looked like she had seen a ghost. The thought brought a sad smile to his face as he reached out with his dirty, calloused hand and gently touched her face.

Somewhere in Rachel's mind, she remembered the telegram in her pocket. Jonathan looked deeply into her eyes as he spoke. "Rachel,"—his voice was raspy and weak—"I'm so thankful to be home. I missed you so much. I…" Jonathan's voice became warbled in Rachel's ears before she saw the porch floor coming up to meet her as Jonathan's arms caught her right before she fainted.

Chapter Forty-four

"A miracle. That's what this is, a miracle from God." Rachel heard the words as if through a tunnel as she slowly came to confused awareness. *What am I doing lying on the couch?*

It was Ellen's voice she heard as she opened her eyes and looked up at her mother-in-law, who was gently wiping her forehead with a cool cloth. Jonathan and his father were standing behind Ellen, anxiously waiting for Rachel to come to. Rachel looked so pale and still. She'd been out for so long that even Ellen was concerned. They all breathed a sigh of relief when Rachel came to. Though exhausted and weary to his soul, Jonathan felt tremendous gratitude that God had brought him safely home to his family. Now that he was home, he realized he missed them more than he thought possible.

"How long was I out?" Rachel asked.

Elias Bailey spoke up. "Long enough to give us all a good scare. That is, I mean after the one we got when Jonathan opened up your door when we stopped by earlier. We thought for a moment we were seeing a ghost." But he was grinning from ear to ear as he looked at his son. He shook his head in disbelief.

Jonathan grinned back. But his heart twisted in his chest as he studied his father. More gray was sprinkled throughout Elias's dark hair. The lines around his eyes and mouth were deeper, etched from too much worrying while his son was fighting in the war. When Jonathan had first opened the door to see his parents, their look of shock and confusion surpassed Rachel's. In return, Jonathan was shocked to see how much his parents had aged. *What in the world happened?* he wondered. *Why weren't they expecting me? And Jennie!* he thought. *All she could do was stand at the entryway of the parlor and stare at me, completely speechless.*

Jennie had come down the stairs just in time to see a man in a shabby coat place her fainted sister, Rachel, on the couch. Jonathan's back was to her. When he turned around, Jennie's mouth dropped open in stunned surprise as Jonathan walked past her, telling her he'd be right back, Rachel had fainted, and he was going to get his parents as if it was just like any other day. But when he opened the door, there stood his parents.

Jonathan was surprised at how much his parents had changed. Even though his mother had fared a little better than his father, she'd lost some weight, and her hair was grayer too. To Jonathan, however, his mother would always be a very pretty woman.

But why had they all looked at him as if they'd seen a ghost? Hadn't they gotten his telegram to let them know he was coming home? Rachel sat up, insisting she felt fine. She couldn't take her eyes off Jonathan. The sight of him overwhelmed her with love and gratitude that God had brought him back to her.

Elias stepped forward to stand beside Ellen, placing his arm around her shoulder. His wife was right. This truly was a miracle. Their boy was alive, although not exactly well, by the looks of him. His heart ached as he looked at his son. Jonathan was so thin he looked like a skeleton. His complexion was that of pale ash. But he was home. The devastating telegram they had received was wrong.

The room went silent. No one could think of anything more to say—not even Jennie, who never seemed to run out of things to say or opinions to express on any matter. Jennie still hadn't spoken a word since she set eyes on Jonathan. Her eyes were as round as saucers. Even Katy the cat, who was standing next to Jennie, never let out one meow but sat quietly as she observed this strange scene before her.

The sounds of Little Jon waking up demanding his breakfast broke the uncomfortable silence. His cries to be held and fed brought Rachel quickly to her feet and with it, another wave of dizziness. "No, no," she said as she held out her hands, motioning to all of them that she felt fine and she just stood up too fast. "I'm fine. Honestly," she said as she looked up at Jonathan.

Their eyes locked. This was the moment they'd all been waiting for. Jonathan was about to meet his son for the very first time. "Wait here," she whispered to Jonathan as she reached up and gently touched his face, feeling the stubble on his unshaven chin in her cupped hand before turning away to go upstairs for their Little Jon.

Jonathan shifted from one foot to the other nervously as he waited. Why did he suddenly feel so scared? Ellen sat down in the chair. Jennie remained standing. Elias stuck his hands in his pockets to hide his nervousness as he softly whistled a tune.

Jonathan's mind quickly filled with questions. *Now that the moment is here, what should I do? Should I try to hold Little Jon right away? Perhaps I should wait until Little Jon is used to the sight of me. Should I—?*

Jonathan turned at the sound of Rachel's voice. "There we go. Whee..." Little Jon's laughter filled the room as he was being lifted up high in the air by Rachel, who was entering the parlor.

Jonathan's breath caught in his throat. He couldn't seem to move as he watched Rachel walking toward him, placing their baby on her hip. Little Jon was all smiles. When Rachel stood in front of Jonathan, he didn't know what to say. He didn't know what to do. The sounds of happy gurgling from Little Jon as he held out his chubby, little arms to his father for the first time brought tears to everyone's eyes. Jonathan reached out his arms to hold his son and pulled him close to his chest as a sob escaped his lips. Never had he ever experienced a feeling of love like this. The completeness in his heart and soul overwhelmed him as tears ran down his face unchecked. Rachel stood close beside him, tears flowing from her own eyes. Elias and Ellen joined them, as did Jennie, until the whole family, minus their beloved Maggie, was huddled together as they allowed their tears to flow freely.

The tears they shed were tears of joy in the miracle of Jonathan's return. The bittersweet tears also flowed for their Maggie, who went home to be with her precious Lord. Maggie had been right. Jonathan did indeed come home.

> Give thanks to the Lord, for he is good; his love endures forever.
>
> Psalm 107:1 (NIV)